MAKING TIME

A QUEER HOCKEY ROMANCE

TAYLOR E. WESTON

TAYLOR E. WESTON

All names, characters, and incidents portrayed in this production are fictitious. No identification with actual persons (living or deceased), places, buildings, and products is intended or should be inferred.

Cover Art by Len Gorbunova
Team Logo by Coldwater Design
Cover Design by Sarah Kil Creative Studio

E-Book ISBN: 979-8-9905681-5-0
Print ISBN: 979-8-9905681-6-7

CONTENT GUIDELINES

This book is a queer romance between two men, written in third person, dual point of view alternating in each chapter.

Potentially sensitive content includes: mentions of financial insecurity, brief mention of a birth parent who is not involved in raising a child, mention of vomiting, confrontation with and mentions of a creepy patron of a strip club who attempts to solicit sex from a main character.

This book contains multiple scenes with graphic, explicit sexual content between two consenting adults.

If you are uncomfortable with any of these, please prioritize your mental health and skip this book.

The luna moth is often associated with new beginnings and transformation.
This one is for everyone who has tried again.

CHAPTER 1
JAMIE
LIKE A DINGUS

Daniel: Welcome back to the Madison Muskies Broadcast, I'm Daniel Cummings, joined by Tabitha Dunkirk. Heading into the third period, the Muskies trail Vegas 3 - 1, after a late period goal from Vegas D-man, Nilsson, slipped over the pad of Muskies goaltender, Berglund. Tabitha, what do you think of the Muskies play so far?

Tabitha: What stands out to me through the first two periods of play is the lack of high-danger chances generated by the Muskies offense. The team only has 10 shots on goal through the first two periods, with more breakdowns in the neutral zone than we're accustomed to seeing with this group. It's in games like this that I'm sure the Muskies are missing having the Sharpe Shooter on their bench.

Daniel: Oh boy, are they ever. Since Aaron Sharpe's retirement at the end of last season, the Muskies have struggled to find an offensive player who can single-handedly score those clutch goals and create the high-danger opportunities. The first line is predictably strong and generating, but the Muskies need more offensive production from their second and third lines.

Tabitha: Three may have slipped past him this game, but Berglund has been good in net for the Muskies. No one can deny the power and skill of the Muskies D-core, led by their top pairing, Jackson and Roberts.

Like you just said, it's the offense that is under fire right now, especially the new captain, Jamie Sullivan.

Daniel: Sullivan has never been a forty-goal per season player in the years since the Muskies drafted him. He provides solid offense, has a great two-way game, strong on the forecheck, obviously well-liked in the locker room, but do you think the coaching staff is looking to him for more this year?

Tabitha: Given the hole left in the wake of Sharpe's retirement, I would imagine they are. Unless one of the rookies steps up, I think all eyes are on Sullivan.

Daniel: Should I pull out my old skates and get out there? I'm not sure if I've told you before, but–

Tabitha: You had a hat trick in the Quebec Peewee tournament, Dan. You only remind us every week.

Daniel: (chuckles) Well, I'm just saying, if the Muskies need offense badly enough, I'm happy to throw my hat in the ring.

Tabitha: Let's see if Sullivan can get the team going out there.

Daniel: I'm Daniel Cummings for the Muskies–don't go anywhere, we'll be back for the start of the third period after this.

"Let's go, boys! Matty, you've got the space! There it is. There it is! You've got Emmy down below–" *Shit*. "Come on, let's get it back!"

Jamie Sullivan grabbed a towel, and wiped it across the inside of his visor. Tossing it aside, he nudged his thigh against his Finnish teammate and linemate, Esa Couri, raising his voice so he could be heard above the roar of the crowd at Culver's Arena. "Once we're in our zone, I'll try to get position in front of the net. Get a screen for you."

Esa didn't take his eyes from the game, but nodded in understanding. "Got it, Cap," he said, his words heavily accented. "We need to score."

Yep. They needed to fucking score.

"Sully, your line's up," their assistant coach Sam Miller called out from behind the bench.

Get your ass out there and get your team a point, Jamie. Do whatever it takes, but there better be another one on the scoreboard by the next time you're going back to the bench.

Jamie swung over the boards, pushing out into the neutral zone with Esa and their other winger, Cooper Bell. Their top D-pair was still on the ice. Mitch Jackson held the puck behind their net, waiting for them to complete their change, and Cody Roberts hung out on the left wing in anticipation of Vegas' brutal forecheck.

The shift started well. Textbook. Just like they'd done it a thousand times in practice.

Mitchy passed to Cody. Cody pushed up the ice, hitting Jamie's stick perfectly as he cut across the neutral zone. Jamie managed to get past Vegas' forward before dropping the puck back to Mitchy, who'd trailed him down the ice.

Jamie skated hard, muscling his way into position in front of the goalie, using his body and stick to push against Tanner Dorren, Vegas' veteran defenseman who was infamous in the league for his dirty play and tendency to run his mouth. At 6' 2", Jamie wasn't the tallest guy on the ice, but he made up for it with a thick body he didn't hesitate to throw around for the sake of his team.

"Looking fucking slow out here, Sully," Dorren grunted, lifting their locked sticks before shimmying to get in position. "Got the C and let it all go, eh?"

Jamie tried to ignore him, popping out to the corner. Cooper fed him the puck. Jamie swung around and surveyed the ice. Vegas had them fully covered *Shit. Nothing.*

Dorren advanced on him, his stick extended to cut off any possible passing lane. He needed to do something.

Do it, Sully. Fucking do something.

He dug his back skate into the ice and charged forward, doing his best to guard the puck. He managed to catch Dorren off guard.

With his vision narrowing on the net, Jamie willed his legs to pick up speed.

Three Vegas guys dropped down to cover him. The window of space Jamie had previously seen was gone, and now he was smothered. He tried to use his body to hold onto the puck, tried to find a teammate to dish it to, but *fuck*.

Vegas took the puck.

He lunged after the player, making one last effort to get it back. Frustration tugged at him, but he fought it. His team needed him to be better.

What the hell was wrong with him? It was like the hockey instincts that lived somewhere between his muscles and his brain had gotten tangled. He was working harder than he ever had, pushing his body to the brink, and *still* nothing was going right.

He'd made it a few feet up the ice when Cody picked off Vegas' attempt to pass up the wall. A wave of relief left Jamie feeling almost lightheaded. At least his mistake hadn't cost his team a point.

He needed to focus. The puck was…*there*. On the left wing with Cooper. There wasn't an open window for Coop to shoot, but if he could get it across to Mitch there was a chance Jamie could hold his position on Dorren long enough for Mitch to take advantage of the open lane to the net.

Cooper passed up to Esa in the middle of the ice. Jamie held his position, skates dug in as he leaned heavily into Dorren's side. Esa faked the shot, and then dished to Mitch. *Come on, Mitchy. Come on…*

He felt the *whoosh* of the slap shot move the air beside him, and heard the *thunk* of the puck against the goalie's blocker. Jamie tried to extract from Dorren, his eyes searching the ice for the rebound. *There,* just to the right of the crease. Jamie lunged forward with his stick, reaching with his off hand, and managed to get a piece of the puck, tapping it back toward the net.

A hard body slammed into him, sending him careening backwards. *Shit*. He flailed his arms, trying to get his footing, but a well-placed elbow from Dorren sent him to the one place he didn't want to be: directly into Vegas' goalie.

They both fell back, the goalie's heavy pads breaking Jamie's fall. Distantly, he heard the whistle, the ref calling the play dead. Jamie tried to scramble to his feet, wanting to put as much distance between himself and the netminder as possible.

"The fuck, man!' Dorren shouted, eyes wide and mocking as he bumped his chest in Jamie's. "You trying to fuck with my goalie?"

"Class act as always, Dorren." Jamie shook his head, trying to skate away. "Acting like your ass didn't shove me into your own fucking net."

Dorren's sneer turned cold. "Hey, at least I'm doing my job," he said. "Major downgrade from the last captain, huh? I'm shocked your old ass hasn't gotten traded."

Any other night he would have ignored the comment. Talking shit was a part of the game. He'd been in the league for eleven years, and had been playing as an openly gay man for the last five. He'd heard it all.

But tonight, Dorren's words hit right where it hurt, and with his team down and all eyes on him to score or do something, *anything* to warrant the white C stitched on his chest, Jamie didn't give a flying fuck about taking the high road.

Both of Jamie's gloves dropped in perfect synchronicity, and he cocked his left fist back as his right hand gripped a handful of Dorren's white jersey.

Jamie had played many roles throughout the course of his professional hockey career: a two-way center matched against the league's top scorers, a loud, authoritative voice in the locker room, a player who'd had consistent seventy-five point seasons and the guy who always knew the best place to get a pastry on the road.

One role he'd never had? Fighter.

The first punch to Dorren's jaw was sloppy, the awkward angle sending a sharp pain up Jamie's forearm. By the time he drew back for another hit, Dorren had reacted, landing a solid blow to Jamie's jaw. He tried to hold his own, he really did, but his left hand was throbbing and all he could manage was to take each hit and think about how badly he'd fucked up.

By the time the linesman pulled them apart, Jamie could feel the beginnings of a bruise spreading over his jaw and knew his punch had seriously messed up his hand. He climbed up from where he'd fallen to his knees on the ice, and ignored the half-hearted applause from the home crowd, keeping his head down as he skated over to the penalty box.

"Number 3 for Madison and number 43 for Vegas, 5 minutes each for fighting."

Goddammit. Jamie felt the eyes of his teammates on him, and gave the bench what he hoped was a reassuring nod.

"Don't see you in here often, Sully." Pete, the penalty box attendant who'd been there since Jamie's rookie year, closed the clear, plexiglass door behind him.

Jaime gave him a strained grin before looking down at his left hand. He flexed his fingers, a sharp hiss escaping him as the bright pain radiated from his middle knuckle and down the back of his hand. Unconsciously, he lifted his right hand to twist and tug at the wet hair curling at the nape of his neck.

A bad habit, he knew, but it was one that had grounded him for years. One that kept his head clear in a game, that helped him move past a mistake.

Dammit Sully. Damn it all.

"They think it's broken."

"How long?"

Jamie couldn't look his best friend, Mitch Jackson, in the eye as he responded, trying to hide the frustration in his voice. "Don't know yet. I'll get x-rays tomorrow and then follow up with the doc."

"The Winter Classic, Sully..." Mitch started, his typically

relaxed face marred with a frown that creased the warm brown skin between his eyebrows.

"Fuck, man. I know." The outdoor game was less than two months away, and Jamie couldn't stomach thinking he might miss the chance to play because of a *stupid fucking fight*.

He'd gone down the tunnel as soon as he was out of the penalty box to get his hand checked out by the Muskies medical staff. They'd strapped him into a brace and sent him to get showered early. He'd hated every second of it. He was supposed to be on the ice with the team.

Depending on what the docs said, he could be out for months.

Mitch shook his head, sweat sliding over his bronze, clean-shaven cheeks. He'd taken off his helmet, leaving the tight black curls that covered the top of his head sticking out in all directions. "What the hell happened out there?"

"You know how Dorren is."

Tossing his game jersey into the laundry cart, Mitch started to work on unstrapping his shoulder pads. "Of course I know how Dorren is, but you know he's always going to say some stupid shit to get under your skin. It's who he is. What I'm *not* used to is seeing you lose it."

The locker room was quieter than usual. A 4-2 loss, even in the first half of the season, had an impact on the room. Their coach, Jeff Hollister, spoke to the team, the usual combination of acknowledging what had gone well while not pulling any punches when it came to how they'd come up short. Hollister had been with the team for the past three seasons, and Jamie admired the hell out of him. He was tough and old school, but respected hard work and effort and went out of his way to acknowledge the guys who were playing well.

As their captain, Jamie was supposed to be making the rounds. He needed to check on the guys, reassure the rookies that this was just one game, and help the team move on.

He couldn't bring himself to get up. He didn't think he could look his teammates in the eye when he hadn't done his part. When he hadn't done what the team needed him to do.

Jamie stared down at the brace strapped around his left wrist. He'd taken the mild pain killers the trainers had given him, but they had barely dulled the throbbing. Usually he'd take the time to wash his hair after a home game, but had barely managed to soap his body with one hand. It had been humiliating to ask Mitch to help him with the buttons of his shirt and tie, but Jamie wanted nothing more than to go home, curl up on his couch, and watch Grey's Anatomy reruns until he fell asleep.

"Want to come over?" Mitch asked. "The kids are probably down, but Layla made chicken and dumpling soup again."

Honestly, hanging out with his best friend sounded like the perfect way to spend the rest of his night, but that wasn't what the team needed. Jamie looked around the room, shaking his head. "Nah. I'm going to take the boys down to grab some beers at Caps. See if we can get our heads straight."

Mitch clapped him on the back. "Good man. Do me a favor and have a few yourself. You need it."

Jamie smiled fondly, inexplicably grateful for Mitch. "Will do. Give the kids a hug for me."

As Mitch wandered off to the shower, Jamie stood up. *He could do this. He could be the captain the guys needed.* Forcing a smile, Jamie pushed his shoulders back. "Drinks on me at Caps tonight, boys!"

He was met with cheers, and, finally, felt a tiny sliver of relief.

Jamie exhaled. Tomorrow morning, he'd come back to the arena to start rehab on his hand. He'd start to fix things. Get back on track. Tonight, he needed to get it together and be the captain he hadn't been able to be on the ice. He'd have a few beers, kick back with the boys, and show them he hadn't completely lost touch.

"Sully! You're up for media!"

He got up, wincing in pain as his bandaged hand throbbed at

this side. Sharon Parish, the Muskie's no-nonsense media relations manager, stood by the door, eyes fixed on her tablet.

"Sullivan," she said, leveling him with an unimpressed look.

"Bad?" Jamie asked.

He'd worked with Sharon for years, although this was the first time he'd ever been on this side of a PR situation. Typically he was one of the guys who was encouraged to bring more personality to his conversations with the media. He wasn't used to facing a room of reporters asking why his play was crap or why he'd decided to fight Dorren, a notorious heavyweight.

"It's not good," she said.

Jamie felt his stomach sink. "Right. I figured."

"Just be the captain," Sharon said, looking directly at him. "Own up and be accountable. They want to see you're still the leader of this team."

Nodding, Jamie lifted his uninjured hand to tug on the still-damp curls at the back of his head. "Right," he said again, because he couldn't tell her that he had no idea what being the leader of his team meant anymore.

"Randall from Muskies Daily. Jamie, how do you feel the season is going so far?"

It was taking every bit of control Jamie possessed to keep his shit together. He tried to keep his facial expression neutral, to keep his posture upright when all he wanted to do was slump down on the table and scream.

"We have a talented team," Jamie began, leaning forward to speak closer to the mics, phones, and recorders lined up along the edge of the table. "We're two months into the season, and so many of our guys are showing up and playing their best hockey. Our record isn't what we want it to be, but I still believe in what this team can accomplish this year."

"Sam, from League News. What is the status of your hand?

You aren't generally known to be a fighter–can you tell us what happened on the ice out there?"

Jamie wet his lips, dropping his gaze to his braced and swollen hand. "At this point I'm being cautious until I get the hand x-rayed and speak to the team doc. As for what happened in the game..." He trailed off. *What the hell was he supposed to say?* He cleared his throat. "Sometimes the wires just get crossed out there. I'm not proud of what happened, but in the moment, I did what I thought needed to be done."

"Veronica, The Madison Gazette. This team saw success for years under Aaron Sharpe's leadership. Now that he has retired, what are you bringing to the team as the new captain?"

Not enough. Nowhere near enough.

"Um, we all know Sharpie will go down as one of the best leaders and players in the history of the national league. I've spent my whole career in Madison, and had the chance to learn from him." He paused, swallowing. "I'm committed to being the best captain I can be for this team, and that means I need to keep stepping up my play. I can't afford to make mistakes like the ones I made tonight. I need to do better for the team and for the fans."

"That's it for the captain," Sharon called out from her spot next to the table.

Jamie forced a tight smile and a wave, leaving the media room. He felt his shoulders relax as he walked down the empty hallway toward the parking garage.

He didn't blame them for asking the questions. What the hell *was* he bringing to his team other than an inability to provide the points Sharpie used to put up every night? Jamie knew he was a good hockey player. He'd grown up, like so many other Canadian kids, working his way up through junior hockey, and at some point he started making a name for himself. He hadn't made it to this point in his career without talent.

But he wasn't Aaron Sharpe. He wasn't anywhere close. No matter how hard he'd trained that summer, no matter how many extra hours he'd put in at the gym, he couldn't seem to become the captain the team needed him to be on the ice.

And now that the season was underway, there was nothing to do but keep showing up and filling his days with hockey. He had to make the time. For himself, for the team, for the fans.

Get to Mitch's house. Don't eat shit on the ice, and get to Mitch's house.

It should have been easy. Or it probably would have been easier if Jamie's brain hadn't been sloshing around in his head every time he took a step. His face was numb–he wasn't sure if it was the cold or the three shots of whiskey he'd downed at last call.

Thank *fuck* for the beanie and long wool coat he wore over his suit. His loafers were shit for walking on the icy sidewalk, but there was nothing he could do about that now.

He was close to Mitchy's. Or maybe not? Caps was over by the university, and he thought he knew the way to his best friend's house like the back of his hand. On a good night the walk took him twenty minutes.

Tonight was not a good night. He should have gone home and right to sleep after the game. Give his brain a break from the clusterfuck in his head.

Twenty-five minutes into the walk, he was still surrounded by student housing. Most of the houses had overgrown yards, bikes cluttering the porch, and political flags hanging in the windows. Madison was one of those weird cities where neighborhoods seemed to bleed from one to another with nothing but a street dividing them.

Shit, he needed to pee. Maybe he could find a bush–

A flash of unmistakable orange and green caught his eye. He blinked, trying to focus on what was in front of him.

It was a snowman, built at the edge of a small front yard. It was short, with an impressively round head and an actual carrot for a nose. But it was the Muskies jersey that caught Jamie's eye, especially the bright white C emblazoned on the chest.

"Aw, come on," he slurred, shuffling through the snow toward the snowman. He circled it, frowning at his name stitched across the back. "Why'd you want to support this guy," he said, throwing his hands out, waving at the white number three on the arm. "This guy sucks! He can't score goals. He can't captain the Muskies for shit! He broke his hand throwing a stupid punch like a…like a dingus!"

Fuck this snowman.

The first kick was clumsy, barely knocking against the snowy base. "You can do better than that," he muttered, resetting his feet. He swung out with his good hand, letting out a loud *whoop* when he made a significant dent in the snowman's face.

"Take that, Snow Sully!" His voice cracked and he stumbled, his footing unsteady on the brittle snow. His stomach roiled and his vision went blurry. The moment it cleared, he kicked his knee out in front of him, hitting the snowman square in the chest.

The whole thing crumbled, landing in a shapeless heap of dirty snow and fabric. Jamie grinned, pleased with his work.

"What the fuck are you doing?"

Jamie glanced up, momentarily blinded by a porch light that had switched on somewhere above him. Stumbling back, he felt his heel hit the slick sidewalk. He swung his arms out, tried to get his balance, but it was too late.

I'm really good at skating, some part of his mind protested as he went down.

Thunk.

Fuck.

CHAPTER 2
TYLER
ARE YOU DEAD?

"Buttercup is the sister," the toddler said, his legs curled under him where he sat on the rug in a pair of indigo tie-dye pajamas. His little hands gripped two hand-knit cats–one white and the other orange. "And Poncho is the brother."

Cradling his now-cold cup of tea in his hands, Tyler Raymond lowered himself to the floor beside his son, Rowan. "What are they up to today?"

Rowan hummed, seeming to consider the question. His brown curls bounced out from his head, tangled and untamed. At three, his imagination was starting to run wild, and Tyler was barely able to keep up with the stories he came up with. "Fishing," he finally said.

"Awesome, kiddo." Tyler snagged a blue bandana from the floor with a heavily tattooed hand, and then flattened it out on the rug. "Check out this pond. Do you think there might be some fish in here?"

"This pond has fishes and whales."

"Whales? Really?"

"Mmhm," Rowan's big blue eyes were wide. "They can be shy, so we have to be quiet."

Tyler nodded, shifting to lean against the end of his queen mattress. The room he and Rowan shared was small, but they'd managed to fit a crib in one corner, as well as a chest of drawers and a few baskets of Rowan's toys.

The last time Tyler had lived in this boarding house, he'd been a senior at the University of Wisconsin, partying away the final days of his college career in Madison. The nine other people who lived in the house had been his family–they'd shared classes and spent weekends seeing DJs in warehouses and camping out at music festivals around the Midwest. There'd always been someone willing to share a joint on the back stoop and dirty dishes piled in the sink. It had been chaos, and Tyler had loved it.

Now he was back, and everything was different.

This is what you wanted, Tyler reminded himself.

He'd recently left his parents' house in Vermont, along with the free childcare and homemade meals that had come with living there. He'd tried to explain how he felt to his mom: how he needed to prove to himself, needed to prove to Rowan that he hadn't made a mistake when he committed to raising his son as a single parent.

So there they were, living in student housing, trying to figure out how to sleep in a house where there was always someone playing music or having loud, bedframe-bouncing-off-the-wall sex.

It was all they could afford at the moment. Tyler had a part-time job at a coffee shop and, when he wasn't working there, delivered groceries. The latter he could do with Rowan strapped into his carseat, and a friend in the house watched Rowan while Tyler worked at the coffee shop.

Between the meager funds and food stamps, they were trying to make it all work. It wasn't much, but it was enough. As long as he had Rowan, it was enough.

"Flat white with oat milk for Bailey!"

Tyler slid the paper cup across the counter, and then turned back to the espresso machine. *Next: dark chocolate mocha, two shots, hemp milk, add cinnamon.* His hands moved instinctively as he checked out the morning crowd.

The Daily Grind was always busy. It was the kind of coffee shop that had waves of patrons throughout the morning: the early-morning exercise crowd became office workers, and then students and remote workers. The buzz of voices and sound of the espresso machine were a familiar soundtrack by this point.

Annabeth, who lived in the same boarding house, agreed to watch Rowan in exchange for cash on the days Tyler worked. He knew her from school–she was sweet, and was working as a freelance artist around Madison, so her schedule allowed her some flexibility.

Tyler frowned down at what he was wearing. His favorite colorful knit cardigan had an egg yolk stain across the front, thanks to Rowan deciding he was a street sweeper in the middle of breakfast that morning. At least the lace-edged camisole he wore underneath had escaped the mess. His hair, which he'd impulsively cut into a mullet a few months ago, was growing out, and he'd clipped his brown curls back from his face with sparkling butterfly clips he'd found in the break room.

"Ty! What's happening, brother?"

Tyler turned toward the familiar voice. He hadn't seen Corey in…Well, it'd been at least four years. Corey still looked like Tyler remembered him: skinny jeans, a deep v-neck tee, homemade jewelry made from hemp string and wooden beads, and his black hair buzzed short. "How's it going?"

"It's so good right now, Ty. I'm serving over at The Oracle for some quick cash, and I've got a one-way ticket to Cape Town in the spring."

"Cool." Tyler finished pouring the steamed milk into the mocha and handed it to a waiting woman, plastering on what he hoped was a convincing 'customer service' smile. "Sounds like a sweet adventure."

"I didn't know you were back in town."

"I just got back a few weeks ago," Tyler replied.

"Do you go out anymore? I see the others from the boarding house all the time."

"I have a kid."

Corey looked surprised. "Oh shit, that's right! You and Falcon had that baby, didn't you? What's she up to?"

"Traveling, last I heard." Tyler thought of his friend, of the way she'd looked up at him with wide, panicked eyes from the hospital bed, her blonde hair wet with sweat. *I don't want this, Ty. I don't want to be a mom. I don't know what I was thinking.* He and Falcon had never been more than friends who occasionally hooked up, but when they'd found out she was pregnant after a casual night together, they decided they were going to try to raise the kid. He'd been terrified, but it seemed like the right thing to do. When she'd said she wanted that, Tyler hadn't said no.

He wiped down the espresso machine. "I think she's teaching yoga in Bali."

"Nice."

The sound of Muse's *Exo Politics* filled the silence that fell between them. Tyler was accustomed to this from the people he used to hang out with, the unspoken questions: *Are you and Falcon still together? Is she in the picture? Why are YOU the one with the kid?*

There had been moments in those first few months when Tyler had been belligerent with anger, so overwhelmed and lonely he'd struggled to keep his crying silent as Rowan, his beautiful, healthy, *perfect* son had slept curled up on his chest. But with every passing day, Tyler came to appreciate the courage Falcon had shown in that moment. She'd been honest. She hadn't been ready.

He'd rather parent alone than with someone who didn't want to show up for a kid.

"We had some good times, yeah?" Corey smiled at him, easy and unburdened.

Tyler remembered. It all felt like a fever dream, so distant from the reality he currently inhabited. He could barely believe that he used to be the guy who had recited poetry in a cramped tent, Corey fucking him while their friend Natasha had been on her knees with her lips wrapped around Tyler's cock. There had been others there, a whole group of them who'd lived a glorious life full of music and fucking and drugs and philosophical discussions they'd all believed would change the world.

It was how his life had been, back then.

He'd called them his family, back then.

When he came back to Madison, he'd hoped to find that same family waiting for him. But somewhere along the way, he'd changed. He didn't fit anymore, not the way he used to.

Turned out they'd been his family for as long as he was the slutty, *always up for whatever* guy. There had always been room for *that* version of Tyler. But Tyler the dad? The one who needed someone to play with Rowan just long enough for him to take a shower?

There hadn't been a place for that version of him.

Maybe it had been naive of him to hope that everything would be the same after four years away. As his mom always said: *Don't waste time waiting for people to be someone they are not.* And his college friends? They were exactly who they'd always been: a gaggle of free-spirited people who chose to live the way they wanted to. Who had no interest in things like settling down or having children.

Corey was still looking at him with an easy-going smile, waiting for Tyler's response like he had nothing but time. "Things have changed," Tyler finally replied, not sure what else to say.

"Well maybe you can come out some time? DNGR is playing in Tim's garage on Saturday."

"Maybe." There was no way in hell he was going to go.

Corey wandered back to sit with a group of people Tyler vaguely recognized. When his pocket vibrated, he put down the jug of milk he was holding, scrambling for his phone. He didn't care what his boss said–Tyler had to check. He had to know that Rowan was okay.

ANNABETH

Is it cool if Rowan watches 28 Days Later?

TYLER

No?!!!! Please don't let him watch that.

Really?

Really.

He looked up at the clock. *Noon*. Only an hour left, and then he could go home.

The stairs creaked beneath Tyler's feet. He moved slowly, exhaustion weighing down his limbs. It was after midnight–Rowan had woken up crying, and it had taken a minute to put him back down.

It had been a good afternoon. Cyrus and Davey, two of the guys who lived with them, had come home with a huge haul of random clothes from the thrift store where they worked, and had helped Rowan build a snowman in the front yard. They'd put some hideous orange and green sports jersey on it, and had even found a carrot for a nose.

It was sweet, really. His friends were great. They were all fun and creative people who lived their lives to the fullest.

And yet, it was painfully clear that they were at different places in life than Tyler. None of them had children, and while Samira on the third floor was in grad school and had a regular schedule, most of the others had jobs with unconventional hours.

They didn't have to worry about consistent meal times or going to bed on time. They weren't used to worrying about sharp objects on the table or laptops on the couch.

He didn't begrudge them living their lives. It wasn't fair of him to ask them to change for him and Rowan.

But fuck, it sometimes felt impossible to get through it all.

He needed to refill his water bottle, and the trek down three flights of stairs was worth it to get the filtered water they kept in a jug in the fridge rather than tap water.

The kitchen was cluttered when he wandered in, but he moved on autopilot to the fridge. He grabbed the pitcher–fucking empty, *again*. It seemed so logical: if you took the last of the water, you were responsible for refilling it.

He'd only brought it up with his housemates about twenty million times.

He filled up the jug and set it on the counter, resigned to wait the seven minutes it would take for the water to trickle through the filter.

His eyes were heavy. At his hip, the baby monitor emitted a soft crackle–the sound machine he always ran in an effort to drown out the noise from their housemates.

Finally, he filled up his water bottle. He'd just turned toward the staircase when he heard a muffled voice in the front yard. He stopped to listen. Their place was in the thick of student housing, so it wasn't unusual to have drunk pedestrians walk by on the weekends.

But this voice sounded angry.

The voice rose in volume. "He can't captain the Muskies for shit!"

What the fuck?

Tyler went to the wide front window, pulling the faded curtain aside and looking out into the front yard. It was dark enough that it was hard to see much, but he could make out an unmistakably large figure in a long coat shuffling in circles around the crooked snowman in the middle of the yard.

Long arms waved in the air, and the deep voice continued, loud enough to be audible through the glass. "He broke his hand throwing a stupid punch like a..." The arms flapped like a bird. "Like a dingus!"

Before he could try to comprehend what the hell they were talking about, the person started to kick and punch the snowman. *Seriously? What kind of asshole hits a snowman?*

Tyler pushed back from the window. He was over it–over this day, over people and their bullshit. He grabbed a broom from the hall closet, flicked on the front light, unlocked the deadbolt on the front door, and stepped out onto the stoop. He closed the door behind himself, careful not to slam it. "What the fuck are you doing?" He shouted, waving the broom above his head.

The figure froze, took a step back, and Tyler watched as their foot connected with the icy sidewalk and they slipped as if in slow motion, arms windmilling wildly before they fell backwards with a dull, muffled *thud.*

"Shit." Tyler picked his way carefully down the wet, sandy stairs and down the front walk toward the crumpled stranger. "Hey." He poked them in the side with the end of the broom. "Hey. Are you dead?"

Nothing.

Tyler got closer, the street lamp illuminating the thick, expensive-looking navy wool coat wrapped around the man's body. Because it was a man–a huge man, with his thighs splayed out in the snow and a thick blonde mustache tracing his upper lip.

He was out cold by the look of his soft, parted mouth and closed eyes. Tyler crouched down, and saw the puff of fog hovering in the air above the man's mouth. *He's not dead. That's good.*

Standing up, Tyler ran a hand through his hair. *Should he call the cops?*

He ran back inside, up the stairs to the first door off the landing and knocked on his roommate's door.

Davey opened the door in nothing but a robe. It wasn't even tied around his waist.

"There's a guy in the front yard," Tyler said, waving his hand toward the stairs. "I think he needs to go to the hospital."

Rubbing his eyes, Davey let out a groan. "Fucking bummer, man. Good luck with that."

Tyler opened his mouth, then closed it again. "Can you take him?"

Davey winced. "No can do. I've got another episode to edit tonight." Davey, in addition to working at a thrift store, was an independent podcast producer.

Frustrated, Tyler ran a hand over his mouth. "Fine. Can you keep an eye on the baby monitor, then? Rowan shouldn't wake up, but if he does, go get Annabeth."

"Got it." Davey took the monitor and closed the door.

Tyler ran down the stairs, grabbed his coat and keys, and muttered a loud, frustrated "*fuck* this guy" as he rushed out into the night.

It was a short drive to the closest hospital, and Tyler drove as quickly as he could while being safe on the slick roads.

In the passenger seat beside him, the hulking, wet man leaned heavily against the window. Tyler had been trying to figure out how to drag the stranger into his car when the man had groaned, grabbed his head, asked "Where the fuck am I," and then vomited all over the sidewalk.

It had taken a while to get the barely coherent man loaded up in his Subaru.

Tyler kept sneaking glances at him. He couldn't help noticing his unruly blonde brows and his full lower lip–but it didn't matter how objectively attractive the well-dressed stranger was. Didn't matter that Tyler had always had a weakness for men who were bigger than him.

This guy was drunk, possibly concussed, and he was single-handedly ruining Tyler's night.

At least he'd stopped throwing up.

"Think you can walk, big guy?" Tyler asked.

The man groaned.

Tyler came to a slow stop at the red-painted curb in front of the emergency room.

"Ready for this?"

A grunt.

Tyler shook his head, got out of the car, and by some miracle he managed to get the man on his feet with his shoulders supporting a heavy arm. "Work with me, you caveman," he gritted out between clenched teeth, his body struggling to stay upright with the weight of the body leaning against him. "You're the one who showed up on my lawn and beat up my kid's snowman. I probably should have left you to freeze. The least you can do is walk, for fuck's sake."

The man finally lifted his head, and Tyler's breath froze in his chest. He could see him now, *really* see the man who'd stumbled into his yard in the middle of the night. In the harsh light filtering out from the automated glass doors he looked like the lead from a black and white Western, with heavy brows over serious, green eyes, a perfectly average nose and that *fucking* mustache that framed a full, soft mouth.

He stared down at Tyler, shaking himself like he was trying to rouse himself from a deep sleep. "I," he started, his voice a dry rasp. He cleared his throat. "I think I'm drunk."

Tyler snorted. "And apparently a fucking genius."

Wincing, his eyes tightened in a squint and he let out a hiss of pain. "Did I hit my head?"

"Yep. After you beat the shit out of my kid's snowman."

Those green eyes got big, looking down at Tyler with an expression of unmistakable anguish. "Oh m'god. I'm an asshole."

"I mean," Tyler began, resuming their slow shuffle toward the front doors. "I'm not going to argue with you there."

"And you're so pretty, too."

A surprised huff escaped Tyler's lips, which were already growing numb from the cold. He almost tripped over his feet when he felt the press of a nose against the top of his head. *What was this guy doing? Smelling him?*

"Behave yourself," Tyler muttered.

"I don't wanna," the man said before letting out a groan, only this time the sound didn't sound pained. It almost sounded…

No. Nope. None of that.

Thank *god* they had finally reached the sliding doors, moving into the warmth of the lobby. He helped the stranger into a chair against the wall, shielding the back of his head from slamming into the sheetrock as he slumped back. Damn *this guy was wasted.*

Tyler went over to the receptionist. "Hey, so I don't actually know this guy, but he hit his head on my sidewalk and seems to be drunk."

After answering some basic questions about what had happened and his impression of the stranger's condition, the redheaded man at the computer looked up at Tyler through copper lashes. Tyler felt his appraising gaze on his face, picking up on the interest directed his way. "Are you going to stay?"

Tyler turned to look at the stranger. The man seemed to be sleeping, head tipped back and mouth hanging softly open. He thought he saw the sheen of drool dripping down the stranger's chin. The beginnings of a purple bruise spread over his jaw. His long, thick legs were sprawled out, and Tyler caught a glimpse of orange and green argyle socks peeking out above his dress shoes.

He had no business thinking about towering, bumbling strangers who had called him *pretty*. There was a kid at home waiting for him. A toddler who Tyler loved with a fierce, unquestioning blaze that sometimes left him breathless; the kind of love that could overwhelm someone.

If his life was different, he might have stayed.

"No," he said to the receptionist. "You guys will take care of him, right?"

The man winked. "It's what we do here."

Twenty-five minutes later, Tyler crawled into his double bed, tugging the heavy pile of layered quilts over himself as he tried to make his body as compact as possible, waiting for the warmth to come. Across the room, Rowan slept.

As he felt the tug of sleep dragging him under, he thought about blonde mustaches and tall men with tree-trunk thighs.

CHAPTER 3
JAMIE
SKETCHMULE RELIEF

"Good morning, you big, silly ray of sunshine."

Jamie opened his eyes and immediately regretted it. He groaned; the fluorescent light above him looked nothing like the cream-painted ceiling of Mitch's guest bedroom.

But that voice… "Mitchy?" His voice came out in a croak.

"I'm right here, Captain Dumbass."

He tried to sit up, only to be blinded by a sharp pain in the back of his head. Gritting his teeth, he forced his eyes to focus, and found Mitch sitting in the corner of a strange, white-walled room. His friend was watching him with a look of concerned amusement as he tried to wet his lips with a sticky, dry tongue. "Where?"

"Hospital."

That was a curtain around his bed, and *shit,* that was an IV in his arm. "What the hell?"

Mitch was wearing his wire-frame glasses and a gray Muskies hoodie and sweats. His eyes crinkled the way they always did when the rookies did something especially stupid. Only now, he was looking at Jamie. "Out of all the idiots we share the ice with, I didn't expect to get a call for you, old man. You're not supposed to be the problem child!"

Jamie took a quick inventory of his body. Left hand: still in pain, still in a splint. Head: throbbing, like he hit the back of it on something, and there was an ache behind his eyes. Jaw: aching, like he'd been punched. Stomach: roiling. Whatever had happened last night, taking those shots was probably part of the problem. As an infrequent drinker beyond the occasional couple of beers with the guys, hard liquor tended to put him on his ass for days at a time. *Idiot, Sully. Fucking idiot.*

"What happened?" His mind–though battered and liquor-drenched–was already racing, trying to piece together apologies to teammates for being such a shit captain, on, and now *off*, the ice.

Mitch got up and ambled over, perching on the edge of the bed by Jamie's covered feet. "The nurse said you slipped on some ice and hit your head. Knocked yourself out for a minute."

"Shit." *No wonder he felt like he'd been sucker punched in the back of the head.* The end of the night started to come back to him: the desperate need to get to the comfort of Mitch's house; the clumsy, crooked snowman wearing the Muskies home jersey, the unmistakable C embroidered on its chest. He knew the walk well, but must have underestimated how drunk he was.

He remembered wondering if it was a Sharpe jersey. There were still plenty of those around the city and in the stands, the legacy of the last Muskies captain undeniable even after his retirement.

But no. It wasn't a Sharpe jersey. There was a number three on the sleeves, and across the back, his own last name. *Sullivan.* The poor bastard who had to follow in the footsteps of a future Hall of Fame forward who'd set a new franchise scoring record. Who'd lead them to a Stanley Cup six years ago. The man who'd effortlessly knit their team into a family. Who'd shown up on his doorstep when the news got out that Jamie's grandmother had passed away. Who'd held him in his long arms while Jamie wept and wept and wept.

"Apparently some guy in a yellow coat brought you in. You were in rough shape, barely able to walk, so he was helping you out."

Jamie blinked, and even that hurt. "Damn it. I fucked up."

"It's not your best look, Sully." Mitch leaned forward. "What the hell's going on?"

"I'm a fucking joke, Mitchy. Can't do the thing I'm paid to do, and now I'm wandering into a fan's front yard and beating up their snowman." Jamie tried to gather his thoughts, to come up with a plan to fix the mess he'd gotten himself into. "My phone?" He asked.

Mitch pointed to the table. "It's there, but it's dead."

Shit. "What do you think I should do?"

Mitch looked at him, his teeth gnawing at his lower lip, and then shrugged. "This is your mess, Sully. I'm here for you, but you've got to figure out the plan."

Letting out a groan, Jamie scrubbed his hands over his face. He'd ruined a kid's snowman–a freaking *kid* who had his jersey–and he didn't think he could live with himself if he didn't try to make amends. *It's what Sharpie would do,* he told himself. "Get me out of here so I can apologize to the kid whose snowman I beat up."

"What even was that, man?" Mitch asked, shaking his head. "Did the snowman look at you funny or something?"

"No," Jamie felt his cheeks flush. "It was wearing my jersey."

"Oh my god." Mitch made what he probably thought was a valiant effort to contain his amusement, but then doubled over, his loud, honking laugh filling the sterile room.

"It's not funny!" Jamie protested, even though he knew it was. It was ridiculous, and embarrassing, and probably a sign that his life was going off the fucking rails.

Mitch took off his glasses and wiped his eyes, his grin so big it creased his cheeks. "There's a lot to unpack there," he said, exhaling loudly. "Let's go find this kid, then."

Of all the ways Jamie could have nursed his hangover, trying to retrace his drunken path through downtown Madison was at the bottom of the fucking list.

The pounding in his head mirrored the throbbing of his jaw where he'd taken a punch during the game. He was nauseous, trying to breathe in through his nose so he wouldn't get sick, and his injured hand ached.

He needed to get to the rink and start his rehab plan. He needed to put something in his stomach and drink some fucking water.

But he knew himself well enough to know he wouldn't be able to relax until he made some attempt at an apology for what he'd done to that kid's snowman.

"This is it."

Jamie didn't recognize the house itself, which was one of those big, three-story monstrosities that barely fit on its lot. Faded siding framed wooden windows that showed signs of decay. A Pride flag flapped on the sagging front porch.

But there, in the small front yard, was a pile of dirty snow and sticks scattered around a bright orange and green jersey.

"Jesus, man. You did a number on that thing," Mitch said, nodding in the direction of the snowy remains.

Jamie felt like the biggest piece of shit to ever exist. "Better showing than I had against Dorren," he muttered.

"Alright, bud. That's enough of that. Let's do this." Mitch led the way up the path.

The front door opened as they reached the steps. A tall, gangly guy with a shaved head came out with a joint tucked into the corner of his mouth. He lit up and took a deep drag, giving Jamie an up-nod. "Sup," he said, blowing the fragrant smoke from his mouth like he was completely indifferent to their presence.

When they didn't move, the guy waved them toward the door. "Just go on in," he said.

Jamie opened his mouth to ask about the guy who had helped him last night, but Mitch was already nudging him forward.

The front door was cracked, and Jamie hesitantly pushed it open. He found himself wondering if it was normal for strangers to show up at the house.

Mismatched couches lined the walls of the living room. Beside the door, a hodgepodge of shoes were piled, and a row of hooks were overflowing with coats.

A woman sat cross-legged on the floor with headphones on, various art supplies and papers spread around her. Her blue hair was up in pigtails. Someone bundled in one of those *can't really tell if it's a blanket or a hoodie* things lay on one of the couches. They looked asleep.

Jamie cleared his throat. No one moved. "Hello?" His voice sounded too loud in the room.

He could make out the murmur of voices down a hallway, and, exchanging a shrug with Mitch, they walked toward the sound.

The kitchen was small, the counters cluttered with dishes, pots and pans. At one of the counter tops, a toddler stood on a chair, obviously occupied with something on a plate in front of them. And next to the toddler–

Oh, fuck.

"You're not dead," the man said, crossing his heavily tattooed arms over his chest.

Jamie stared. A lot of the night was blurry, but this face, this man, was branded in his memory. He had wild brown hair cut short in the front and long in the back like the frontman of an eighties rock band the morning after a bender. Sharp, dark eyes. Heavy lashes. A gold ring through his nose. He looked so far removed from the men Jamie spent his days with at work, like he was another species of human entirely.

"Ah, no," Jamie managed to say. His voice came out in a low rasp. "Not dead."

The gorgeous man, who wore nothing but holey socks, plaid

boxers, and a baggy knit sweater that hung off of one shoulder, didn't say anything else. Jamie couldn't take his eyes off of him–the slender lines of his body, the way his mouth seemed stuck in a soft frown, and his tattoos.

Black, precise lines were scattered over his pale skin without any sort of discernible pattern. A flower on his left kneecap. What looked like an ancient mask with empty eyes and an extended tongue on his right shin. An intricate geometric design started on his thigh and disappeared under the hem of the boxers he was wearing.

There were symbols on his long fingers, the word *compromise* in clear print on the side of his hand. And the one that had inexplicably left Jamie with a dry mouth: a moth of some sort at the base of his throat, outstretched wings curving below his Adam's apple.

He looked between Jamie and Mitch, his expression unreadable.

Finally, Mitch stepped forward, extending his hand. "I'm Mitch," he said, his voice as warm and kind as always. "This is my friend, Sully. He wanted to stop by."

"To apologize," Jamie rushed to add. He frowned, shoving his hands into his pockets. "I wasn't in my right mind last night and I…I'm so sorry."

"Papaaaaa!"

The toddler on the chair turned toward the tattooed man, small hands outstretched. Jamie felt himself smile at the round cheeks and brown hair that looked so much like the man standing in front of him. Then the kid caught sight of Jamie and Mitch, and his blue eyes went wide.

The man hoisted the kid up into his arms. "Hey kiddo," he whispered, the softening of his voice matching the transformation of his face. "We've got some visitors."

The boy smeared his hands across the man's cheeks, leaving a trail of what looked like smashed bananas in their wake.

Before he realized what he was doing, Jamie reached for a roll of paper towels he saw on the counter. Tearing one off the roll, he handed it to the man, who took it from him. The man's soft frown deepened, but he offered a quiet, "Thanks."

"Hey, buddy," Jamie said, turning his attention to the kid. He'd always wanted kids–he'd dreamed of coming home to a family like Mitch's, of having a house full of shouting and laughter and toy trucks on the floor, of so much joy and chaos.

Unfortunately, in order to have *that,* he needed to find a partner who'd sign up for a life with a professional hockey player who was gone for almost nine months out of the year.

Based on his dating experience since he'd started his career, that man didn't exist.

The kid grabbed a handful of the man's sweater. Jamie could barely make out his whispered words. "These guys are pretty big, Papa."

Jamie stifled a laugh behind his hand. The tattooed man let out a soft breath that Jamie thought might be a laugh. "Yeah, they are." To Jamie and Mitch, he said: "This is my son, Rowan."

Mitch took a step closer, raising his hand in a wave. "Hi, Rowan. I'm Mitch." He shot Rowan a conspiratorial grin. "Did you know, I'm actually a papa, too."

"Papa, does he have a kiddo?" Rowan spoke against the man's unshaved cheek, obvious excitement in his little voice.

Mitch smiled. "Three of them, actually. My daughter Stef is right about your size."

"Wow."

"Um." Jamie cleared his throat, turning his focus to the tattooed man. "What's your name?"

"Tyler."

Tyler. Jamie's eyes drifted shut for a moment. It was the perfect name for him–he couldn't explain why, just that it fit the hard, challenging set of his jaw, the way his eyes watched them like he wasn't sure if he was assessing a threat or not.

It fit the man who had all but melted when his son had called him 'Papa.'

Jamie cleared his throat, clearing his thoughts. "Tyler," he said, the name slipping from his lips on a heavy breath. "I'm sorry again for last night, for disturbing you and your life. There aren't any excuses for my behavior. And thank you for taking me to the hospital. You didn't have to do that, and…Well, thank you."

"Is your head okay?"

"Yeah, it's fine," Jamie said, waving his hand dismissively. "Is there anything I can do to make things–"

"Hello, lovely people!" A willowy young woman wearing a rainbow beanie and a variety of patterned fabrics wrapped around her body swept into the cramped room.

"Morning, Annabeth," Tyler said quietly.

"I'm so glad you're entertaining visitors again," she said, walking around Tyler to peer at the countertop. "A little sexual release will help with all of the…" She wrinkled her nose and waved her hand in front of Tyler's face. "Gunk," she finished.

"Papa, what's sketchmule relief?"

Jamie watched Tyler's face tighten. "Seriously, Annabeth," he muttered. "These guys are…I don't actually know who they are. Their names are Mitch and Sully."

"Oh, hello," the woman waved absently to them. "Your vibe is too corporate for my tastes, but the glasses and the mustache are nice."

What the fuck was happening? Jamie felt like he was stuck in a bizarre dream.

"We play hockey," Mitch offered. "For the Muskies."

There was absolutely no recognition on any of their faces. Annabeth frowned at them. "I don't trust men who play games. And aren't muskies a fish?"

Well, then. They weren't fans. That was…Reassuring. Some anonymity felt nice amid the clusterfuck that was his public persona.

"Someone made food," Annabeth said, grabbing a plate from the counter behind Tyler. "I just love how generous people are." She paused at the door. "Happy trails."

Jamie watched Tyler. He saw the pinch of his eyes as he stared at the counter where the plate had been, the way those beautiful, tattooed hands flexed against Rowan's back.

"That was your breakfast, wasn't it," Jamie asked, softly.

Tyler nodded, his face falling in defeat. "I'm trying to find a new place," he muttered.

Jamie didn't know what to say. It was hard to imagine trying to raise a kid in an environment like this. He knew from years of having teammates with little kids how much they needed routines and calm surroundings.

"Is it just you?" Jamie asked, unable to help his curiosity.

Tyler nodded. "Just me and Rowan."

"Do your moms still rent their attic out?" Mitch asked.

Jamie turned to Mitch. *Oh, damn. That was a good idea.* "Yeah, and I think their last tenant was getting ready to move out. I'll ask." He faced Tyler, who was watching the two of them with that careful, guarded expression. "My moms have a place about five minutes from here, and they rent out an apartment in their attic."

Tyler's expression was flat. "Oh."

"I'd be happy to ask if it's available," Jamie went on.

Tyler stared at him. "I'm sorry, but you're a stranger who just walked into my house and the only thing I know about you so far is that you have some sort of complicated beef with the snowman my son made and you like to smell hair."

"I–" Jamie blinked. "What?"

Tyler shook his head. "Never mind."

"Wait, what is this about smelling hair?" Mitch's expression was much too amused for the current situation.

"Mitchy, give me your phone." Jamie reached out a hand and his best friend obliged without further comment. Jamie typed in Mitch's password, and quickly navigated to a search engine. When he'd found what he was looking for, he flipped the phone around so Tyler could see it.

He watched dark eyes look between the screen and Jamie's face, his serious expression unchanging. Finally, Tyler nodded.

"Okay. At least you're not some creep pretending to be a professional athlete."

Jamie sighed. "Would you consider the offer about the apartment?"

"You really don't have to–" Tyler started.

"Honestly, they'd love to have you live there. They're both retired teachers and love kids." Jamie chuckled. "They harass me all the time about giving them grand babies."

Tyler's dark eyes flashed with something. It was brief, only visible for a moment, before that mask of indifference settled back into place. "Okay," he said. "I mean, if it's actually available, then I'll check it out."

As they exchanged numbers, Rowan picked his head up from Tyler's shoulder, looking back and forth between Jamie and Mitch. "Are you warriors?" His face was scrunched up like he was thinking really hard.

"They're hockey players, kiddo," Tyler said, handing Jamie back his phone.

Rowan looked up at his dad. "What's a hockey player?"

"It's a game," Tyler explained. "They wear skates and hold long sticks and try to get a disk into a goal."

As if choreographed, Jamie and Mitch made quiet noises of protest. "I mean," Jamie began, "it's a little more complicated than that."

"It's a really intense game," Tyler went on. "Sometimes their teeth get knocked out."

Rowan turned to gape at Jamie. "Do you have all your teeth?"

"Row…" Tyler started.

"Actually," Jamie began, feeling a smile tug at his mouth. "I'm missing a few." And then he reached up and pulled one side of his mouth to the side, revealing an obvious gap in the back of his mouth.

Rowan stared, transfixed. "Can you eat chips?"

Jamie laughed. "Yeah, I can eat chips just fine."

His eyes lifted at that moment, catching Tyler staring at his face. It was a quiet moment, nothing remarkable about it, except for the way Tyler looked at him with what might have been curiosity.

Like maybe, just maybe, Jamie wasn't the only one who felt something.

CHAPTER 4
TYLER
BANG. BANG. BANG.

There were days where parenthood felt like a noble endeavor, an opportunity and experience bestowed by the gods. Like a fragile, gentle thing that deserved care, attention, the lightest touch.

There were also days when it felt like Tyler had been thrown into a fighting pit armed only with four hours of sleep and a kitchen towel.

"I'm a kitty, Papa," Rowan wailed, his wide blue eyes brimming with tears. "And kitties don't eat sweet potaybados!"

Tyler ran a hand over his face, trying to hide his frustration. Sweet potatoes had been one of Rowan's favorite foods up until five minutes ago, when his son had informed him that kitties did not, under any circumstances, eat them.

Now the scramble he'd made with pork sausage, eggs, spinach and sweet potatoes sat untouched on the plate, and he had a hungry and raging three-year-old on his hands. Rowan had woken up at 5:45 that morning, and Tyler hadn't had a chance to do anything more than brush his teeth and throw on a thick, baggy sweater in a color palette that reminded him of a Vermont autumn. Rowan was still in his mismatched pajamas: jack o'lantern-patterned pants and a long sleeve shirt with a rainbow butterfly print.

They needed to leave in twenty minutes so Tyler could deliver groceries for two hours, and then they were going to check out a potential new place to live.

It still didn't feel real that the man who'd knocked himself out in Tyler's front yard just happened to be a professional hockey player with a lead on a place to live. He'd fully prepared himself for Sully's offer to be lip-service, the kind of thing someone who has everything says to the poor single dad.

He hadn't expected anything when he'd called the number Jamie had given him, but then a woman had picked up on the first ring. Dotty had been warm, friendly, and let him know their last tenant had just moved out when she married her fiancé. Tyler had learned that Dotty and her wife, Sandra, were retired school teachers who loved kids.

It was hard to imagine it all working out. Sure, what they asked for in rent was affordable, but he'd need to figure out child-care if he wasn't living at the house with Annabeth anymore. He'd looked at some of the local daycares, but most of them had a waiting list.

He didn't know how it was going to work, but he was trying. *They* were trying.

"Row," he said gently, walking over to stand beside the wooden learning tower where Rowan was glaring daggers at his plate. "All of the kitties I know *love* to eat sweet potatoes."

Rowan bared his tiny, white teeth. "They do not!"

Okay. Time to pivot. "I can offer you some apple sauce or a scrambled egg."

"No!" Rowan's wavy brown hair–a mirror to Tyler's–flew out from his head as he shook it back and forth with a vehemence that signaled the approach of a meltdown. "Kitties only eat muffins!"

There weren't any muffins.

Resigned, Tyler scooped up his son. "Let's go get some clothes on, kitty. We've got an adventure to go on."

Later that afternoon, Tyler pulled up at the curb of the address Dotty had sent and stared.

They were obviously undercharging on rent. The house was beautiful, the yard well-maintained even in winter. The Victorian was painted a dark blue with green trim on the windows, and looked like it had recently been updated.

"Papa, it looks like a castle," Rowan said, his breath hot on Tyler's cheek.

"It really does," he replied.

He'd only knocked once when the door opened, revealing two women, standing side by side with sincere smiles on their faces.

"You must be Tyler and Rowan! Come on in," one of them said. "I'm Sandra, and this is my wife Dotty."

Tyler gave them a grateful smile and walked into their bright, comfortable living room. Sandra was broad-shouldered and tall, with an ample chest and shoulder-length blonde hair streaked with gray. Tyler immediately recognized pieces of Sully in her face.

Beside her, Dotty was a shorter Black woman with short hair and a beautiful, bright smile. A gold necklace rested around her neck, and she wore a crew neck sweatshirt with a big green fish on the front.

"Thank you so much for showing us the spot," Tyler said.

"Well, aren't you just the sweetest," Dotty said, looking tenderly at Rowan. "Can you tell me who you have with you today?"

Rowan looked down shyly at the well-loved stuffed sloth he held. "This is Bunny," he said softly.

Sandra looked delighted. "Bunny! Was there a mixup at the zoo on naming day?"

Rowan giggled. Tyler felt himself relax.

"No, this is Bunny for Bunny Wailer!"

The older women seemed to think about it for a second, before recognition dawned on Sandra's face. "Bunny Wailer! Do you like listening to The Wailers, Rowan?"

Rowan nodded. "They're my favorites."

"That is too much fun," Dotty said, shaking her head with a smile. "Well, let's show you guys the place." She led them back out to the front stoop, where there was a second door off to the side of the small porch. "This is a separate entrance for the apartment."

Tyler had trouble keeping himself from staring as they guided him through the attic apartment. It was small, sure, but there was a complete kitchen that opened to a living area, and two small bedrooms with a shared bathroom off the hall. It even had a tub and shower combo.

There were plenty of windows, and mid-morning light streamed in. The wooden floors were scuffed, the fixtures dated, but it was *perfect*.

A few minutes later, they sat in the living room downstairs. Sandra had made them all tea, and, after checking in with Tyler, had offered Rowan a plate of sliced apples, cheese, and some rolled turkey lunch meat.

"Any questions for us?" Dotty asked, settling onto the couch next to her wife.

"I don't think so," Tyler said, his head reeling. "The place is beautiful, and the rent is incredibly affordable."

Sandra shrugged, looking at Dotty with a soft, tenderness in her eyes. "We don't need the money. With Jamie's generosity and our pensions, we aren't trying to do more than cover taxes."

Tyler frowned. "Jamie?"

"He probably introduced himself to you as Sully, didn't he?" When Tyler nodded, Sandra rolled her eyes. "His name is Jamie. Jamie Sullivan. The nicknames are a hockey thing. They all call him Sully."

Jamie. His name was Jamie.

"Got it," Tyler said.

"We'd love to have you and Rowan stay here," Dotty said gently.

Tyler felt his eyes burn, and he pressed his teeth down on his bottom lip. Just the thought of getting out of the boarding house, of being somewhere quiet and private, of giving Rowan more stability, felt like more than he could process at once.

"Thank you," he started. "I want to say yes. Your place is beautiful, and it's exactly what I've imagined for us. But I don't know if I can say yes until I figure out childcare for Rowan. A roommate at the boarding house watches him for me while I work at the coffee shop. If I'm going to have to start paying more for childcare, I need to know before I commit to a new place."

Dotty and Sandra looked at each other. They were obviously having one of those ridiculous, silent conversations people who'd spent years together managed to make look effortless.

Sandra was the first to look back at Tyler. "I have an idea, and I want you to know that my wife and I have reached a point in our lives where we don't do anything we don't want to do."

Tyler felt himself smile at that. Rowan was fully occupied with his snack, munching away at an apple slice.

"We love kids," Sandra went on. "If you'd like, we could watch Rowan while you get your feet under you."

Tyler blinked, certain he'd misheard. "What?"

"I keep waiting for Jamie to settle down with a nice man and have babies of his own, but in the meantime, we would be happy to watch Rowan."

Sandra nodded with a fond smile on her face. "Hockey keeps him too busy most of the year, and he's gotten it in his head that no man will stick around for a guy who's practically married to his job."

Tyler's brain did a little stutter step. *So Jamie was a queer professional athlete with soft blonde curls and a slutty mustache. That was…* Fuck.

There was no time for that.

What these two women were offering him? It was beyond comprehension. Saying yes to something like this, from strangers? They were strangers, and yet they'd asked Rowan about his sloth.

They'd looked him in the eye and engaged with him like they really cared.

And they'd even asked Tyler before offering Rowan a snack.

"What would you charge?" He asked. "For watching Rowan?"

Sandra shook her head. "Nothing. Really, it would be a gift to us."

"Can I think about it?"

The two women nodded. "Of course. We'll hold out on posting the apartment for a few days while you decide."

Tyler thanked them both for the tour, the tea, and the snacks. As he buckled Rowan into his carseat, he looked back over his shoulder at the big, blue house.

It was so easy to imagine it being their home.

He'd pulled out onto the road when his phone buzzed in the cup holder. He glanced down. *Mom.*

Ignoring the tightness in his chest, Tyler answered, putting the phone on speaker.

"Hey, Mom," he said.

"Hi, darling," she responded, her voice full of love and home. "What are you up to today?"

"Mimi?" Rowan called out from the back seat. "Papa, is that Mimi?"

"Rowan, sweetie!" Tyler could hear the smile in her voice. "I miss you so much, bug. Both of you."

"Where's Pop Pop?"

Tyler loved Rowan's name for his dad. It was the same name his sister's kids used, and fit his thin, sweater-wearing dad to a T.

"Pop Pop is taking the dogs for a walk with Marley and Hazel," Tyler's mom said, mentioning two of his sister's three kids. "Sebby is napping, so I'm getting some cleaning done and thought I'd give you two a call." Tyler heard the unmistakable sound of water running in the background. Probably the lunch dishes, he thought. "We miss you, you know. I know you felt like you needed to go, but–"

"Mom," Tyler cut in. They'd had this conversation over and over again, both before and after he'd left Vermont.

His parents were loving, generous people who loved being grandparents. Tyler wouldn't have survived with a newborn without their support.

But as he'd come out of the haze of learning how to parent an infant, Tyler had come to realize just how much his parents did. Not only for him and Rowan, but for his sister and her three kids. She worked as a pharmacist in a rural hospital, and her husband was a fireman. Between the two of them, they worked long hours and relied heavily on their parents for childcare.

In addition, his parents ran a small bed and breakfast just down the hill from Stratton Mountain Ski Resort, which required constant upkeep. Asking them to take care of Rowan on top of everything else felt like too much.

Tyler had a degree in creative writing, and work experience ranging from coffee shops to a lucrative job as a stripper he'd had during his last two years of college.

Other than helping out at the bed and breakfast, he hadn't been able to find steady work.

On top of that, he hadn't been able to escape the gnawing guilt that he was cheating, somehow. That living in his parents' house, barely working, and relying on their generosity was somehow skipping out on the real work of being a dad.

So he'd left. Packed up his Subaru with trash bags full of their things, in spite of his mother's insistence that they stay. She'd pleaded with him, reassuring him how caring for her four grandchildren was all she'd ever wanted, but still, Tyler felt like he needed to go.

"We're doing okay," he said finally, glancing at Rowan in the rearview mirror. There was a sleepy smile on his face as he played with Bunny. "We're figuring it out, one day at a time."

His mom was quiet for a moment. "Your room will always be ready for you," she added. "Just in case. If you need to, you can always, always, come home."

The conversation wrapped up quickly after that. He told his mom he loved her, and then hung up, the silence weighing heavily in the car.

He peered into the backseat again, his shoulders slumping when he realized Rowan had fallen asleep.

Tyler was going to figure it out.

Tyler woke up to Rowan's cries.

His brain wasn't even aware of his legs climbing out of his bed and taking two steps to reach Rowan's crib.

Tiny fists glowed in the orange light of the salt lamp, rubbing furiously at his eyes as the whimpering cries built into wails.

Tyler shook the sleep off slowly, sluggishly, as he picked Rowan up and cradled him against his chest. *Bang. Bang. Bang.*

He looked up at the ceiling.

Fucking Samira.

Or, more accurately, Samira fucking.

Tyler tried to rationalize with himself. This was the shittiest part of their situation. There was no reason why Samira *shouldn't* be having what sounded like very athletic sex in the middle of the night. Most of the people in the house were up at that point, either getting off work or entertaining their own company.

It was Tyler and Rowan who were out of place. They were the ones who didn't fit.

Rowan's cries quieted, his body slumped heavily against him. Carefully, Tyler carried him to his bed, laying him down beside him. Rowan curled into Tyler's side, sighed, and seemed to drift back off to sleep.

Tyler grabbed his phone, pulling up the phone number Sandra had given him.

He knew he should wait until morning, but he needed to act now before he changed his mind. Before he convinced himself that what the women were offering was too good for them.

TYLER

If the apartment is still available, we'll take it.

CHAPTER 5
JAMIE
A MULLET, FOR FUCK'S SAKE

"Sully!"

Jamie blinked, glancing up from where he'd completely zoned out on one of the stationary bikes at the Muskies practice rink. He waved at Pauly, who'd just walked into the training room with Cody, who had noise canceling headphones pulled tight over his shaved head.

Jamie had come in early to do x-rays and sit down with the team doctor. The verdict was clear: his hand was broken, and even if everything went perfectly, he'd still be out of the lineup for four to five weeks. After that, he met with Morgan, the team trainer, and got started on a rehab plan for his hand. Unfortunately, her directive was equally harsh: *Don't move it, come in for treatment, and we'll see.*

He had to be back for the Winter Classic, which would take place early in the new year. He couldn't fucking miss it, not after how shitty his start to the season had been. He owed it to his team, to the fans, to be back and better than ever.

Practice would start in an hour, which meant most of the guys were starting to roll in to go about their varying warm-up routines. Esa Couri, Jamie's winger on the second line, flopped down on the mat and started talking loudly in Finnish to Onni Koskinen, their young backup goalie and a fellow Finn.

The bike vibrated beneath him. His quads hummed, muscles primed and warm.

This was all normal. It felt normal, at least. The team coming together in the training room, getting ready for practice. Warming up their bodies while casually socializing, gravitating toward the little friend groups that inevitably crept up on such a large team.

Jamie had spent years with many of the guys in this group. He'd been drafted alongside Hugo Andersson, a thin, lethally fast Swede, and Mitchy, who had, at eighteen, quickly become his best friend. He'd roomed with Zach Baker for his first four years on the team, and they'd bonded over tracking down the best bakeries on the road in search of the ultimate cinnamon roll. The past few seasons, Jamie's house had even become the de facto living space for the young rookies–this year he had Onni, their backup goalie, and Oliver Campbell, their third line winger, living in his basement.

Now, though? Jamie was their captain.

Jamie had been an alternate captain for the past four seasons, and had worn the A proudly. Being a leader was something he'd always taken seriously. It was a responsibility and an honor to be a voice who commanded respect on and off the ice. And then, when Sharpie announced his retirement, all eyes had turned to Jamie.

The letter C on his chest, combined with the large contract he'd signed last season…it was a lot. A lot of pressure and a lot of scrutiny. More than what Jamie had been expecting.

He knew he deserved it.

He'd been off his game for the first few months of the season. He was fully aware of that. But he didn't know how to turn off the panicked voice in his head that screamed at him to *do more, work harder, score goals,* every time he set foot on the ice. The stress had bled into his play like an infection. He was taking shots he'd never have taken before. Trying to beat defenders one on three–odds even the best players in the league couldn't handle.

Jamie was a good player. He knew that. But he needed to be better, for his team and for the Muskies fans. He was their captain now, and he needed to earn it. Every day, every practice, and every game.

Injuring his hand in a losing fight was just icing on the cake. The bruise on his jaw was a painful reminder of his mistake, and his left hand was wrapped up in a velcro brace, cradled in his lap while his other gripped the bike handle. At least he could still do *some* cardio.

Oliver, who they all called Ollie, climbed onto the bike next to his, a huge, uninhibited smile splitting the younger man's freckled face in two. "Morning, Cap."

Jamie had left the house before the two rookies had gotten up. "Morning, kid."

"How's the hand?"

Shrugging, Jamie held it up. "Broken, but could've been worse. Four to five weeks."

"Bummer, man." Ollie's legs started working the pedals, his floppy brown hair hanging down on his forehead. "Have to say, it was kinda badass to see you fight Dorren. Not sure it was worth the broken hand, but..."

Rather than respond, Jamie reached over and lightly shoved Ollie's shoulder with his good hand. "If you keep that up, I won't make that grilled chicken you like so much."

Ollie mimed locking his lips, but his eyes still danced with amusement.

Kids these days.

Jamie followed the team to the locker room, but while everyone got on their pads and skates, he headed to the showers. Afterwards he tossed on a team hoodie and a pair of sweats with his clean, white Nikes, and started toward the stairs, planning to watch the team practice from the stands, where he could see the flow of things on the ice.

Watching practice was horrible. Jamie felt like he was losing his mind, his muscles twitching as he imagined working through the motions with his teammates on the ice. All his reflexes were firing with nowhere to go, and when he realized his fingers were curled like he was gripping an imaginary stick, he tore his gaze from the ice.

He pulled out his phone and opened one of his social media apps.

While many guys in the league had sworn off having a personal, online presence, Jamie hadn't. He liked taking pictures on his phone–it was silly, he knew, but he liked playing with light and colors, even though he was a total amateur. But being on social media also meant he saw everything the fanbase said about him.

When he was playing well, a picture of Mitch and Cody smiling on the team plane would get comments like: *Nice power-play goal, cap!* Or *Keep it up, #3!*

This morning, those same people had flocked to a photo he'd put up of the lake from his back porch. Now, the comments were: *Waste of cap space,* or *Put this guy on waivers.*

There were also about a hundred versions of: *Biggest captain downgrade in NHL history* and *#bringsharpieback*

His phone rang.

There was only one person who called him rather than texting. "Hey, Mom," he said, leaning back in the uncomfortable stadium seat.

"Jamie, that lovely young father and his son are moving in this afternoon. Can you come over and use all those muscles for something other than bumping into boys on the ice?"

Jamie sighed, shaking his head. "I'm injured, remember?"

"Bring over the rookies who live in your basement," his stepmom, Dotty, cut in. "Ollie's been getting bullied on the boards. He could use the extra workout."

"And carrying boxes is going to help?" Jamie asked, chuckling.

"Sure couldn't hurt," his stepmom said. "We'll make a pan of something to feed everyone."

"I'll ask them after practice," Jamie said. He watched the rink, the blur of bodies flying down the ice in perfect unison, hating how far away he was from the action. He was supposed to be down there with the guys. "So Tyler's going to move in, then?"

He could hear the fondness in his mom's voice as she replied. "He sure is. Sent us the deposit and everything." She paused. "He seems like a wonderful young man. And that Rowan is a sweetheart."

Jamie smiled, remembering the little brown-haired kid who'd asked if he was a warrior. "Yeah, he is." Before he could stop himself, he thought of Tyler. The way the overhead lights in the tiny kitchen had illuminated his lashes, his sharp eyes, and the artwork covering his skin.

"I'm glad your spot was open," Jamie said.

"Us too," his mom said. "Let me know what the boys say. Love you!"

"Love you, Jamie!" Dotty's voice echoed.

"Love you both." He hung up, tucking his phone into his pocket, and settled in to watch practice.

"They're here!" Jamie's mom stood at the front window, watching the street with her hands braced on her hips. Turning back to the room, she gave them her best, no-nonsense teacher glare. "Be nice. Tyler's a little skittish, but he's a good one. I can tell."

Jamie rose from the couch, wincing at the stiffness in his back. Not skating was kicking his ass. With any luck, he'd be cleared to skate again, without a stick, in the next week.

Beside him, Oliver and Onni stood up.

Oliver had brown wavy hair that took about half an hour of careful grooming in the morning, and alarmingly blue eyes that had fans falling over themselves to buy his jersey. He knew he was cute, too, but he was so fucking nice it offset any potential annoyance. He'd had a strong start to his rookie season, earning a spot on the third line.

Oliver was never seen without Onni. They were a bit of an unlikely duo–Oliver's loud, vibrant personality and charisma couldn't be more different from Onni's stoic quiet.

Onni had the kind of build that guys in the league spent years trying to achieve. Being six-three helped, sure, but he had wide shoulders and thighs that could crush a coconut between them. He had white-blonde hair that he wore buzzed close to his head, and, when he smiled, he revealed a small gap between his two front teeth. He was coming in as their backup goalie, but everyone knew Anders was approaching the end of his career. A lot of hope rode on Onni panning out to be a beast in net.

The two young guys hadn't hesitated to help when Jamie had asked them. Ollie looked like all the kids nowadays–joggers, a black hoodie, and a canvas coat that looked like it was intended for someone who worked on a farm instead of a fashion statement. Onni was a bit more refined in a green fleece and brown beanie.

They dutifully followed Jamie's moms out onto the porch. It was cold, and a bitter, slicing wind cut through Jamie's own down coat, but at least some of the snow had melted.

Jamie watched the old Subaru pull up beside the curb. The small trailer behind it had a cheerful, rainbow-colored representation of a beach on the side. *Charleston, South Carolina,* it said.

The driver's door opened, and Tyler climbed out. He didn't seem to notice them, rushing around to the backseat. After a moment, he emerged with Rowan in his arms.

Jamie couldn't look away.

It didn't make sense. None at all.

If he'd been walking down State Street and seen Tyler walk past, he wouldn't have spared him a second glance. Everything about him–the shaggy hair, the tattoos and nose piercing, his clothing–was the opposite of what Jamie was typically attracted to.

He'd always picked men who were meticulous in their appearance. Clean-shaven, classically handsome faces with square jaws and full mouths. Men with tailored clothing, office jobs, and strong opinions about wine pairings at dinner.

Tyler wasn't…He wasn't that.

He had a mullet, for fuck's sake.

Today, Tyler wore a mustard-yellow puffy coat that was much too big for his frame. It hung open, revealing the purple, washed-denim overalls underneath. A pale lavender beanie sat crooked on his head, and his hair was curlier than Jamie remembered it being.

Tyler was halfway up the front walk when he looked up. He froze, staring up at the assembled group on the porch.

"Um," Tyler began, adjusting Rowan on his hip. "Hi."

"Hello!" Dotty called out, waving.

His eyes lingered on Jamie. "What's going on?"

"We thought you could use a hand," Jamie's mom said. She pointed to the little door leading up to the attic apartment. "Those are some steep stairs."

Tyler surveyed their group, his dark brows knitting together. "Oh, that's really nice of you," he said, already backing up. "But I think we've got it." He said the words with finality.

Jamie watched him circle around the vehicle to the back of the trailer. He whispered something in Rowan's ear and then set him down on the curb. The toddler immediately began to cry, hands reaching up and grabbing at the hem of Tyler's coat.

Jamie started toward them, but his mom reached out and put a hand on his shoulder. "Let him," she whispered.

"Hang on, kiddo," he heard Tyler say, with a frantic edge to his voice. He fiddled with the trailer door. "We've got this, okay? Me and you, Row. Me and you."

Rowan's cries grew louder. The trailer opened, and from the porch Jamie could see a hodgepodge of boxes and furniture crammed into the small space. Tyler reached up, grabbed the end of what looked like a chest of drawers, and pulled.

It didn't move.

He tried again. Nothing.

Jamie felt a sharp pang in his chest. He watched the moment Tyler gave up, his whole body visibly deflating as he stood there by the trailer. He picked up Rowan, cradling the boy against him and murmuring softly.

Jamie wanted to look away, to tell everyone gathered on the porch to give Tyler some privacy. But then Tyler turned to them with a brittle, tight smile. "We'd appreciate the help," he said.

Jamie ached for him.

Onni and Ollie did most of the heavy lifting, while Jamie or his moms held doors open along the way. Jamie was relegated to carrying things he could hold with one hand–a potted orchid, a bag of stuffed animals, or a duffel over one shoulder.

His mom convinced Tyler to stay upstairs with Rowan so he could tell them where to put their things. There wasn't much–a bed, a wooden crib, a chest of drawers, a few cool baskets where they kept toys, and a folding card table. Two mismatched wooden chairs, a beanbag chair, and a worn loveseat couch rounded out the last of the furniture.

Dotty had gotten Rowan to play on the floor where they'd set up the toys, freeing Tyler up to start unpacking. He didn't go far, though, casting frequent glances over at his son.

Jamie set himself up in the kitchen, pulling dishes out of a box and setting them on the counter. Tyler joined him quietly, putting dishes up into the wooden cabinets.

Jamie was surprised when Tyler broke the silence. "Your moms are nice."

"They're amazing," Jamie said, smiling.

"How'd they meet?"

"They worked together for years," Jamie said. "They were close friends. As soon as my mom noticed her feelings changing, she went to my dad and told him." Jamie couldn't remember much about the days leading up to his parents' separation. He'd been thirteen and solely focused on hockey. Then one day, they'd sat him down, his mom had come out, and his dad had voiced his support for her. He could look back on it now and recall the hurt his dad had felt, but at the time, it felt amicable. "My parents sold our house and found new places," Jamie went on. "Mom and Dotty quietly dated for a long time before they were open about their relationship. During that time, my dad met someone, and they've been together since then. I've got a few younger half-siblings, too."

Tyler had stopped putting away dishes, and was leaning against the counter, listening intently to Jamie. The tattoo of the moth around his throat looked darker than usual.

"It was hard for my parents to break up, I think. To walk away from something certain–maybe not perfect, but reliable and safe. But life got better for both of them after my mom came out. My dad's second wife loves him to pieces. Mom found something beautiful with Dotty." Jamie shrugged, not entirely sure why he was sharing all of this with Tyler.

There was a wistful look on the younger man's face, like there was something about what Jamie said that spoke to him. Like maybe he understood.

Jamie wondered what his story was. Where he came from, how Rowan had come into his life. His gaze trailed down over the moth, over the tattooed hands. He wondered if the tattoos had their own stories too.

He wanted to know.

He was curious. Captivated.

Tyler was beautiful, Jamie realized. An other-worldly, inaccessible beauty, like a famous singer on a faraway stage.

Only Tyler wasn't far away. He was *right there,* in front of him, with a smidge of dust on his pale cheek.

The meal they shared was predictably loud and boisterous. Dotty had made her pot pie, which she served with roasted broccoli and a salad.

Jamie's mom had sat right next to Tyler, and within minutes she had Rowan giggling and bouncing on her knee. Tyler seemed to have relaxed slightly, a hesitant smile on his lips as he watched Rowan and fielded questions from Jamie's mom.

Dotty was a rabid Muskies fan, asking Ollie and Onni questions about their division opponents and what they were working on in practice. Jamie felt a fond warmth as he sat there with his family–his blood family and hockey family blending together, and now, the new addition of Tyler and Rowan.

"You went to school here?" His mom asked Tyler. When he nodded, she went on. "When did you graduate?"

"A little more than three years ago."

"And Rowan's mom?" Dotty asked.

Jamie watched Tyler's face carefully. If he hadn't, he would have missed the way his lips pressed together for a second before he responded. "She was a friend from school. She decided she wasn't ready to raise a kid, and is off living her life." Tyler paused, and his expression softened as he looked at Rowan. "I wouldn't change it for anything. Having him."

Jamie tried to imagine what it must be like for Tyler, parenting on his own. Every time Jamie had imagined being a father, it had been with someone he'd chosen by his side. Someone he loved and trusted.

He couldn't imagine doing it any other way.

"Is it nice coming back to see your friends?" His mom went on.

Tyler hesitated before responding. "Yeah," he said slowly. "It's good."

"Do any of them have kids?"

"No."

Jamie's mom looked sympathetic. "That can be hard," she offered. "Not knowing people who have children. When Jamie was little, I spent a ton of time at the library. It was a good place to meet other young parents."

Tyler tried to tuck a piece of hair behind his ear, but it slipped right back down onto his face. "I…the library is a good idea. I haven't had time, I guess."

His mom looked over at Jamie then, her blonde brows raised in a silent question. It was obvious she was trying to tell him something, but Jamie couldn't figure out what. He mirrored the same look back at her. She sniffed, looking unimpressed.

"Many of the players on Jamie's team have young families," his mom said, and…*Right*. Jamie got it now.

"My best friend Mitch," Jamie jumped in. "The guy who was with me when we came by your place? He's got three kids, and his wife, Layla, is awesome." He caught his mom's encouraging nod. "I go to dinner at their house most weeks when we're playing in town. Would you and Rowan want to come with me? It could be cool to meet some people with kids."

Tyler stared at him. His mouth opened, then shut. His eyes shifted to Rowan, and then back to Jamie. "Um," he said.

"They're great," Jamie went on. "Their kids are great."

Without breaking eye contact with Jamie, Tyler reached out and brushed a knuckle over Rowan's cheek. "Okay," he said quietly.

The rest of the meal went quickly. Rowan started rubbing his eyes, and Tyler excused himself and Rowan to go upstairs. He thanked them all for the meal and the help with the move, and then, with a hint of hesitation, looked over at Jamie.

"Will you text me?" he asked. "About the dinner."

Jamie smiled. "Yeah. I promise."

What he got back was just the shadow of a smile, but still, it was something.

CHAPTER 6
TYLER
THIS IS A KID HOUSE

"Where are we going, Papa?"

Tyler adjusted his hands on the worn leather of his steering wheel as he turned onto Campus Drive. The afternoon light was just starting to fade, gray clouds hanging low over downtown Madison. "Remember those hockey guys who came over to say hi the other morning?"

"The big ones?"

"Yeah, them," Tyler bit back a smile, thinking of how ridiculous the two massive strangers had looked in the chaos of the boarding house. "We're going to Mitch's house to have dinner with his kids."

"Will Jamie be there?"

"Mmhm."

"Is Jamie our friend?"

Tyler had to think about his answer for a moment. He hadn't had to navigate new friendships with Rowan yet. There had been his family, and then the old acquaintances and friends in the boarding house.

This was different. Jamie was different.

Who was Jamie to them?

Jamie, who had handed him a paper towel to wipe the banana

from his face the very first time they'd met. Who had shown up with an injured hand and helped them move into their new place. Who looked at Tyler like he was trying to understand him.

"I hope so," Tyler finally responded.

They'd been living in the attic apartment for four days, and Tyler had felt himself slowly relax into their new, improved space. It was quiet, spacious, and Rowan even had his own room. Tyler was able to cook without guarding their plates of food. If dishes piled up in the sink, he had no one to blame but himself.

He'd been worried the first time he left Rowan with Sandra and Dotty for his morning shift at the coffee shop. His eyes had burned when he'd left a crying and confused Rowan with the sweet women, and he'd almost called in sick to work.

But then, as he was walking through the back door of The Daily Grind, he'd gotten a text from Sandra.

SANDRA:

He's doing great. In case no one else tells you today, you're a wonderful father.

She'd sent a picture of Rowan smiling as he played with blocks on the floor. The relief Tyler felt had made his knees weak. None of the parenting books he'd read in the months leading up to Rowan's birth had prepared him for the overwhelming love and terror he felt on behalf of his son. And now, to know that Rowan was okay, that Tyler hadn't completely broken him by leaving—*that* was priceless.

He thought about the community he'd hoped to find with his college friends. He never would have guessed that he'd find what he'd been looking for in two sweet, older women who had opened their lives to Tyler and Rowan. He knew he wouldn't be able to rely on their generosity forever, but for the moment, it was saving him.

He still wasn't sure what the hell he'd been thinking when he agreed to this–having dinner at the home of a professional hockey player. He probably had nothing in common with these people.

But he wanted to meet more people with families. He wanted to give Rowan the chance to play with other kids.

And maybe there was something about Jamie that had compelled Tyler to say yes. Maybe it was the way his hazel-green eyes crinkled in the corners when he smiled.

"This'll be fun," Tyler said, glancing back at Rowan in the rearview mirror. His son was fully occupied with Bunny, making the sloth's arms wag from side to side as he sang quietly under his breath.

The words were as much for himself as they were for Rowan.

As he pulled into the long driveway of the Radio Park home, Tyler realized he was *nervous*. With the exception of surface-level conversations with other parents at the park, this would be his and Rowan's first time socializing with another family.

Tyler would be fine. He always was. But Rowan? *Fuck*, he wanted it to go well for him.

Tyler parked beside a newer pickup truck, and made quick work of getting Rowan unstrapped from his carseat, Bunny held tightly in his little arms. He made sure Rowan's wool beanie covered his ears, grabbed the backpack full of toddler emergency supplies he took everywhere now, and carefully walked up the sanded walk to the front door.

The house was big–an older home with deep green siding offset by a stone wall. Tall windows shone golden in the evening light, and he could make out the shapes of well-manicured shrubs along the far side of the snow-covered lawn.

Damn, hockey players must make good money.

Tyler felt Rowan's hand tighten on the collar of the thick wool sweater he'd spent way too much time picking out. He wanted something nice that wouldn't sacrifice his personal style, pairing the sweater with jeans, a single stone pendant necklace, and three silver rings.

"Stay close, Papa?"

He kissed Rowan's cold cheek, a fullness in his chest as he

inhaled the soft scent of the mild, herbal soap he used to wash Rowan's brown curls. "Always, kiddo."

They'd barely reached the front stoop when the door opened, revealing a tall blonde woman with pale pink cheeks, wearing a fuzzy white sweater and wide-legged jeans.

"Hey! Tyler and Rowan, right?" Her voice was warm, a perfect compliment to her girl-next-door beauty. "I'm Layla, Mitch's wife. Come on in and let's get those coats off."

Tyler didn't get a chance to take in the entryway beyond the golden light and the comfortable warmth of the air around them. Wordlessly, he let Layla take his battered, yellow down coat. She gave them space while Tyler crouched down to help Rowan out of his coat and hat, like she instinctively knew a little kid in a new place would need some time to adjust.

Rowan let Tyler tug off his snow boots, clinging to Tyler's faded jeans as he nudged off his Doc Martens. Carefully, Tyler lined their shoes up with the haphazard row of others in varying sizes.

"Can I get either of you something to drink? Dinner is ready, so as soon as the kids get washed up we can sit down. Mitch," she called out as they followed her into the modern, high-ceilinged kitchen. Rowan held tightly to Tyler's hand, his other arm holding Bunny against his chest. "They're here!"

Footsteps thundered below them, and grew louder. "Slow down, you wildebeests," a deep male voice shouted. A chorus of giggles filtered up in response.

A door on the other side of the room slammed open and three kids skidded to a stop next to Layla. The smallest reached her arms up, and Layla swooped her into her arms, settling her on one of her slender hips. "This is Tyler and his kiddo, Rowan. Can you all say hello?"

"Greetings, people who are new in our home!" The tallest one had her black hair in two perfectly symmetrical fuzzy puffs on the sides of her head. She had her mom's height, Mitch's bronze skin and eyes that squinted when she smiled, and wore a rainbow hoodie and matching leggings. "I'm Henri. I'm the oldest. If Rowan would like to play with us, I'll make sure he's safe."

"She's a really good lifeguard," the little boy standing beside her said, a grave expression on his face, which was a lighter brown than his sister. "When we play construction site, she's always the foreman." The dark brown ringlets that hung down to his ears bounced as he looked up at his mom. "Forewoman, mama? Is that right?"

Layla seemed to consider the question. "Forewoman sounds good to me, Jack."

The little boy nodded.

"Do you want to introduce yourself?" Layla whispered loudly to the kid in her arms. Tyler could hear the colorful plastic beads at the end of shoulder-length box braids click as the little girl shook her head. "This is Stef. She takes a minute to warm up." Glancing back, she shouted again. "Boys, get your booties upstairs or you can eat canned food with the cats!" Turning back to Tyler, she rolled her eyes. "Honestly, the two of them are like kids."

Heavier footsteps, and then two big, now-familiar men came through the same doorway. Mitch was dressed down in a black sweatshirt and green, team-branded joggers. He made for his wife, wrapping his arms around her from behind and turning her face to kiss her.

Tyler averted his eyes–not because he had any problem watching people kiss, but because this house, this family, the warm, domesticity that surrounded him, felt like a knife wedged between his ribs.

It was exactly what he'd longed for, what he was hoping to create in their sweet attic apartment. It was what Rowan deserved more than anything in the world.

"Tyler."

His eyes followed the low voice. There was Jamie, right there, standing at the edge of the group like he wasn't sure where to go. His hands were shoved into the pockets of a pair of dark jeans, and an off-white dress shirt with the sleeves rolled up was clinging to those big, broad shoulders. Even his hair was tamed, blonde curls pushed back from his face, and his mustache was neat and trimmed.

Effort. He looked like he'd put real effort into looking nice.

"Hi, Jamie," he said, the words coming out as a question.

"Hello again, Tyler," Mitch said. "Glad you made it for a visit, Rowan."

Rowan buried his face deeper into Tyler's shoulder.

"Wash hands, and then we eat." Layla said, clapping her hands together. "Mitch, make sure they use soap."

There was a flurry of activity then. Tyler didn't have time to feel out of place or uncertain before Layla came up beside him, explaining the meal.

"So we've got beef sauce with tons of sneaky veggies," she said, pointing to a large pot on the stove. "I think this batch has zucchini, carrots, spinach, and beet greens in it. Then there's penne pasta, some roasted broccoli and cauliflower, and I have some pear sliced up for the kids." She placed a gentle hand on Tyler's wrist. "If there's anything you need for Rowan, whatever he needs to have a complete meal, don't hesitate to ask. This is a kid house, and the most important thing is that the two of you feel welcome here."

"It looks amazing," Tyler said, and he meant it. It was the kind of thing he'd make at home, and finding a meal like this out in the world sent such a visceral wave of relief through him he felt his eyes burn. Being somewhere with people who had kids, who *thought* about what was convenient and nourishing, Tyler realized how much he'd missed this since leaving home.

"I set up a booster seat next to your spot," Layla went on.

As Tyler grabbed a plate, he felt someone slide up beside him. "Here," Jamie's voice was quiet. "Hand me Rowan's plate. You've got your hands full."

Tyler caught Jamie's fond, soft smile as he looked down at

them. "Thank you," he said, worried that he might actually start to cry.

Jamie followed Tyler's instructions, listening to Rowan's quiet request of "One more, please," when it came to adding the slices of pear to his plate. He carried the plate over to the table, placing it on the colorful plastic mat between two empty chairs. When he came back to the kitchen, he offered Tyler another one of those hesitant, gentle smiles. "You're up next, Ty." His eyes widened, *so* green in the bright kitchen, and a blush darkened his cheeks. "Sorry, I mean, Tyler."

He watched Jamie closely as he served his plate. With Rowan tucked in his arms and the voices of a loud, loving family surrounding them, Tyler felt himself wonder, imagination adrift, if their lives were about to change for the better.

Dinner had been full of loud conversation and laughter. When the kids got restless, Layla got up and wandered into the open living room, pulling a plastic tote out to the center of the room. "Henri, want to help get the tracks set up?"

Mitch could barely wipe the three siblings' hands and faces before they raced over to the box of wooden tracks, bridges, buildings, and trains. Rowan watched them carefully from his booster seat.

"Papa," he whispered.

"Yeah, kiddo?"

"Can I go play with them?"

Tyler felt his heart melt. "Of course. I think they'd love to play with you."

His son's blue eyes looked up at him. "And you'll be right here?"

"I'll be right here," Tyler echoed, planting a soft kiss on Rowan's forehead.

He watched, emotions tangling in his chest, as Rowan walked

hesitantly over to where the other kids were setting up an elaborate, interconnected track. Henri handed him a curved piece, and, with Bunny in one hand and the track in the other, the rest of the world seemed to fade away.

Leaning back in his chair, Tyler let out a relieved sigh.

"You okay?" Layla asked from across the table.

Tyler nodded, reaching up to run his hands through his hair. "This is his first time doing something like this. Playing with other kids in their house. It's…it's amazing."

Her smile was kind. "We'll have to do this more often, then." She reached out to Mitch, who sat beside her, interlacing their fingers and sharing a smile.

Jamie shifted in the chair next to him, bracing his furry forearms on the table and leaning toward the other couple. "Is there dessert for the grownups?" He whispered.

Layla laughed, nodding toward the kitchen. "Top shelf of the pantry."

A gleeful grin split across Jamie's face, giving Tyler a glimpse of the missing molar near the back of his mouth. He turned to Tyler. "Want something sweet?"

Tyler shook his head, unable to hide his amusement.

Jamie returned a moment later with his cheeks bulging, that same innocent joy still making his green eyes dance.

"So," Mitch said, leveling a look across the table. "You settled in with Dotty and Sandra?"

"Yeah. They've been great."

"They're the best," Layla said, taking a sip of her white wine. "Even if they constantly badger Sully about giving them grandkids." She shot Jamie an apologetic smile across the table. "I'm all for having kids if you want them, but getting nagged about it all the time really does get old."

Tyler looked at Jamie in time to see him shrug, still chewing a mouthful of something.

"So this hockey thing," Tyler started. "It's a big deal here?"

Layla burst out laughing. Mitch buried his face in his hands. Jamie's brows shot up.

"You're my new favorite person," Layla said, still laughing. "See, Sully? Not everyone in this town cares that you broke your hand starting a fight you had no chance of winning."

"So, I take it you don't follow professional hockey?" Mitch asked.

"Nah," Tyler said. "I knew people who played back in Vermont, but I've never really been into sports."

Mitch nodded in understanding. "Well, the team here is a pretty big deal. We won the Cup six years ago."

"The cup?"

Jamie let out a sound like a wounded animal. "He doesn't know what the Cup is!"

"What?" Tyler started laughing too, unable to help himself when Layla's bright, loud laughs filled the air around them.

"The Cup is *the* trophy in hockey. It's the ultimate prize for the best team in the professional league." Mitch explained. "Wait, but now I'm confused. Why did you make a snowman wearing one of his jerseys, then?"

Tyler frowned, thinking back to the night he'd first met Jamie. He remembered the brightly-colored sports jersey they'd put on the snowman. *Oh no*. "That was yours?" He turned to Jamie.

Jamie's cheeks were pink. "Yep. That's me. Sullivan, number three, worst captain in Muskies history."

Mitch and Layla both jumped in to protest, reassuring Jamie that he was just adjusting, that his play wasn't that bad. Tyler barely listened to them, instead watching Jamie's face.

He could almost see the burden of responsibility heavy on his broad, slumped shoulders. If the pained pinch of his blonde brows and the soft frown on his face were any indication of what the man was thinking, it looked like this weighed on him.

Maybe the anger Tyler had so quickly brushed off as a drunk stranger losing control was actually pain and disappointment directed at himself.

"What's the deal with the fish?" Tyler asked, wanting to steer the conversation away from Jamie's obvious discomfort.

"We're going to let Sully take this one," Mitch said, grinning across the table.

Tyler looked to Jamie for an explanation. He rolled his eyes, letting out a loud sigh. "It took me about three years of being on the team before I could pronounce the full name." He pulled out his phone, scooting closer to Tyler's chair. "Here, check this out."

A hard thigh pressed against his leg for a second, only to quickly retreat. Tyler sat there, in a bit of a daze, as Jamie's body heat warmed his left side. His breaths were shallow in his chest, every part of him hyperaware of the man sitting next to him.

Physical intimacy had always been easy for Tyler, a way to form connections with other humans. Before Rowan, he had regularly found himself in the arms of strangers–dancing during concerts, or sharing kisses or touches without a second thought.

Now, with Jamie beside him, he was hesitant. Nervous, even.

He looked down at Jamie's phone. There was a picture of a man holding a fish that had to be at least four feet long. "Holy shit," Tyler whispered.

Jamie let out a soft, gentle laugh that had absolutely no place coming from a man Jamie's size. "Muskie is short for muskellunge. It's the largest member of the pike family, found in freshwater lakes in the Northern U.S."

Tyler couldn't help the grin that spread. "That is a mouthful."

Jamie's smile grew. It was an overly large smile, one nobody in their right mind would classify as attractive. But on this man, on his particular face, Tyler thought it was beautiful.

Jamie's eyes lifted at that moment, catching Tyler's stare. It was a quiet moment, nothing remarkable about it except for the way Tyler's entire body stilled, waiting, anticipating *something*.

He couldn't breathe.

There was nothing but *green* and *moss* and *that fucking mustache.* Nothing but *god I think I want something, someone just for me, for the first time since becoming a father.*

"You guys should come check out a game sometime." Mitch's voice rang out, too loud across the table. Tyler glanced over, catching the pleased smiles on his and Layla's faces.

He felt Jamie shift beside him, felt the slide of his arm across his back as he scooted his chair away. The room felt colder now, and Tyler had to suppress a shiver.

"I, um." Jamie cleared his throat. "I'd be happy to get you some tickets."

"You don't have to," Tyler rushed to say. He didn't want Jamie doing things out of obligation.

"We get tickets for family and friends all the time," Jamie said, and there was a glimpse of that smile again. "Think about it?"

Tyler opened his mouth to respond.

"Papa!" Rowan jogged over to the table. "Potty?"

"Down the hall on the left," Layla said, pointing.

Tyler ushered Rowan down the hall, helping him use the step stool conveniently positioned by the toilet. As they washed his tiny hands, Rowan looked up at him. "These kids are good at playing."

Tyler smiled at his son. "I'm so glad to hear it, bud."

"Are *you* having fun, Papa?"

"I am," he replied, and he realized, meeting his son's trusting, brave, blue eyes in the mirror, that it was the truth.

CHAPTER 7
JAMIE
THE PEOPLE'S CAPTAIN

The Daily Grind was busy, a winding line filling the front of the coffee shop. Jamie let the door close behind him, scanning the room. The team was on the road–a short trip down to play St. Louis–and while Jamie had begged to go, he'd been reminded that he had an appointment with a local specialist the team doctors had found. After doing his rehab on his hand and getting some cardio in at the practice rink, Jamie had gotten tired of pacing his house.

It was easy to pick Aaron Sharpe out of the crowd. He was as tall as Jamie, with dark brown hair he'd grown out since his retirement. It was long enough that sometimes, like now, he pulled it back in a little bun at the back of his head. *Stupid bastard could pull anything off and still look good.*

"Look here," he said when he saw Jamie, his Québécois accent still as strong as ever. "It is my son all grown up." He pulled Jamie into a hug, clapping his back with a big, warm hand. "I see you are still experimenting with this mustache?"

Jamie shoved Sharpie away, shaking his head even as he smiled. "Good to see you, old man."

Sharpie grinned and joined the end of the line. "So, this is where the cool kids are getting their coffee these days?"

"Matty recommended it."

"He is playing well," Sharpie said, gazing up at the menu, which was neatly printed on chalkboards hanging from the ceiling. "All of you are."

Jamie scoffed.

Sharpie turned to him, looking at Jamie in the same calculating way he always had. It was a look Jamie swore could see right through his skin. "We will deal with you later," he said finally, returning his attention to the board. "What are you getting? Wait." He held up a hand. "Let me guess. Hot chocolate with some fancy drizzle on top, yes?"

Jamie scowled, but didn't argue.

There was a gap in the line, and Jamie's breath hitched.

There, behind the counter, was Tyler.

Jamie had thought about him, caught himself imagining his competent, slender hands, his tattooed thighs, that *fucking throat*...

And now he looked–*fuck*, he looked beautiful.

He wore a sheer black top that plunged down to his sternum. A cardigan sweater in a patchwork of colors hung from his shoulders. And then there, on his chest, the distinct round bumps of nipple piercings.

It hit him then, like hunger pains in the morning after a game–*Tyler* was what he wanted.

The timing of it all was terrible. Inconvenient.

But *fuck*. Just...Fuck.

Tyler was affectionate with his customers, reaching a hand out to brush a wrist, winking at a red-haired woman when he handed her her coffee. As they got closer to the counter, Jamie started to overhear their conversation.

"If you like a dark roast then I recommend the Midtown," Tyler said to a younger woman in a denim jacket, leaning her elbows on the counter. "It's got a real full-body flavor I think you'll enjoy."

Jamie's jaw throbbed. He hadn't realized he was clenching his teeth, and tried to force himself to relax. They'd reached the front of the line, and his hands itched at his sides. He wasn't sure what he wanted to do with them. Touch Tyler? Grab his hips and give his mouth something to do that wasn't flirting with every single customer?

Calm the fuck down, Sully.

Tyler's brows shot up when he saw Jamie. "Oh, hey," he said, something uncertain in his voice.

"Hi."

Beside him, Sharpie cleared his throat loudly and bumped him with his shoulder.

"This is Sharpie." Jamie pointed his thumb at the man next to him. "Aaron. Aaron Sharpe. My captain. I mean, the last captain." Jamie laughed then, the sound panicked and way too high-pitched to be natural. *Jesus, man.* "He's the people's captain."

Sharpie stared at him like he'd lost his mind.

Tyler cleared his throat. "Nice to meet you," he said quietly. "What can I get started for you guys?"

"Americano for me," Sharpie said, going for his wallet.

"I'll take a mocha," Jamie said, feeling his face heat.

Tyler's fingers flew over the tablet. "Do you want the seasonal crumble topping?"

"No, thank you."

"He is lying," Sharpie said, exasperated. "Give him twice the normal amount, and then his sweet tooth might be happy."

"Seriously?" Jamie turned to Sharpie, indignant.

Sharpie looked completely unfazed. "What, I am wrong?"

Jamie heaved a sigh. He'd forgotten what a pain in the ass his old captain was. Turning back to Tyler, he offered him a smile. "The topping would be great," he admitted.

"He likes that too," Sharpie went on. "Topping."

"What the fuck?" Jamie hissed, feeling his face and ears burn.

Sharpie just shrugged, looking pleased with himself.

Tyler looked like he was trying to hide his own amusement as he looked alternately at the two men. "That'll be twelve eighty-five."

"I should make you pay," Sharpie muttered as he handed over his card. "You're the one making big money now."

"You've made more in your career than I'll ever see in my bank account," Jamie shot back.

He looked at Tyler, wanting to say something. He wasn't ready to walk away from him. Not yet. "You look nice," he said, immediately wishing he could take the words back. Not because he regretted saying them, but because Tyler looked so much better than *nice*. There were so many words that would do a better job of describing how Tyler looked to Jamie then. *Beautiful. Breathtaking.*

Tyler stared at him. "Um, thank you."

Jamie felt Sharpie's hand on his arm guiding him away. "If I let you stay there any longer, I am afraid of what you will say to that poor, pretty man."

They found an empty table, and Jamie sat down, burying his face in his hands. "Oh my god," he groaned.

"That was bad."

"I know."

"Have you always been shit at flirting?"

"I wasn't flirting."

"Okay," Sharpie said, like he didn't believe him. "But you know him, yes?"

Jamie glared at his captain, but then told him the whole story. He told him about the game and the fight and the shots and the snowman, how he'd hoped it was wearing a Sharpie jersey, only to find his own name on the back. About the ER and the hangover, about the tattooed dad and the adorable kid living in chaos.

"Now he and his son live with my moms." He finished.

"You like him." Sharpie's expression was amused. "Ask him on a date."

Jamie looked up at that. "I can't do that."

"Why? Are you worried about what people will say about you being gay?"

"No, it's not that." He'd been out for years, and other than the occasional comment online, people seemed to forget about Jamie's sexual orientation. He'd had boyfriends here and there over the years, but he hadn't found someone who would stick around through the madness of the season. "I don't have time to date anyone."

Sharpie frowned at him. "Explain."

"Drinks for The People's Captain!"

Sharpie let out a barking laugh. Jamie groaned, dragging his hands over his eyes. "Kill me," he muttered, feeling the heat of embarrassment climb up the sides of his neck.

As Sharpie walked over to get their drinks, Jamie took a chance and glanced over his shoulder at the counter. Almost like he could feel Jamie's eyes, Tyler looked up from where he was busy making another drink.

He flashed Jamie a smile, a teasing, amused smile, and Jamie *knew* he was seeing something rare and precious, that Tyler didn't let just anyone catch a glimpse of his dimples.

Sharpie slid a mug across the table. It looked incredible, the swirl of whipped cream dotted with crumbles of cookies and drizzled chocolate. Jamie took a sip, groaning at the rich sweetness on his tongue.

"I want to tell you this is disgusting, but you get very cute, like a big blonde baby, whenever you eat a sweet treat." Sharpie waved a hand in front of him. "Now tell me again why you cannot have a boyfriend."

There was no point in responding to the first comment. "I have no time during the season," Jamie said, running a hand through his curls. "Between the practices and travel, I don't have the time to give someone what they deserve."

Sharpie took a sip from his own drink. "This is bullshit," he said, looking right at Jamie. "We are home for lunches, for long mornings, and sleeping. We go home after practice. We are busy, but we are around. When I was captain, yes, there were many demands on my time. Yes, it was hard for my family. But the minutes I was home added up, and having important people who waited for me, who needed me for something other than scoring goals? I think it saved me." He reached across the table and put a hand on Jamie's shoulder. "It is good to remember there is a world outside of hockey. More important than that, *you* are a person outside of hockey."

Jamie dropped his head. "Before my hand," he started. "I was giving hockey everything. More time, more training, more effort than ever."

"Why? You are very good already."

"But I'm the captain now!" Jamie exhaled, frustrated. "I need to be better."

"You need to be Sullivan–number three, good on the forecheck, very stubborn, silly mustache, bad taste in music, pastry man. The boys love you, just the way you are. That is who the team needs." Sharpie leaned back in his chair, crossing his arms over his chest. "Now tell me what Coach is saying about the power play. It is looking…iffy."

They talked about hockey for a while. Jamie missed Sharpie. He'd always valued his direct commentary and eye for the game. They laughed about Emīls, their fourth liner fresh from Sweden, who still got lost in the stadium. Olaf Sandersson, one of their assistant coaches, had started driving him to games and walking him to the locker room.

It was easy to talk to Sharpie. There was an unspoken understanding of the pressure that came with a captaincy. The way people looked to him for answers when the team struggled. The way his play was under a microscope.

But Sharpie had always worn the pressure well. He'd been a steady, sure presence for years. He'd put up consistent points. Won awards. And when he'd been the first of the Muskies to hoist the cup, the world had sung his praises.

They'd long finished their drinks when Sharpie said he needed to head out. "You take the dishes. Maybe you will get the chance to say something *nice* to the pretty man." He shot Jamie a grin. "Maybe he believes in giving second chances to big boys with silly mustaches."

"Asshole," Jamie muttered fondly, but still accepted the offered hug from his old friend.

"You will find it," Sharpie said softly. "You will figure it out, yes?"

Jamie nodded, overwhelmed with gratitude as Sharpie walked away. Grabbing both of their mugs, he walked up to the counter.

Tyler straightened as Jamie approached. "Hey," he said, pausing where he was wiping down the counter.

"It was great," Jamie said, setting the mugs down carefully. "The mocha. Really tasty."

Tyler smiled. "I'm glad to hear it."

A woman with at least ten different facial piercings came up to Tyler and bumped him with her hip. "Take your break. It's slowing down and I'll be fine up here."

Tyler glanced over at her. "You sure?"

She looked pointedly at Jamie before looking back at Tyler like he'd lost his mind. "I'm sure."

Jamie watched as Tyler worked his lip with his teeth. "Um, you probably have somewhere to be," Tyler muttered. "I usually just sit and chill for fifteen minutes." He waved a hand toward the tables.

"I've got nowhere to be," Jamie said, a little kernel of something blooming in his chest. "If you don't mind the company?"

Tyler stared at him. It was a calculating look, like he was trying to figure out what Jamie's angle was. "If you want," he finally said. "I'm going to make myself a drink real quick."

Jamie stood there, hands shoved into his pockets, as Tyler made himself a drink. His hands moved quickly, decisively, and Jamie had the offhanded thought that Tyler could be a savvy stickhandler with hands like that.

The coffee shop was loud, full of the low rumble of voices layering on top of each other. But the hum of conversation faded as soon Tyler walked out from behind the counter.

What Jamie'd thought was a blouse was actually the top of a

short silk dress that barely reached Tyler's mid-thigh. Below that, black fishnets encased his tattooed legs.

A sound slipped from Jamie, something a little bit broken and completely out of his control.

"Come on," Tyler said, walking toward the back of the building like Jamie wasn't on the verge of keeling over.

Jamie willed his legs to move, following Tyler around the tables to a round booth in the back corner of the coffee shop. Jamie noticed he still wore the black Doc Martens that he favored. His eyes traced up slender ankles, calf muscles and knees covered in fine dark hair.

Oh.

Jamie was fucked. Completely, and utterly, fucked.

They sat down at an empty table along one of the walls, and Jamie watched Tyler closely. He cupped his mug in both hands, blowing gently over the surface of the green drink. Jamie had shared a locker room with plenty of men who had tattoos, but he had never been presented with the opportunity to openly look at someone who was as covered with ink as Tyler.

"Did they hurt?" He asked.

"The tats?"

Jamie nodded.

"Yeah. But it's a good kind of hurt. When you sign up for pain, there's something heady about it."

Jamie thought of bag skates and summer training sessions when he'd pushed his body to the brink. When his quads trembled, spasming, and he still had to push through for five more reps.

He knew a little something about that kind of pain.

"Maybe I should try it," he offered.

Something sparked in Tyler's eyes, and he leaned forward, bracing his elbows on the table. "What would you get?"

Jamie considered the question. "The obvious answer would be something to do with hockey." He chuckled at Tyler's unimpressed look. "What? I really do love it. I know it's a cliché, but I fucking love hockey. It's my favorite thing in the world."

A little smile played on Tyler's lips. "I admire that," he said softly. "I think it takes a lot of courage to love something like that. To go all in without constantly keeping an eye on the exit."

"Do you love anything like that?"

Tyler's long fingers spun his mug in a slow, careful circle. "Rowan, but that's different. Loving a child isn't a choice, really. Loving him is the same as breathing or waking up. It's a part of me." He frowned, shaking his head. "Before I had Rowan, I used to write poetry. I had a wild life, lots of partying and live music and loud friends and sex, and I tried to put words to my life. At that time, I loved it."

Poetry?

Jamie remembered struggling through sonnets and Shakespeare in high school, and a poem by Mary Oliver about geese. But other than that, outside of the endless rhyming children's books he'd read to teammates' kids over the years, he didn't know a damn thing about poetry.

"Are your poems out there in the world?"

"Nah. It was just something I did for myself."

"That's so cool."

Brown eyes blinked at him, thick, heavy lashes casting a shadow on his pale skin. "It was a different time in my life. Everything is different now."

"So, do you still write?"

Tyler's eyes sharpened, and the laugh that fell from his mouth was harsh. "There's no time for the things that used to inspire me. Everything I wrote was inspired by hookups in tents at music festivals and being high under the stars. I don't miss that life–not at all–but without those things I don't know what the hell to write." His throat bobbed as he swallowed. "And I miss the writing. That, out of everything, is what I miss."

The statement echoed between them.

Jamie opened his mouth. Closed it. Pressed his lips together, unsure how to respond.

He watched as Tyler's expression shuttered. Eyes still open, still looking right at him, but the window of light peeking through them had closed.

Wait, Jamie wanted to say. *Don't go yet.*

He wanted more of Tyler. More admissions and more sincerity and more of those teasing grins.

"Have you thought about the hockey tickets?" Jamie asked, not wanting their conversation to end. "There's a game on Saturday night."

Tyler looked down, sipping at his drink. He set the mug down, and there was a thin line of pale green foam tracing the curve of his upper lip. "Sure," he said. "That's really generous of you to offer them."

Jamie's tongue slipped from his mouth, tracing his own lips subconsciously. Belatedly, he realized it was his turn to talk. *That's generally how conversations work, Jamie.* "Of course. Yeah. It's no big deal. If you want to go, I can text you the tickets. And there's parking nearby so you won't have to walk too far."

"Will you be playing?"

"No." Jamie held up his braced wrist. "Not for a few more weeks."

He thought maybe Tyler looked disappointed.

"I'll text you," Jamie went on. "The details. For the tickets."

Tyler grabbed his mug and flashed a quick, crooked smile at him. "Thanks for the company," he said, and then Jamie watched him go back to work. Watched him smile and laugh with the baristas behind the counter, watched him put the mug away in the dish bin until he finally decided he should leave.

As Jamie walked out the door, he thought about what Sharpie had said.

You are a person outside of hockey.

CHAPTER 8
TYLER
THE STEADY, UNYIELDING SHORE

"Come on, Row. Let's get your coat on."

Tyler was exhausted. Rowan had been waking up in the middle of the night and struggling to go back down. The endless loop of trying different things–night lights and chamomile tea and stories and even a spray bottle of water he'd taken to calling "monster spray"–was wearing Tyler down. None of it was working.

The last thing he wanted to do was leave the house.

When Jamie had originally offered the tickets at Mitch and Layla's house, Tyler hadn't taken him seriously. But then Jamie had shown up at The Daily Grind with his serious, handsome face and ordered the sweetest thing on the menu.

It had been unexpectedly nice, spending his break with the hockey player. There was an edge to their conversations, like they were both feeling the other out, searching for something before they shared too much.

Tyler hadn't meant to say what he had about writing. About poetry. Nothing about Jamie had indicated that he was the kind of man who understood the ache of losing a creative practice.

And yet, Tyler had opened his mouth, letting those vulnerable words fall between them, and Jamie had listened. He'd watched

Tyler intently, and behind the concentrated frown there was a softness that promised gentle understanding.

It was too much, having that kind of ease and chemistry with someone so unexpected. Tyler had retreated, terrified by the ease he felt in Jamie's presence. There wasn't time for him to indulge in fantasies. There wasn't time to imagine *what ifs*.

He needed to focus on finding another job, something that paid better than delivering groceries. He was trying to make it work, but no toddler could tolerate going between a car seat and a grocery cart for hours on end. No amount of Bob Marley or toys could curb the meltdowns that typically started about an hour into his two to three hour shifts.

He needed to find a long-term childcare solution. He needed to update their health insurance. He needed to find time to sew a patch onto Rowan's pants that had ripped at the knee.

Tonight, he was going to take his son to a hockey game, because their landlords' son–who Tyler definitely *hadn't* been thinking about non-stop–had been kind enough to give them free tickets.

That was all.

Half an hour later, Tyler used the pass Jamie had included with their tickets to park in a garage near Culver's Arena. There was heavy traffic, but eventually they had parked and joined the flood of people walking toward the arena.

Rowan was already whining and wriggling in Tyler's arms, but was also too nervous to walk with the throngs of people around them.

This was Rowan's dinner time, so they'd have to make do with the snacks they'd packed from home in the stands. Tyler's backpack was stocked with some fresh fruit, a bag of cherry tomatoes, and some sliced sausage.

Everyone was decked out in orange, green, and white. Beanies and scarves and hockey jerseys worn on top of hoodies. It was loud, an air of excitement making the night feel warmer than it actually was.

"No outside food or liquids," the older woman working the entrance informed Tyler, his backpack open on the table in front of her. "You can either throw them away or take them back to your vehicle, sir."

"Papa, where's Jamie?"

Tyler shifted Rowan on his hip, the sound of the crowd around them pressing in on him.

"This is my son's dinner," Tyler said, trying to keep his voice level.

The woman shrugged. "I don't blame you for wanting to bring something for your kid, but the rules are the rules."

Tyler closed his eyes for just a moment, forcing out a breath. "Throw it out, then," he said, trying for a smile. "It was my fault for not knowing."

Rowan was fussing and fidgeting by the time they found their seats. They were close to the ice, a few rows back from the clear glass that circled the edge of the rink. Fans wearing jerseys sat on either side of them, talking animatedly with their friends and well on their way to finishing large cups of beer.

He'd put orange noise-canceling headphones over Rowan's beanie as soon as they'd entered the arena. His son's eyes were huge as he stared around them, and Tyler was struck by the fact that this was probably the most people Rowan had ever been around at one time.

Tyler tried to force a deep breath. If he could go back in time, he'd say no to the tickets.

The game was about to start, but Rowan was hungry. It was slow moving against the crowds going to their seats, and it took longer than he wanted to find a spot that sold brats and fries. He'd loaded up on pickled onions, which Rowan now happily munched on.

By the time they'd gotten back to their seats, the game was underway.

"Okay, kiddo," Tyler said, sitting back in the seat and getting

Rowan settled on his lap. "Let's figure out what this hockey thing is all about."

Apparently, hockey was about deafening noise, huge bodies hurtling around on ice skates, the scrape and resounding *smack* of the puck on sticks, bright lights, and an announcer bellowing an overly-dramatized play-by-play.

Rowan held the bratwurst like a banana and devoured the whole thing.

Tyler had been to a hockey game or two back in high school, but remembered almost none of the rules. An older man sitting next to them must have been able to tell they were clueless as to what was happening on the ice, because he started pointing out players to them.

"Our goalie is good," he said, pointing to the huge and heavily padded man standing in the net closest to them. "Anders Berglund. He's getting older, but hasn't lost a step. We've got a new guy backing him up this year. A rookie from Finland, Onni Koskinen."

Tyler remembered the tall, pale, young guy who'd helped them move into the apartment. It was hard to imagine him out there with all that padding on.

The man pointed out Mitch, who skated like he'd been born on the ice. He explained the different lines, and then, without prompting, "Our captain is out right now. Injured his hand in a fight he never should have been in." He sighed heavily, shaking his head. "He's been brutal this year."

Tyler frowned. "What do you mean?"

"Our last captain, Sharpie? He was one of the best players in the league. A top scorer, and one of the main reasons we won the Cup. Now, with Sully in his spot, we just don't have the same offensive generation. He looks awkward on the ice. I dunno, something's up with him. Between you and me, if he doesn't get it together, I think we should trade him at the deadline. He's older, has a big contract, and maybe he's lost it. Maybe it's better to move on with someone young."

Tyler stared at the man, trying to reconcile the Jamie Sullivan who had sat with him on his break with the hockey player this man described. He'd never gotten any indication from Jamie that he didn't take his work seriously–if anything, Jamie seemed like the kind of person who was completely consumed by their work. Like hockey was *who* he was.

Listening to this fan, he thought he maybe now understood the tight set to Jamie's mouth and the tension he seemed to carry in his shoulders.

"Where's Jamie?" Rowan asked, rubbing his brat-greased fingers on Tyler's cheek.

"Not sure, bud," Tyler said. He ran his eyes over the bench of guys in the green and orange uniforms, scanning the people in suits behind the players. He didn't think he saw Jamie, but he also could barely make out the features of the men through the plexiglass.

Rowan whined and kicked his feet at the seat in front of them.

Someone on the Muskies team scored, and the man next to them cheered.

Tyler pulled out his phone with the intention of checking the time, but he froze when he saw a string of text notifications from Jamie.

JAMIE:

Did you find parking okay?

Hope you find your seats. Let me know if you need help.

I'm up in the team box for the game, but can probably come down if you need any help.

I'd recommend the k-bab place on the east end of the concourse if you are hungry. They're a part of a pilot program where they buy produce and meat from local farmers. IDK. Seems like you'd appreciate that.

And finally, only a minute ago:

JAMIE:

I hope Rowan's having fun.

And you. I hope you're having fun, too.

For some reason, Tyler's chest felt tight.

"Papa," Rowan whined. "I'm hungry."

Tyler pocketed his phone. "There are more fries."

Rowan's lower lip jutted out and his eyes welled up with tears. "Nooooo." He reached up, grabbing big handfuls of Tyler's loose hair and yanking, hard.

Hissing, Tyler bit back a curse. Around them, the crowd roared. Someone must have scored again, but Tyler couldn't bring himself to care about goals or games. Right now, he had a toddler who was up past his bedtime, stuck in an environment that was, objectively, overstimulating.

He dislodged Rowan's little hands and gathered his son into a tight, all-consuming hug. A quick glance up at the game clock showed there were still twelve minutes remaining in the second period.

Fuck.

His knee bounced. He forced it to still.

Jamie had gotten them these tickets. It was such a nice thing to do–Tyler knew that. He guessed they were good seats, too, expensive seats, that he wouldn't have been able to afford.

But Rowan didn't understand any of that. Rowan was just a kid who was tired and overwhelmed, and that made the choice easy.

Standing up, Tyler gathered Rowan in his arms and grabbed his backpack.

It was a battle to get to the car, Rowan squirming and crying and melting like he always did when he stayed up too late. Tyler tried to stay steady, to keep his voice soft and calm. If Rowan was a raging sea, it was Tyler's job to be the steady, unyielding shore. Consistent. Strong.

Reliable.

The night was cold, biting at bare skin, a stinging, brutal touch. Tyler kissed Rowan's nose, holding him close, and then began to sing. *"Don't worry,"* he started, voice coming out a little rusty. *"About a thing. 'Cause every little thing, is gonna be alright. Singing don't worry, about a thing. 'Cause every little thing, is gonna be alright."*

"Three little birds, up with the rising sun," Rowan sang back, his voice high and small as he mixed up the words. He got them wrong every time, and it was one of the many tiny, precious parts of parenthood that Tyler held close and coveted.

They sang back and forth as he carried Rowan to the parking garage. As Tyler was buckling him into his car seat, Rowan said: "Papa, I wanted to see Jamie tonight."

Tyler kissed Rowan's warm, red cheek. "I know, kiddo."

"Can we have him over for a playdate soon?"

Kids, man. Fucking kids. "He's a pretty busy guy, but maybe we can ask."

Rowan fell asleep almost immediately, but Tyler didn't fully relax until they'd gotten home and Rowan was safely tucked into his crib, holding Bunny in one hand, and the other gripping the edge of a soft, old quilt.

Tyler had an old beanbag chair wedged into a corner of Rowan's room, where he'd sit while he waited for Rowan to fall fully asleep.

Once Rowan's breathing became even, Tyler crept out of the room, leaving the door cracked.

Exhaustion overwhelmed him then. He retreated to his room,

changing into a pair of sweatpants and a soft crewneck. Still in his wool socks, he padded into the hall bathroom, digging through the basket of their shared toiletries for his face wash and lotion. He flossed and brushed his teeth, staring blearily at his reflection in the mirror.

He spat out his toothpaste, cupping his hands under the tap and scooping cold water into his mouth. He swished, spit again, and then he was back in his room, crawling under the covers, hating how cold the cotton sheets felt.

He grabbed his phone from where he'd tossed it onto the duvet, curling up on his left side and pulling the heavy blankets over himself.

Five unread messages. *Five.*

He ignored them for the moment, navigating to his online banking profile. His chest grew tight as he looked at his balance.

Fuck.

They were a week out from the end of the month, and he was going to be short.

He was trying to do everything he could. He got food stamps. He'd maxed out his number of shifts at the coffee shop–they weren't willing to move him up to full time. He was pushing how much he could deliver groceries with Rowan tagging along.

And even with all of that, it wasn't enough.

There was an option. One he'd been hesitant to explore now that he had Rowan. But maybe it was what he needed. Maybe it could take away some of the financial stress.

In the morning, he'd ask Sandra and Dotty if they'd be up for a little more time with his son.

Decision made, he finally opened the unread messages.

JAMIE:

Please let me know if you guys need anything.

Not to be a creeper, but I just looked down at your seats and you're not there. Everything okay?

Tyler, please don't hesitate to ask if there's something you need.

Okay. Guess you really left.

Have a good night, then.

Tyler closed his eyes. He needed to respond. He *should* respond, but sleep tugged at his eyes. He didn't have time to think about someone else. He knew it was shitty to not reply, but right then, he couldn't bring himself to worry about Jamie.

Dropping his phone, he let out a slow, deep breath.

Tomorrow. He'd text Jamie tomorrow.

CHAPTER 9
JAMIE
GO GET THE CAT

"Good win, boys."

Jamie stood at the door of the locker room in his suit, slapping the slick, sweaty hands of his teammates as they trooped in from the ice. It had been close, but with Bergy standing on his head in goal they'd managed to close out the game with a 3-2 victory at home against Washington.

It hadn't been pretty, but a win was a win.

"Fuck, that was brutal." Mitch tossed his helmet down in his stall, peeling the soaked jersey from his back. He turned to Jamie, a frown on his face. "See anything from up top that might help?"

"We're getting isolated trying to get the puck through the neutral zone," Jamie said, shoving his hands into the pockets of his gray slacks. It didn't feel right, being clean and dry and buttoned up while the team, *his team*, bore the evidence of a battle well-fought. "I think working up the walls a little more in practice could help."

Mitch nodded.

"Cap," Liam Olsson shouted out.

Jamie wound his way through his teammates to the tall, long-limbed Swede. He was young, only in his early twenties, and still had the shadow of acne scars on his red cheeks. Blonde hair stuck out straight from his head. "Good work out there," Jamie offered, clapping a hand to Liam's shoulder pad.

Liam shook his head. "I'm getting beat on defense. Playing second line is different. More quick."

"You're holding your own," Jamie said, even though he'd seen how tough the matchup had been for Liam, who was playing up on the second line to fill in for Jamie. "How about I stick around after practice tomorrow and we can run some drills to get your footwork a little cleaner?"

The relief was obvious on Liam's face as he smiled. "You are very good captain, Sully."

"Not much of a fighter, though," Cooper called out from his stall down the wall, his grin teasing as he unlaced his skates. "Let Carter do the dirty work next time, eh?"

"Fuck off," Jamie mumbled, but as the team broke out into laughter around him, he didn't mind being the butt of the joke. Cooper wasn't wrong–letting Carter Belanger, their tough as nails fourth line center, take care of the fighting would have been the responsible thing to do. The teasing was fine with Jamie, *good* even. If it meant the boys were together, that the team was finding their stride, he'd throw himself under the bus every time.

"Oi, Cheerios!" Matt Lee was one of the first out of the shower, his dark hair damp. "We playing 'Chel at your place?"

Oliver Campbell and Onni Koskinen looked at each other and then, as expected, looked at Jamie, twin questions on their faces. They frequently hosted the rest of the younger guys on the team for NHL Xbox tournaments.

Jamie sighed. "How many times do I have to remind the two of you that, just because you live in my basement, it doesn't mean I'm your dad."

Oliver grinned while Onni flushed pink and looked sheepish. The two rookies had moved into his basement right before training camp. Oliver was coming out of Canadian juniors, while

Onni was coming over from playing in Finland. The basement was already set up like an apartment, with a separate kitchen, a comfortable living room, two bedrooms with a shared bathroom, and, most importantly, its own entrance.

Jamie loved having the rookies there, but he also didn't want to be woken up in the middle of the night when the kids came home from partying.

"If I crash on the couch, does that mean I can get in on Sully making breakfast tomorrow morning?" Matt went on.

Onni scowled, looking up from where he was carefully situating his goalie pads. "No. Sully breakfast is special. Just for us."

"Not fair!" Matt turned to Jamie. "Is he serious?"

Jamie felt a smile tug at his mouth and shrugged, leaving the kids to sort it out.

"Are you still beating yourself up?"

Jamie glared at Mitch. "No."

They walked together down the corridor from the locker room to where the families waited. Mitch had showered and changed back into his suit.

"I don't know why you think you can get away with lying to me. The mustache gives away all of your secrets."

Scowling, Jamie shoved him in the shoulder. "Fuck off." Then, after a moment: "Does it look bad?"

"My god, man. The mustache looks great. Tyler was looking at it like he wanted to eat it off your face."

"What?" *Mitch couldn't really mean that.* There was no way Tyler had been looking at him like–

"Not my best choice of words," Mitch said, huffing out a laugh. "But the other night, at dinner? That man looked at you like he wanted you. *Carnally.*"

Jamie stared at his friend, trying to ignore the rising heat on the back of his neck as his mind tried to come to grips with the word 'carnal' in the same sentence as Tyler. "Jesus, Mitchy. What have you been reading?"

"I have an extensive vocabulary!"

"Is that what you and Layla text about on the plane that gets you all fidgety? Wanting each other 'carnally'?"

"Who does my husband want carnally?" Layla stood in front of them, blonde hair pulled up into a sleek ponytail and a stylish green sweater hanging off one shoulder. She looked immaculate, as always. Henri, their eldest daughter, was chasing one of Sergei's kids behind them, while Jack was on the floor with his nose in a book.

"Sully's talking about you, baby," Mitch said, pulling his wife into a deep kiss. "He's just jealous there isn't a man in his life who wants him the way we want each other."

When they pulled apart, Layla cocked a brow at her husband. "You're a menace, but your passing looked better tonight. Don't forget to look for your shot on the power play–you're on the first unit for a reason."

Jamie grinned. "Listen to your wife, Mitchy."

"Yeah, yeah," Mitch said, leaving them to say hi to his kids.

"Did Tyler and Rowan make it to the game?" Layla asked.

Right. He'd managed to shove that out of his head. The messages sent with no reply, the seats empty.

All he'd wanted was to do something nice for Tyler, but somehow it had backfired.

"They made it," Jamie finally said. "I got them great seats in the lower bowl, and I sent him a bunch of recommendations for food, but they left about halfway through the second period."

Layla let out a loud sigh, looking at Jamie with her lips pressed together.

"What did I do?" He asked.

"Objectively," she began, "getting someone lower bowl tickets is a really nice thing to do."

"But?"

"Sully, this is a late night for a little kid. Stef stays home with the nanny when the games start this late. When they're that age, one late night can mess up their sleep schedule for a week. And it's loud down there. I don't know if you've been up to the WAG's suite, but there's a whole back room, where we bring toys and books, that is shielded from the noise of the arena. Some of us even bring a Pack n' Play for the little ones to nap. It's a lot for a little kid, especially one who's never been to a game before."

Jamie stared at her. He reached his right hand up, tugging at the hair on the back of his head. "Damn it," he muttered, shaking his head.

Layla put a hand on his arm. "If you're going to do things like this–" she raised her brows knowingly– "for someone with a young kid, you've got to think about the kid. That's what he's thinking about all the time. If you want him to give you the time of day, think about the kid."

Jamie nodded, not sure what to say.

"He seems like a good guy," Layla added. "And into you, too."

"I don't think that's on the table," he said, flexing the fingers of his injured hand. He felt a twinge of pain and winced. "I don't even know if he's queer, and every time I talk to him I feel like he's barely tolerating me."

Layla smiled at him. "I mean, you could ask him. Tyler seems like someone who takes time to warm up to people. He's probably trying to keep himself safe."

An hour later, when he pulled into his three-car garage, he checked his phone. No response. Nothing.

He let out a loud, frustrated groan, slapping his good hand against the dashboard. Sure, Layla had made a good point about getting them tickets for an evening game. And maybe picking the lower bowl, where the crowd was even louder, hadn't been the right call.

But even with all of that, he couldn't pretend the radio silence from Tyler didn't hurt.

If Oliver or Onni noticed Jamie's shitty mood the next morning at breakfast, neither made a comment. The boys did the dishes like they always did, thanked him for the food, and then retreated to the basement to do whatever the hell they got up to before heading to the rink.

The team was flying out on a seven day, four game road trip later that afternoon. Normally, Jamie would go for a run in his gym, sit in the sauna, and then do a round of laundry before packing. But without the team schedule driving him, he wasn't sure what to do with his time.

He washed his sheets. He mopped the dark tile floors in his kitchen. He walked down to the lakeshore, careful of the slick steps, and checked the ice. It wasn't quite ready to skate on, but another hard freeze and it would get there.

Finally, after reorganizing his pantry, he flopped back on his couch with his tablet to watch the most recent game tape. He grabbed the pad of paper he kept on his coffee table to take notes in, groaning when he remembered his injured writing hand. He grit his teeth, ignoring the little flare of pain as he gripped his pen.

He'd gotten through the first period when a loud *ding* interrupted him. Grabbing his phone, he read the notification on his screen:

DOTTY:

Come over and see your mother. We know you're probably home moping. She made muffins.

Jamie looked up at his empty, quiet house, at the spotless kitchen and the almost heavy absence of anyone else.

Normally, he was too busy to feel lonely. Now, without hockey, it was inescapable.

JAMIE:

See you soon.

Tossing the tablet aside, he got up, grabbed his keys, and headed out the door.

He showed up at his moms' place with a drink holder balanced in one hand, and didn't bother knocking. "Hey," he called out, as he pushed through the front door.

"We're in the kitchen!"

Jamie slid out of his tennis shoes, and padded into the blue kitchen in his socks. His mom was at the stove with an apron tied around her waist, and Dotty stood at the sink in her yellow rubber gloves, doing dishes.

He set the drinks on the counter and went to his mom first, giving her a kiss on the cheek. "Hello, dear," she said, smiling up at him.

He went to Dotty next, wrapping an arm around her shoulders. "Can I help?" He asked.

"Sit down and entertain your mother," Dotty said, her tone teasing. "Tyler is out with Rowan, and now she's bored."

"Dammit," he muttered. He'd been hoping Tyler was there. He'd picked up one of those green drinks for him–a matcha, he'd learned, after asking the barista for "one of those pale green frothy drinks." He wanted to talk to Tyler, to apologize for getting him tickets to the late game, for not thinking about the impact on Rowan. But he also wanted to ask Tyler why he'd said yes, and why he hadn't responded to any of Jamie's messages. He wanted to look him in the eye again, to see for himself if he'd imagined what he'd hoped was attraction between them.

His mom turned away from the stove, putting her hands on her hips as she looked discerningly at him. "What's that face about?"

Jamie leaned back against the counter, drumming his fingers against the granite edge. "I can't get anything right with this guy."

"With Tyler?"

He nodded.

"Do you want to get things right with him?"

Jamie let out a frustrated sigh. *That was the question, wasn't it?* "Yeah," he admitted, and rather than relief at the admission, he felt...*Fuck*. He was terrified. "There's something there, I think. I don't know what, really. Maybe I'm imagining it, but, I mean... Have you seen him?"

His mom raised a blonde brow at him. "We've got different wiring, Jamie. To me he looks like an adorable, grumpy, black kitten covered in stickers."

Dotty snorted. "Sandy, my god," she said, her back still turned to them.

Jamie felt himself smile, shaking his head at his mom. He pointed a finger at her. "I'm going to tell him you said that."

"What? I like cats." Her cheeks dimpled as she pointed a wooden spoon back at Jamie. "Also. They went to the children's museum downtown. Do with that information what you will."

"Right." Jamie stood there, unsure of what to do. "So, you're saying I should..."

"For the love of–" Dotty whirled around, her gloved hands covered in suds. "Go! Go get the cat!"

The Madison Children's Museum was situated on a corner one block away from the state capitol, and the whole building was shaped like an elongated triangle. Jamie'd never actually been inside, but had driven past a few times.

He passed the cafe in the bright atrium, glancing up at the life-sized cow hanging from the ceiling, and the vibrant colors covering every surface.

He found Tyler and Rowan standing at the bottom of a staircase beside a wooden slide. Rowan was in a tiny pair of Vans, tie-dye sweatpants, and a sweater with flowers embroidered on the sleeves. Tyler crouched in front of him, a purple blouse with bell sleeves tucked into a pair of distressed jeans. He also wore Vans, though his looked much more battered than Rowan's.

Again, Jamie was confronted by just how *different* Tyler was from the people who surrounded him in his day-to-day life. He was different and vibrant and Jamie was fucking *entranced.*

"Papa, look!" Rowan's eyes got big and he grinned, waving both hands at Jamie as he approached them. "It's Jamie!"

"Hey, buddy," Jamie said, bending down and extending his uninjured fist.

Rowan grabbed his fist, then looked up at Jamie like he wasn't sure what to do with it. "Like this," Jamie said, demonstrating with his splinted hand how to gently tap their knuckles together. Rowan bumped his tiny fist against Jamie's. Jamie smiled, inexplicably proud. "Nice work."

"What are you doing here?" Tyler asked. Jamie was relieved to see that Tyler looked more confused than annoyed to see him. There were purple bags under the younger man's eyes, and somehow exhaustion made him even more hauntingly beautiful.

"My mom. I came to the house hoping to talk to you. She told me you were here." Jamie took a step toward him, handing him the drink he'd brought along. "I got this for you. I hope it's okay. I can go if–"

"No," Tyler said, softly, taking the to-go cup and looking up at Jamie with a guarded look on his face. "Thank you for the drink. It's..." He let out a quiet exhale, and his gaze dropped to the floor between them. "It's good to see you."

"Ohmygod," a young voice said behind them. "Dad, is that Sully?"

"Honey, I don't–" An adult voice started to reply.

"It's you!" An older kid–probably around eight or nine years old, dressed head to toe in branded Muskies gear, stared at Jamie. "Ohmygod, it's really you."

Jamie shot a quick apologetic look at Tyler, but he was just watching the situation unfold with a confused expression on his face. "Hey," Jamie said, extending a hand to the young fan. "How's your day going?"

The kid's hand gripped him tightly. "This is the best day ever. Dad, look!"

A man, who shared his son's dark, feathery hair and round cheeks, approached and gave Jamie a grateful smile. "Danny, you might want to let go of Sully's hand. Don't want him hurting that one too!"

Jamie winced. The man paled a little. "Sorry," he whispered. "That was…"

"It's all good," Jamie said, putting his smile back into place. He turned his attention to the kid, who'd let go of his hand and still stared at him like he wasn't sure if he was dreaming or not. "Now, Danny, what do you say I sign that hat for you?"

Danny's mouth dropped open. "Seriously?"

"Seriously." This time, he didn't have to force his smile.

Jamie fished out the permanent marker he kept in his back pocket, doing his best to hide the discomfort in his hand as he signed the brim of the kid's hat and got the dad's email address so he could send them some free tickets later in the season.

Rowan, who'd been quietly standing with his hand in Tyler's, chose that moment to chime in. "Did you know Jamie is my friend?"

Be still my fucking heart.

Danny looked impressed. "That is so cool, man," he said to Rowan with the kind of sincerity that probably meant he was used to hanging out with little kids. "He's my favorite hockey player in the whole world."

"Mine too," Rowan replied.

"Okay, Danny, let's let Sully enjoy his day at the museum," the dad said, extending a hand for Jamie to shake. "I really appreciate it," he said softly. "And we're rooting for you. The whole city's rooting for you."

Emotion filled his chest. "Thanks, man," Jamie's voice came out raspy and rough.

He watched the father and son walk towards the door. It was one of hundreds of interactions Jamie'd had with fans around Madison. Outside the arena, at the Children's Hospital where the team visited and volunteered, when he went to get his oil changed, or when he went to escape the midseason cold at Olbrich Gardens.

"Jamie, have you seen the snake road?" Rowan grabbed onto his hand, tugging his fingers toward the staircase. "There's a secret entrance behind the grandmother tree. Lemme show you."

With one last look at Tyler, Jamie turned to follow Rowan. He knew they needed to talk. He wanted to apologize and he was still frustrated by Tyler's silence and lack of response. But right at that moment, Tyler was here with Rowan, and the best thing he could do was be there, in the present, with both of them.

The next half hour flew by. Jamie had crawled on hands and knees through a handmade replica of a pond with a ceiling of lily pads, had "eaten" a pizza Rowan had made in the play-kitchen, had collected yellow yarn balls of "pollen" from throughout the building while pretending to be a bumblebee, and had finally collapsed on the cushioned floor of a hollow tree beside Tyler.

Jamie was sweating.

"You and Papa need to rest," Rowan informed Jamie and Tyler, hands perched on his hips. "You're babies. I'm going to get you lunch from the garden." With those parting words he marched out of the tree.

Damn, that kid was adorable. "Do we need to follow him?" Jamie asked between heavy breaths.

"There's a pretend garden right outside. He'll be fine."

"Cool." He looked at Tyler, at his angular shoulders, sharp elbows resting on his knees. At his long fingers and the ink etched upon his skin. "The game last night," Jamie started. "I'm sorry if I put you in a tough position. I wasn't thinking about how late it was for Rowan or how loud it is in the lower bowl."

"Oh," Tyler reached up, pushing his waves back from his face.

"Yeah, that wasn't ideal. But I also didn't say anything, so that's on me."

Jamie shifted his legs, crossing them in front of him. "Why didn't you?"

"Say anything?" Jamie nodded and Tyler was quiet for a moment. "You did a nice thing for us. You've done so much–getting us in touch with Dotty and Sandra, helping with the move. I don't know, I didn't want to seem ungrateful."

"That's–" Jamie cut himself off, smoothing a hand over his mustache. "You've got Rowan. That's a huge job, Tyler. I won't ever think you're being rude if you tell me something doesn't work for the two of you."

Tyler's gaze sharpened, his mouth turning down at the corners. "You're talking like…" He trailed off. Tyler stared at him. Even in the dim light of the hollow tree, Jamie could make out the crooked angle of one of his incisors, and the chapped texture on his full lower lip.

Jamie didn't look away. "Like what?"

"Like you want to stick around."

Jamie couldn't lie. Not then. Not with Tyler right there in front of him, not with his walls still fully in place. "I would," he finally said. "I'd stick around."

"I haven't dated anyone since Rowan." The admission was soft, almost inaudible over the muffled sounds of children playing around them. Tyler looked up, like there was something in the air above them that was helping him make sense of his thoughts. "But sometimes I dream about it. About having something in my life to remind me there's more to me than just being a parent." He shook his head sharply. "And see, even just *saying* that out loud makes me feel so nauseatingly guilty. I'm not supposed to need more than this." He gestured around himself. "Being a dad, having a healthy, happy kid, and making enough to support our life. That's supposed to be enough, but sometimes I'm so lonely. Sometimes it feels like I don't exist. Maybe it's selfish, but I miss flirting and secret smiles and real, human intimacy."

Jamie stayed quiet, hanging onto every word.

Tyler exhaled, finally locking eyes with Jamie. "I can't think about myself yet. Not until we're really settled in here." There was a shadow of worry that crossed his face. "Because right now, if I think about letting someone into our life, and all of the things that could go wrong? It's one thing for me to get hurt, but what about Rowan? What if he got his hopes up and then they didn't stick around? I can't silence the voice in my head that tells me I'd be a shitty dad if I set him up for that kind of hurt."

Jamie thought he saw a flash of moisture in the corner of Tyler's eyes before he ducked his head. He was hit with the desire to pull Tyler into his lap, to wrap him up in his arms and tell him he wasn't alone. To offer him whatever comfort as he could. "I think you're an amazing dad," was what he said instead.

"You're just saying that."

"No, I'm not." Jamie had seen countless teammates interact with their kids over the years. He admired many of them as fathers. Others, however, who were dismissive or harsh with their partners and children, he'd barely been able to watch around their families. "You remind me a lot of Mitch. He shows up for his kids with his whole heart. He loves them loudly, without holding back, and he puts their needs first whenever he can."

But Mitch had Layla. He had a teammate.

Tyler? He had his mom and Dotty in his corner now. They were helping some with Rowan. But was anyone taking care of Tyler?

Tyler crawled over to the entrance, peeking his head out of the hollowed tree. Jamie couldn't avert his eyes from the curve of Tyler's ass, the jeans stretched taut. Jamie's eyes snapped away when Tyler retreated, returning to his seat, an unguarded, beautiful smile curving his mouth.

"He okay?" Jamie asked.

"He's singing to the veggies, happy as can be."

The carefully neutral expression Jamie had come to expect from his face had slipped, leaving a playful, almost *devious* smirk in its place. The quirk of his lips was the kind of lazy smile you'd expect from someone confident, who knew just how hot they were. Like he *knew* everyone in the room wanted him.

This was Tyler. It was obvious, then, just how guarded he'd been up until that point. How little of himself he'd let slip through the cracks.

Jamie wanted more of this version of the man who'd accidentally stumbled into his life. He wanted all of him.

CHAPTER 10
TYLER
TOY VEGETABLES

Tyler didn't know what the hell he was supposed to do with the hockey player sitting on the floor in front of him. He'd come all the way to the children's museum, he'd played with Rowan, and he'd apologized, even though Tyler was pretty sure *he* was the one who owed Jamie an apology for the unanswered messages.

Then he'd looked Tyler in the eye and said: *I'd stick around*.

Seriously, who the fuck was this guy?

It was too much. Tyler wasn't ready for a man like Jamie to say things like that to him. But still, there was something about him that had Tyler opening his mouth, had him admitting the gripping fear that he was failing as a father if he considered bringing a partner into their life.

And Jamie? This stranger–although he couldn't even claim that anymore–had, with all the confidence and certainty in the world, assured Tyler that he was a good dad.

Tyler wanted to be the kind of parent who didn't need anyone to tell him that. He aspired to be confident in himself, to be certain he was doing the right things for Rowan. But still, hearing it said out loud meant something.

Actually, it meant *everything*.

Across from him, Jamie bent one of his long legs, shifting his weight. Tyler tried not to stare at those thighs, at the body so different from his own he wondered if they were actually the same species.

Tyler wanted to know more about him. The curiosity gnawed at his throat, wanting to catalogue and document all the pieces of Jamie, to understand how he was built, the things that sustained him. Even though Jamie wasn't for him, *couldn't* be, maybe Tyler could enjoy their time together. Maybe, for a little while, he could just be a man in the company of another man.

"If you had a day," Tyler began. "One that was all yours, what would you do?"

Jamie frowned. "At this time of year?"

"Yeah."

Jamie slumped back, his heavy brow furrowed. "If it was cold enough and the ice was good, I'd get my ice fishing hut set up out on the lake. I'd grab a six pack of Spotted Cow, pick up a burger and cheese curds from Culver's, put on some Brandi Carlisle, and fish. Not sure if I'll be able to manage to get it set up with this," he paused, waving his splinted hand, "but it's my favorite way to unwind in the winter."

"Really?" Tyler felt himself smile. "Fishing?"

"Ice fishing," Jamie retorted. "It's not the same."

"I'll take your word for it." Tyler was ravenous for more. "Chocolate or vanilla?"

"Chocolate."

"Order at a Chinese restaurant?"

"Egg drop soup and General Tso's Chicken."

Tyler hummed. He was grinning so hard his cheeks hurt. "Good choice."

"Go-to hype song?" Jamie asked, his own teasing smile catching the dim light.

""Naturally.""

Jamie barked out a surprised laugh. "Selena Gomez? Not what I expected."

"What did you expect?"

"Honestly? Someone I'd never heard of."

Tyler laughed then, letting his head fall back. *Fuck*, it felt good to do this. To have a playful conversation with someone.

Rowan marched back into the tree, his arms overflowing with large, toy vegetables made out of felt. "Papa, Jamie, I have your lunch," he announced. He dropped the whole pile on the middle of the floor. "Papa, you get beets, and Jamie, you get carrots."

"What about you?" Tyler asked, shifting forward to look curiously at the pile of pretend produce. "What's your lunch?"

"I had cabbages," Rowan said, looking at him like the answer was obvious.

Tyler saw Jamie cover his mouth to hide his grin, and he felt his own smile stretch his cheeks. "Of course," he said. "Cabbage makes an excellent lunch."

Tyler grabbed a beet, pretending to bite into it. Across from him, Jamie did the same.

It was odd, sharing this with someone else. It was so outside of the scope of what parenthood was typically like for him. These were the moments that belonged to him and Rowan. Just the two of them. And now there was a large intruder with a blonde mustache licking his lips and humming like the felted carrot was the most delicious thing he'd ever tasted.

It felt *domestic*.

"I've got to head out soon," Jamie said, and he sounded apologetic. "Meeting with the doc for my hand. But," he suddenly looked nervous. "I wanted to see if you'd like to come with Rowan to the practice arena this weekend. The team is home this weekend, and Mitch'll have the kids there to give Layla a break. I'm not sure if you know how to skate, but we have a ton of gear if you and Rowan wanted to try it."

Tyler blinked at him. It was…Fuck, this was exactly the kind of thing he was hoping to add to their life. Rowan had loved playing with Mitch and Layla's kids.

"I work Saturday," Tyler said, apologetic.

Jamie was nonplussed. "Sunday morning is off for them, if you're up for it."

"Rowan's never skated," he said. "Is that alright?"

"Of course," Jamie grinned, a dimple divoting his cheek. "There's nothing cuter than a kid learning how to skate. I'm a legend at teaching them. Helped teach all of Mitch's kids."

Tyler worried his bottom lip for a moment. "Is it safe?"

"He'll be in a helmet," Jamie reassured. "I'll take care of him."

Tyler believed him. He couldn't explain why, but he trusted Rowan would be safe with Jamie. Something about this man who commanded such physical presence and strength also promised gentleness. Protection.

Tyler exhaled. "We'll be there."

Jamie's face lit up with a pleased smile and Tyler felt something inside of him melt, just a little bit. "Thanks for letting me join you guys," Jamie said. "I really had a great time."

"It was good to see you," Tyler said, like he was admitting something he couldn't quite believe. "Rowan, can you say goodbye to Jamie?"

Rowan ran over from where he'd found a cloth baby doll in a corner of the hollow tree. "See you soon, Jamie?" He asked, looking between Tyler and Jamie.

Tyler's heart broke, just a little bit. He gave his son *everything*, and yet he could see the way his blue eyes lit up at the possibility of having another loving grown-up in his life.

Just another reminder that he could try to give everything, and it would still never be enough.

"We'll see him next weekend, kiddo," Tyler said gently.

"Hug?" Rowan asked, his eyes on Tyler.

Tyler glanced at Jamie, who nodded deferentially to him even though his eyes were soft. "Ask him," he said to Rowan, "and if he says yes, then you can hug him."

Rowan turned to Jamie and threw his arms open. "Hug?" He repeated.

Jamie knelt down and opened his arms. "I'd love one, bud."

Tyler had to look away as the hockey player circled his arms around his son's small shoulders. He couldn't stand to see the way Jamie watched him, his eyes holding questions Tyler wasn't ready to answer.

Soft velvet dragged across Tyler's bare, sweaty shoulder as he ducked through the black curtain into the dressing room.

Even if four years had passed since he'd set foot in The Blue Barn, everything about the strip club remained the same.

He'd picked up stripping on the weekends his junior year of college. The money had been too good to pass up, and he liked it. He loved to dance, and the hard, physical work required to maintain his strength and flexibility was a good balance to the rest of life.

When Tyler finally understood the reality of his expenses in Madison–especially knowing he needed to start saving for a long-term childcare solution for Rowan–he panicked. He'd hoped the coffee shop job and delivering groceries would be enough to cover their living expenses. He'd considered taking on another day job, but he didn't want to sacrifice more of his time with Rowan.

Tyler had asked Sandra and Dotty if they'd be up for keeping Rowan's baby monitor one night a week while Tyler worked a late shift at the club. It wasn't ideal, but they were right downstairs in case Rowan woke up.

Tyler had been transparent with them about his work and his financial situation. Even on a slow night, he'd make enough money dancing to double what he'd made each week delivering groceries. To their credit, the retired women had met him with nothing but love and understanding. "She's a night owl anyway," Sandra had said with a kind smile, pointing at Dotty. "She can work on her crosswords with a hockey game on her laptop."

He was still trying to figure out a way to thank them, to fully express his gratitude for how much they were helping him and Rowan.

"How's the crowd tonight?" Tyler asked Gio, another dancer who went by the stage name George of the Jungle. Gio sat at his station with a mascara wand in one hand and a vape pen in the other. He had flawless brown skin, and wore his thick hair swept back from his face. His body was bare except for a pair of tiny, glittering shorts, and his skin sparkled with the body glitter they were encouraged to wear. He'd met Gio when he first started dancing at The Blue Barn in college, and had been relieved to see a familiar face when he returned.

Gio made a noncommittal noise. "Average. There's a bachelorette party on the left who are on their second round of shots, and a few suits in the back who are repeats."

Tyler wrinkled his nose. "Is Handsy Dan out there?"

"Thank fuck, no." Gio shuddered. "He always did have a thing for you, didn't he?"

Tyler tried to play off his indifference, but they both knew Gio was right. Handsy Dan was the name the dancers had given a regular who'd been around for years. He was an older man who sat in the back of the room, and had a nasty habit of getting handsy with the dancers and waitstaff. Handsy Dan relentlessly propositioned the dancers for paid sex in the VIP room, but he wasn't going to find anyone at The Blue Barn willing to risk their job or a solicitation charge.

Apparently, last year the dancers had brought up banning him, but he was an old friend of Eddie, the owner, and they were told to *deal with him*, whatever the fuck that meant.

Back when he was still in college, Tyler had shown up at work to find an envelope of cash at his station with a single white rose. It wasn't the cash itself that was the problem–he didn't mind taking extra cash from customers. There were some respectful regulars who understood the professional boundaries in place. But when the other dancers had seen the flower, though, they'd warned him that the cash was from Handsy Dan. Then it happened again. And again.

Every time, Tyler gave the cash back.

Every time, he threw the flower in the nearest trashcan. Putting up with Handsy Dan was just a part of the job. Tyler was used to it.

He stood in front of his station mirror, pulling the sweaty bills from the waistband of the white jock he wore. He took in the gold highlighter on his cheekbones, the precise eyeliner across his upper eyelids, and the mascara darkening his already thick lashes. He surveyed his body: the toned, lean muscle he'd inherited from his mom's side, the silly chicken tattoo on his left hip he'd let a friend do for practice, the dark hair trailing below his belly button.

It was odd, now, to do something so sensual with his body. Tyler barely had time to remember that he was an adult with sexual desires. He was finally coming out of the baby haze, when he'd been sleep deprived and so wrapped up in surviving that he'd barely considered his own needs.

He was starting to remember, now.

He counted the cash from his first solo stage dance of the night. 164 bucks–good for this time of night. He rolled the bills and stashed them in his backpack. Before the night was over he would work the floor a few times, as well as join a few group numbers and perform another solo stage dance later. He'd have to tip out the staff at the end of the night, but he wasn't worried about that yet.

Tyler had moved through his individual routine as he always did. The lights hot on his bare skin, the stage sticky under his hands and knees. He was on autopilot, engaged only enough to make eye contact with the blurred faces in the audience and draw them into the fantasy he was creating. Even though it had been years since he'd been on stage, the movements came back with ease, and Tyler used his time on stage to think through his to-do list for the upcoming week.

He needed to grab groceries–*sponges, fuck.* He needed some new sponges. Maybe when Rowan was napping tomorrow he'd have time to sweep, and he needed to check the coupons for what meat was on sale this week. Christmas was right around the corner, and Tyler had already been squirreling away time to work on a few homemade gifts for Rowan.

He was sewing a vest and a little backpack for Bunny out of an old, ripped pair of corduroy pants, as well as knitting Rowan a new hat with cat ears on top. He'd learned to knit and sew years ago, and it was both affordable and easy to work on during his breaks at work.

His mom would send them a package of goodies from Vermont, with thoughtful, handcrafted toys for Rowan.

Part of his motivation for picking up some nights at the club was to cover holiday expenses. This would be the first holiday he and Rowan had spent on their own, and he wanted it to be perfect. He wanted to create magic for Rowan.

He ran a towel over his sweaty hair, yawning.

"Troy, you're up on the floor." Freddy, their floor manager, poked his head into the dressing room. "George, you're on stage in two."

Tyler took a long drink from his water bottle and reapplied some clear lip gloss and deodorant. He pulled on the tiny pair of denim shorts the dancers wore out on the floor. He checked himself one last time in the mirror.

There he was. Troy, the alt-grunge, tatted dancer. For a moment, he wondered what Jamie would think of Troy. If his eyes would still darken, if he'd still say: *I'd stick around,* if he knew.

But there was no reason for him to find out. Even as Tyler got to know Jamie better, they were just two men who happened to meet, who now shared the connection of Jamie's moms. Nothing more.

He stood up from his station, bumped his fist against Gio's, and went back to work.

CHAPTER 11
JAMIE
BABA BARLEY

Jamie tugged at the hem of his red sweater, frowning at his reflection in the rearview mirror. He ran his fingers over his mustache, attempting to straighten a few of the stray hairs that refused to fall into place.

Fuck. He should have gone with the green quarter zip. Would Tyler think he was trying too hard? A sweater and black jeans felt casual compared to the suits Jamie wore to games.

They'd had a bit of milder weather, which had left only a few clumps of dirty snow at the base of the trees and exposed the brown grass in his moms' neighborhood. Jamie dodged a crusted bank of ice at the edge of the sidewalk and jogged up the steps to his moms' house.

He'd barely knocked on the side door when the interior door opened, revealing Tyler with Rowan on his hip, their brown mullets a mirror to each other.

"How's it going, guys?"

Tyler's smile was tired. "We're good."

Jamie held up a paper bag. "I brought presents. Can I show you?"

Rowan's eyes got huge, and he squirmed out of Tyler's arms. "Jamie, I want to see!"

Jamie had texted Tyler earlier, checking to see if he could bring them both some team gear to wear. Tyler had emphatically told Jamie he didn't have to, but had ultimately agreed. Now, Jamie pulled out a kids-sized, green home jersey–one of his–and handed it to Rowan. "I was thinking you could wear this, if you want."

Rowan looked up at him, breaking into a big, toothy smile. "Is this yours, Jamie?"

Jamie nodded, feeling his chest warm.

Rowan touched the number three on the back, then the stitched letters above. "What does it say?"

"It says Sullivan, and then my number: three."

"One, two, three," Rowan counted with his fingers. "Papa, put it on me, please?"

Tyler helped Rowan pull the jersey over the thermal shirt he already wore. "You look good, kiddo," he said, pressing a kiss to his forehead.

"So," Jamie began, fishing the last two pieces of clothing from the bag, "I mean, obviously, you don't have to take this if you don't want to. I just thought…" He cleared his throat. "Anyway. Here's one of my jerseys." He held up one of his jerseys that matched what Rowan was wearing. "Or this." He returned to the bag, pulling out one of his oldest team crewneck sweatshirts. The team logo was faded, and he'd cropped it so, on *his* body, it hit a few inches above his bellybutton. "Thought you might like this."

Tyler's eyes brightened, his mouth curving up into a grin. "That," he said, pointing to the sweatshirt.

Five minutes later, Jamie watched Tyler strap Rowan's carseat into the back of his truck. Tyler's hands moved quickly, although Jamie was having a hard time ignoring the way his black skinny jeans hugged his ass.

Once Rowan was situated with Bunny and a handful of blueberries for a snack, Jamie pulled out of the driveway.

"Jamie?" Rowan called from the back seat.

"Yeah, bud?"

"Can we listen to Baba Barley?"

Jamie glanced at Tyler. "What?" he whispered.

Tyler smiled, shaking his head as he pulled out his phone. "He means Bob Marley," he said softly.

"Oh my god," Jamie laughed, and something warm and fucking *big* tangled in his chest. "Yeah, we'll get some Baba Barley for you." To Tyler, he added, "That's the cutest thing I've ever heard."

Once Bob Marley was playing, the rest of the drive was quiet. Rowan's small voice sang from the back seat, and Jamie's face ached from grinning.

They parked in the player's garage, and Rowan clung tightly to Tyler's hand as they walked into the practice arena. It was where the team spent a lot of their time, including meals, training, meetings, and some of their medical staff had offices there.

"Mr. Sullivan!" Tanya, the security guard, gave him a fist bump. "How's the hand?"

"Cleared to skate this morning, so that's good," Jamie replied. "This is Tyler, and his son Rowan."

Tanya practically beamed as she introduced herself. "Well, aren't you all the cutest? Lovely to meet you both."

Jamie led them down the hallway to the locker room. It was mostly empty at this time of day, but he knew Mitch and his teammate Sergei were bringing their kids to skate.

Jamie had done a poor job concealing how much he cared about this going well. Mitch had only teased him for a moment, before laying off with one of those smiles that said he saw right through Jamie. "It's a sweet thing to do," he'd said. "The kids and I will be there."

More than anything, Jamie wanted to make sure Rowan had fun.

The boy was up in Tyler's arms, watching his surroundings with those big, curious eyes. It was probably overwhelming, being somewhere new, but he seemed to be hanging in there.

When Jamie opened the locker room door, children's laughter

echoed off the low ceilings. Without thinking, he placed a hand on Tyler's lower back, nudging him down the hallway.

Tyler looked back over his shoulder, his eyes wide.

Shit. Jamie drew his hand back. "I'm sorry," he said, his voice a whisper. "I don't know what I was–"

"It's okay," Tyler said, his brown eyes searching Jamie's. "You just surprised me."

"Sully!"

Mitch's kids came running down the hall, followed closely by Sergei's youngest daughter.

"Hey, gang," Jamie said, smiling down at the gaggle of kids, who were already geared up in skates and helmets. He'd helped teach Stef how to skate last year, and now she toddled along on her skates just like her older siblings.

"Dad is making us stretch before skating," Henri said, scrunching up her nose. "Stretching is boring."

"Stretching keeps you from getting hurt." Jamie didn't try to hide his amusement. "Come on. I'll put some tunes on and we can make it fun!"

Then, it was chaos. The younger kids ran circles around the adults. Jamie introduced Tyler to Sergei, who shook his hand with the sort of stoic, rough politeness Jamie was used to from him. Sergei's teenage boys strapped into hockey gear as they exchanged conversation in rapid Russian.

It took a while to get Rowan in his skates and helmet, but Jamie and Tyler worked together. Once Rowan was geared up, Jamie and Tyler sat side by side and laced up their skates.

Jamie missed hockey. He missed the stench of the locker room after a game and the late night flights when all he wanted was to be in his own bed. He even missed the crushing pressure that settled on his shoulders every time he stood in the tunnel before a game, waiting at the back for the rest of the team to hit the ice before he followed.

His first step on the ice was strong, decisive. An exhale fell from his mouth, and there was a sense of tangible relief at being back on the ice. Back where he belonged.

He didn't go far, looping back around to offer a hand to Tyler, who still had Rowan in his arms. The kids, led by Henri, had formed a train, zipping around the ice while holding on to each others' jackets. Mila, Sergei's wife and a retired figure skater, was doing effortless double axles along the walls, while her older sons battled for a puck in front one of the nets.

Jamie watched fondly as Tyler got his feet under him, and moved carefully along the side wall with Rowan in his arms.

"Faster, Papa!" Rowan's cheeks were already pink, and his eyes were bright.

Tyler shook his head. "No can do, kiddo."

"Please?" Rowan's lower lip jutted out, absolutely adorable behind the helmet cage.

"How about I teach you how to skate?" Jamie circled in front of Tyler, holding out his hands.

Rowan's little brows knit together. "Will I fall down?"

"Probably," Jamie offered. "But my job is to be the captain, and the captain's job is to keep everyone on my team safe."

"Am I on your team?"

Jamie smiled. "Yeah, buddy. You're a Muskie now."

Rowan stretched his arms out, and Jamie reached for him, catching Tyler's eyes over Rowan's head. "I've got him," Jamie said softly, hoping his words were enough to reassure Tyler that Jamie took the care of his son seriously.

When Tyler nodded and smiled, Jamie felt like he was on top of the world.

"Step, step, step, step," Jamie said, holding tightly to Rowan's body where he stood between Jamie's spread legs. He glided forward slowly, keeping Rowan upright as he got used to balancing his weight on the skates.

Rowan was doing great, giggling when he slipped onto his bottom and learning to hold his arms out to the sides to help him balance.

"Okay, now," Jamie said, checking that the ice was clear in front of them before returning his attention to Rowan. "You're going to keep your knees soft–"

"Like mushy bananas," Rowan interjected.

Jamie chuckled. "Like mushy bananas, and I'm going to give you a little push and see how it goes. I'll be right behind you, every step of the way. Ready?"

Through the cage, Jamie saw Rowan's brows tighten as he nodded his head. "I'm brave. I'm a Muskie. I'm ready!"

Jamie let out a whoop as he gently pushed Rowan forward, watching as he stayed upright for one, two three, four and–

"I got you." Jamie caught the kid as he started to tip to the left. He picked Rowan up, shifting him to his hip so he could look at his flushed and beaming face. "Holy cra–cow, kid! You were cruising!"

"Yeah!" Rowan raised his fists, a huge smile on his face. His smile somehow grew when he looked back over Jamie's shoulder. "Papa! Did you see me? Did you see? I'm a Muskie!"

Jamie spun on his skates, coming face to face with the beautiful man who wore Jamie's cropped sweatshirt like it had been made for him. It hung from one of his shoulders, the arms too long, but it was a look Tyler pulled off effortlessly.

It was Tyler's smile then, as he skated smoothly towards them, that left Jamie winded, the breath punched out of his chest. It transformed his whole face–eyes squinted, cheeks creased and dimpled–like there was so much joy inside him it had burst out all at once.

There was nothing calculated or practiced about it. It was honest happiness, and Jamie wanted to bottle it up in a jar to save, to treasure and protect it because he knew, he just *knew* that he was one of the lucky ones who got to see Tyler like this.

In a daze, Jamie handed Rowan over to Tyler, who listened

with rapt attention as the boy described his first time on the ice. Jamie just watched him, watched *them,* and he wished… He didn't know what exactly he wished for, only that it felt reachable in that moment. Like if he asked, Tyler might share some of that happiness with him.

His gaze dropped to Tyler's mouth, and *fuck,* he wanted to kiss him. He wished he could lean over and press their wet, cool mouths together.

A thought crossed his mind then. What if he'd just met Tyler at the coffee shop? What if he'd seen him, felt the organic pull of him, and asked him on a date?

It never would have happened that way. Tyler wasn't Jamie's type, hadn't been until he landed in Jamie's life with his adorable scowls and hard brown eyes that sometimes turned soft like browned butter. He'd never liked tattoos on men before, but the dark ink on Tyler's pale skin looked like it had grown there, like the artwork was a part of him.

He watched Tyler skate, Rowan laughing and clinging to his neck. Tyler's hair fluttered around his ears, his lavender beanie perched on his head.

Jamie wanted him. His body fucking wanted him, to the point of distraction. But Tyler didn't have time for dating. He definitely didn't have time for someone like Jamie.

It seemed unlikely that Tyler, whose time was already stretched so thin, would understand that the Muskies were like a family. If Jamie's ex-boyfriends hadn't been able to handle how much of Jamie's attention was occupied by his team, it was hard to imagine this beautiful, vibrant man who deserved *everything,* settling for so little.

It was hard to imagine him settling for Jamie.

CHAPTER 12
TYLER
DUCKING. DUCK.

Before having Rowan, Tyler had believed his friend community would always be there. That they were the kind of people who could transcend the phases of life. Even when Falcon was pregnant, their friends had seemed excited to welcome a baby into their midst.

Of course, things didn't turn out that way.

Now, he found himself in a professional hockey locker room where the kids all helped each other with their gear. One of Sergei and Mila's boys, Sasha, had offered to unlace Rowan's skates, and now Stef and Rowan were both dragging around a pair of sticks they'd found in Jamie's locker.

This was the kind of thing Tyler hadn't let himself want. But now that he was here, in the room, his heart ached.

The Muskies were a family.

It was amazing, really, seeing Jamie here. It was his job, sure, but it was obviously so much *more* than that. Jamie looked perfectly at home surrounded by the small group of his teammates. Mitch had brought enough snacks to feed all the kids. Jamie pulled the tops off of strawberries for Rowan, and Tyler stared at Jamie's mouth.

Fuck, that man's mouth.

Jamie's mouth was going to haunt him. The way his lips drew together in a frown that softened every time Rowan called him Jamie. That thick blonde mustache–would it tickle his skin if they kissed? Would it catch against the shadow of afternoon stubble around Tyler's mouth?

Tyler felt a part of himself wake up, alert and buzzing and hungry–really fucking hungry.

It was getting harder to remember all of the reasons why he didn't have time for *somethings* with green-eyed hockey captains.

Especially when Jamie was gentle with his son. Especially when he pretended to feast on carrots with them at the Children's Museum. Especially when he used those big, steady hands to teach Rowan to skate.

Or when he'd placed a hand on Tyler's lower back.

Rowan started rubbing his eyes. Tyler needed to broach the subject of leaving to Jamie, who was laughing loudly with Mitch about something. He didn't want to bother him, didn't want to pull him away from this moment with his teammates.

As if reading his mind, Jamie looked over at Tyler, glanced at Rowan, and his mouth tipped up into a soft, understanding smile. "We should probably get going," Jamie said, reaching over and hugging Mitch. "Gotta get these guys home."

Tyler was speechless as he packed their things. He said goodbye to Mitch, Sergei, and Mila, and then Jamie was ushering them down the hall toward the entrance.

Rowan grabbed his hand, like he always did, but then he reached out for Jamie's hand too. Tyler's chest tightened, and he watched Jamie smile down at Rowan like he really, truly cared about him.

The drive home passed quickly, Rowan talking a million miles a minute about skating and the kids and how cool it was when Mila did the splits. As Jamie pulled to a stop in front of their place, Rowan let out a loud yawn.

"Papa?"

Tyler unbuckled his seatbelt and looked back. "Yeah, kiddo?"

"Can Jamie come inside and read me a story after supper?"

Tyler turned to Jamie, who was already nodding. Careful to keep his voice a whisper, he asked: "You sure?"

Jamie's smile crinkled the corners of his eyes. He nodded again.

"Okay, Row."

"You don't have to do the dishes," Tyler said for what felt like the hundredth time.

Jamie just shrugged, his hands covered in soap. "I know."

Tyler sighed. He'd made them a quick supper of black bean tacos and leftover roasted veggies. It was simple, but Jamie had raved about the meal.

Jamie had also refilled Rowan's water bottle, gotten a napkin wet to wipe the smeared beans from Rowan's cheek, and insisted on doing the dishes.

Tyler had protested, but Jamie hadn't been deterred. *Fucking stubborn hockey captain.*

At that point, Rowan was exhausted, and, with Jamie trailing behind them, they'd started their typical bedtime routine.

Getting a toddler ready for bed with an audience, especially one as exciting as Jamie, proved to be challenging. At least Jamie tried to be helpful, telling Rowan that Muskies had to be good teammates and listen to their papas. There had been a brief meltdown over brushing teeth, but they'd gotten it done.

Jamie looked huge in their home. His shoulders almost filled the hallway, and the old wood floor creaked every time he moved.

Now, Rowan climbed up to the pile of pillows on Tyler's queen bed, flopping back in his yellow and green striped pajamas. He patted the bed beside him. "Jamie sits here. Papa, you sit in your spot." He patted the other side.

"You sure about this?" Jamie asked quietly.

Tyler shot him a smile. There was no point in protesting now.

Jamie had proved himself, and who was he to argue if Rowan wanted him there? "You heard the man. Get up there."

They barely fit. Tyler could tell Jamie was trying to not take up too much space until Rowan grabbed a handful of Jamie's sweater and insisted he "get cozy."

Jamie read "The Very Hungry Caterpillar," and they all laughed at his dramatic interpretation of the page where the caterpillar ate its way through about seventeen different foods.

When Jamie closed the book, Rowan's head was resting on his shoulder.

Tyler felt…He didn't know what he felt. Whatever it was, it was warm and full and it scared the shit out of him. Like he was hovering right at the edge of a dream where all he had to do was jump, and everything he'd ever wanted waited out of sight below.

"Thank you for the skating, Jamie," Rowan said around another yawn. Tyler scooped him up into his arms, smiling as he felt Rowan's little body sink into his hold.

"Of course, buddy." Jamie got up from the bed. "I had a blast hanging out with you."

"Feel free to head out if you want," Tyler said softly to Jamie. "Or you could hang out on the couch. It shouldn't be too long."

Jamie nodded, running a hand through his blonde hair.

It took a minute for Rowan to settle, as he was predictably wired from an eventful evening. He was humming and talking to himself in his bed, so Tyler settled down on the beanbag chair, pulling a fleece blanket over his legs.

Hopefully, Rowan would go down fast.

Hopefully, Jamie would still be there.

His phone vibrated in his pocket, and he pulled the blanket over his head before he pulled it out.

JAMIE

I'm hanging on the couch. No rush.

TYLER

Thank you for today.

JAMIE

Of course. It was my pleasure.

TYLER

Why are you doing this?

He probably could have been more tactful in his delivery, but he needed to know. Everything about Jamie was throwing him off balance. He was showing up in their lives like he wanted to be there, participating in activities with Rowan and giving Tyler his old sweatshirt. The sweatshirt was soft, and he already knew he'd never want to take it off.

People didn't just do things like that, right?

JAMIE

I can go if you want.

TYLER

That's not what I said.

I'm here because I want to be.

But why?

This is hard to text.

Try?

Okay.

We met because I was a ducking idiot.

Ducking.

Duck.

FUCK

Tyler buried his face into the crook of his elbow, stifling his laughter so he wouldn't wake Rowan up. There was a giddiness in his chest, a nervous anticipation that was both terrifying and exciting.

You okay over there?

Shut up.

Lol.

I'm trying to say that I'm interested in you.

I don't know.

Maybe it's just me.

Tyler's heartbeat pounded in his ears. This was on him now. He'd been the one to draw the boundaries. He'd been the one, over and over again, saying there wasn't enough time.

All of that was still true. Nothing had changed, but…

It's not.

?

It's not just you.

Tyler stared at his screen, waiting, waiting, waiting.

Nothing.

No response.

Had he misunderstood what Jamie meant? Oh god, what if he'd just proclaimed interest in someone who was just trying to be nice to a struggling single dad?

Rowan had fallen asleep a few minutes ago. Tyler locked his phone, pulled off the blanket, and carefully tip-toed to the door. He opened and closed it carefully, and then ducked into his room, grabbing the baby monitor from the milk crate he used as a bedside table.

Jamie was sitting there on the couch, his expression unreadable as Tyler came to a stop in front of him.

Before he could second guess himself, Tyler grabbed a throw pillow and threw it at Jamie's face.

The pillow fell onto Jamie's lap. He looked up at Tyler, panic and confusion on his face. "What did I do?"

"You didn't respond!" Tyler huffed out a breath, tucking some of his hair behind his ears. "I said *It's not just you* and then you didn't respond!"

Jamie's shoulders dropped. "Sorry," he said. "I just wanted to look you in the eye while we had this conversation."

Tyler sighed, flopping down on the other end of the couch. He kicked his legs up, wishing he'd changed out of his jeans, but grateful for the comfort of Jamie's soft sweatshirt. "Okay, then. I'm here now."

Jamie crossed his arms over his chest, watching Tyler with a careful attention that made his stomach flip. "I didn't know if you were…You know." Tyler's expression must have conveyed his confusion. "If you were queer," Jamie clarified.

"Bi," Tyler offered, quietly.

"That's good," Jamie said, running his tongue over his lower lip. Tyler stared at the movement, and wished…He wished a lot of fucking things. "So, what should we do about this?" Jamie asked.

"I don't know," Tyler answered honestly.

"What do you *want* to do about this?"

Tyler let out a disbelieving laugh. *What a ridiculous question.* "I know exactly what I would have done if this was happening three years ago. But now? I don't know how to do something like *this*–" he gestured between them "–while doing *that*." He pointed down the hall, the helplessness of the situation catching up with him. "I just don't have the time or space for someone else."

A part of him had expected Jamie to argue, but the man just nodded, his expression kind, understanding. "I have hockey," he murmured. "You have Rowan."

"Exactly."

Jamie sighed. "Okay, then."

No. Wait. Don't give up on me so easily, Jamie. I know I can be an asshole, but please, fucking please fight for this.

"Want to pretend?"

Jamie's thick blonde brows knit together. "Pretend what?"

Tyler's fingers fiddled with the curled seam of the sweatshirt, anything to avoid looking right at Jamie. "That things are different," he said softly. "Just for tonight?"

"No."

Tyler felt his body stiffen, and his head snapped up to stare at Jamie.

Jamie held up a hand, leaning toward him and looking right into Tyler's eyes. "I don't need to pretend anything is different, Tyler. The way things are is just fine by me. Your life, my life. They're both full and busy and a bit out of our control. If I was going to kiss you, it would be because, in spite of everything else, I want you. As you are." He shook his head. "When I kiss you, I want it to be for the two of us. For you, and for me."

Yes. Please, I want that.

But Tyler had to be realistic. "I don't have time for–"

"We've already covered that, Tyler," Jamie challenged, voice dropping. Like he was *daring* Tyler to go after what he really wanted.

"So, what do we do?"

Jamie studied him. "Maybe the time you don't have could be a match for the time I don't have. Maybe we could not have time, together, and it would be okay. Maybe it would work for us."

Tyler opened his mouth to protest, but then closed it. It wouldn't ever work, right? Couples had to make time for each other. They had to make each other a priority. There was a formula for what worked.

Except, in reality, there were a million exceptions to that. He thought about Layla and Mila, the wives of professional athletes whose work took them away from home for over half the year. He didn't know Mila well, but Layla? She was someone who clearly loved her husband and, even more than that, had her own life, and interests that she'd cultivated on her own.

"I just don't know, Jamie," Tyler finally whispered, and he didn't try to hide the way his voice wavered, vulnerable and uncertain.

Jamie nodded, a sad but understanding smile on his face. "Okay. Take as much time as you need to think about it. I'll be doing rehab on this stupid hand and thinking about how much I'm blowing my first season as the captain."

Tyler scoffed, reaching out his foot to nudge the side of Jamie's thigh. *Hard*. "None of that bullshit. Your team loves you. Even now, when you haven't been playing, it's obvious those guys look to you as a leader. They need you, Jamie. Get your head out of your ass and show up for yourself the way you show up for them."

Jamie's mustache twitched, his eyes crinkling in the corners as he shot Tyler a playful grin. "Did you seriously just captain me?"

Tyler laughed. "You're damn right I did." And then he added, "Are you sure? You really want me as your neglectful boyfriend?"

Jamie's smile softened, and *fuck,* Tyler wanted to know what those lips felt like. He watched as Jamie shifted, leaning toward him and tucking a piece of hair behind his ear. "I think you're exactly what I want," Jamie said, his voice gentle. "I'm going to head out and let you get some sleep."

Jamie stood, shaking out his legs before moving to the door. Tyler followed him, not entirely sure what was going to happen next as Jamie slipped back into his tennis shoes.

When Jamie straightened and turned to face him, Tyler took a step forward, hands reaching out. "I want a hug," Tyler said, flushing as he realized it hadn't come out as a question.

Jamie obliged, moving like he'd been waiting and ready to gather Tyler up against his strong chest and hold him tightly. Jamie smelled like deodorant and a faint hint of clean sweat that reminded Tyler of naked skin.

"Take your time," Jamie repeated, the words a low murmur

against Tyler's hair. "And whenever you want to talk, you tell me, okay? You tell me you're ready, and I'll be there."

Tyler nodded, pressing his cheek against his firm chest, and the world was so quiet, then, quiet enough to hear the echoing *thump-thump, thump-thump* of Jamie's heart.

"Today was amazing," Tyler whispered into the soft fabric. "Thank you for teaching Rowan to skate."

Jamie hummed above him. "I had fun, too."

Tell him you're in.

Tell him he's already proven himself, proven that there was enough time for them. Tell him all the excuses are falling through your fingers, weak and without merit.

Tell him you're ready and you want to fall.

No. Not yet.

CHAPTER 13
JAMIE
JUST BE SULLY

Jamie pulled his beanie down as a sharp, cold wind whipped around the corner of the modern, stone house. He rapped his knuckles against the door again.

"Come on, Sharpie," he muttered under his breath, shifting on his feet in an effort to keep his blood moving.

Finally a shadow passed behind the door. As soon as it opened, Jamie crowded in, not waiting to be invited. "Took you long enough," he said as he nudged his boots off beside the pile of shoes by the front door.

"You know I retired to get away from you, right?" Aaron Sharpe shook his head with an amused smile. "I am supposed to sleep in, spend time with my beautiful wife, and enjoy some peace and quiet. Instead I am sewing these sequined and sparkly dance costumes, learning K-pop dances, and barely have time to exchange more than a high-five with Celina, now that she's working."

Jamie followed his captain–even retired, Sharpie would *always* be his captain–into the sleek slate and tile kitchen. "Coffee with all the sweet crap in it, no?" Sharpie always teased Jamie in a way that made him feel seen, like his former captain really, truly knew him.

He watched Sharpie make coffee, grumbling under his breath as he poured hazelnut creamer into one mug while leaving the other black. Once they both had their coffees, Sharpie led them over to the leather L-couch where they'd spent hours and hours talking over game video and the team and, well, anything. Jamie had always been able to talk to Sharpie about anything.

"How's the hand?"

"Close," Jamie said. The brace was just a precaution at that point. He was still doing PT daily, and was now putting in an hour of conditioning on the ice in addition to some light stick work without contact. Unless he did something else idiotic, he'd be cleared to practice in time to join the team on the road after Christmas. He'd get a few games under his belt before the Winter Classic, when all eyes would be on the Muskies. On *him*.

Sharpie watched him carefully, his expression concerned. "Why are you stressed?"

Jamie scoffed. "I'm always stressed."

"You're still worried you are not a good captain," Sharpie said, tilting his head to one side. "Why?"

"I'm not like you!" Jamie scrubbed his free hand over his face. "I'm not putting up points like you did. And the harder I try out there, the worse I get. I'm better than this, Sharpie, but I don't know how to get there, and I'm fucking scared I'm taking the team down with me as I try to find my game again."

"You really think this way?" Sharpie looked confused, affronted, even. "And here I thought I raised you better than to believe that crap."

"I'm not a good captain, Sharpie."

Sharpie scoffed. "I call bullshit. You are not like me, and that is okay. The team knows this. Management knows this. The fans know this. And still they chose to make you the captain."

Jamie's hand found its way to the back of his head, yanking on the curls there. Finally, he managed to get his voice working again. "I don't know what to do," he admitted, the words coming out rough. "When I get back out there, I have to be better. I can't be this bad. Not for the fans. Not for the guys. I want to do right by them so fucking badly, Sharpie, and I don't know what to do."

Sharpie leaned over, one of his hands landing heavily on Jamie's shoulder. The firm squeeze was so familiar, something he'd done countless times in the locker room. "Management asked me who should be the captain, you know. When I started talking to them about retirement."

"Yeah?"

"Of course. And I told them they'd be crazy to pick anyone other than you." Jamie opened his mouth, but Sharpie shushed him. "Before you ask me why, I will tell you. You are a pro. I know that is a silly thing to say, but there are hundreds of guys in this league who are skilled enough to work *just* hard enough. Not you. You show up every day with effort and commitment to work–not for yourself, but for the team. The guys respect that. They admire that. And on the ice, you may not have the most points or goals, but you are pulling some of the toughest matchups against the top lines in the league. You are doing everything out there to create opportunities for your teammates. *That* is being a captain."

"But you–"

"I was myself. Now it is your job to be yourself. They signed you, knowing exactly who you are. They made you captain, knowing exactly who you are. All anyone needs you to be is Sully. Just be Sully."

Jamie sank into the cushions. "You make it sound easy," he muttered, but already he was recalibrating, rebuilding the story he'd told himself about his role on the team.

Just be Sully.

"Now that we've solved this crisis," Sharpie said, his mouth curving into a smile. "We need to talk about getting you a boyfriend. You need to relax, and sex will help." His eyes widened. "What ever happened with the pretty boy from the coffee shop?"

Jamie absently fingered the phone in his pocket as he told Sharpie about Tyler. About the push and pull, about the tiny moments of intimacy between them. About how much he cared about his son.

How badly he wanted Tyler to take a chance on him.

So far, there hadn't been any more messages. It had only been a few days since they'd talked, but he couldn't help the anxious need to know where they stood. He wanted to know what Tyler was thinking. If they had a real chance.

When they'd sat there together on the couch in Tyler's small, comfortable house, Jamie had felt like they were on the edge of something. Tyler had been right there with him, ready and willing to jump.

Jamie was ready.

It felt good, after months of shaky confidence on the ice, to feel so certain about something. To be confident in himself, in his ability to show up for someone else and make it work.

He knew it wouldn't be simple or effortless, but the best things in life rarely were.

Nothing about Tyler felt like an obligation. They would figure out a way to include each other in the quiet moments of their lives. Jamie could easily imagine it: sitting on the floor playing with Rowan, or visiting The Daily Grind on an off-day. Tyler joining him for family dinner at Mitch and Layla's house.

If there was a way to be with Tyler, he would find it.

When his phone buzzed, he almost dropped his coffee in an effort to get it out of his pocket. Sharpie laughed, but Jamie ignored him, eyes quickly scanning the message.

TYLER

I'm in.

Jamie felt his heart rate kick up. His fingers tapped quickly on the screen.

JAMIE

Where are you?

Getting ready for work. I picked up an afternoon shift.

The coffee shop?

No.

Jamie paused. *Did Tyler have another job?*

"I've got to run," Jamie said, standing up and jogging over to the sink to rinse his mug.

Sharpie just looked amused. "Thank goodness. I am so busy, as you can see."

Jamie dried his hands on a towel and walked back to his captain, pulling him up from the couch and wrapping him in a hug. "Love you, Sharpie. Thanks for keeping my head straight."

Sharpie clapped his back. "Ah, Sully, there is no straightening out your head."

"What?"

"You are gay, Jamie. Very gay."

Snorting, Jamie withdrew. "I don't miss you at all."

"No?" Sharpie grinned. "Then stop showing up at my house."

"Pain in the ass."

"Man-child."

Jamie shut the door behind him, bracing himself against the wind as he ran to his truck.

Tyler had given him an address for a strip club.

It was out on the west side of town past Middleton. Jamie never had a reason to go out that way, and had to consult his phone as he pulled into a large parking lot surrounding a moderate-sized commercial building with tan siding.

He knew he was in the right place when he saw Tyler's old Subaru parked in the back corner.

Jamie approached the front doors, frowning up at the driftwood sign, which read: *THE BLUE BARN.*

A well-built man in a black t-shirt stood in the sparse entryway. "ID," he barked in a low voice.

On autopilot, Jamie fished his license from his pocket, handing it over.

The man looked surprised. "Oh, shit, man! You really are Jamie Sullivan."

"Hi," Jamie said, not entirely sure what he was doing there.

"How's the hand?" The man leaned over to look at Jamie's hand, like maybe he could *see* the state of his injury. "You feeling good?"

Jamie offered him a smile. "Yeah, feeling really good."

"So stoked to have you here, man. Head on back. No cover for the afternoon, and thirty-five bucks for a dance until six."

It took Jamie's eyes a moment to adjust to the dim room. A high ceiling. Low lighting tinted red and pink. A bar along one wall, shelves of bottles glinting behind it. Low tables, cushioned chairs, and a round stage.

He took a deep breath, forcing his hands to relax.

So. Tyler worked in a strip club.

Cool. This was cool. *He* was cool.

Maybe half of the seats were filled. Jamie found a spot off to the right of the stage, and tried to get comfortable as he waited. Maybe he should have asked someone if they knew where Tyler was, but he needed a moment to himself.

Newer country music played over the speakers, and he noticed other subtle nods to a country-Western theme around the space.

A yellow spotlight flashed on, illuminating the middle of the stage. Loud guitar filled the room. Someone in the front row whistled.

And then, there he was.

Tyler strutted–there was no other way to describe the way he moved–to the front of the stage. His arms and chest were bare, and a pair of denim overalls hung by one strap. His nipple piercings flashed in the light. He wore a pair of unlaced work-boots on his feet, and a wide-brimmed cowboy hat on his head.

Holy fuck.

Jamie watched, mouth open, his body hot and skin buzzing, as Tyler started to dance. He wasn't breathing, didn't know if he remembered how.

There was music. There were cheers. Lights flashed on and off, and spotlights sliced through the darkness, criss-crossing the stage. But none of that mattered to Jamie.

Everything else in his head had evaporated at the sight of Tyler. Any coherence was reduced to a static haze that sounded suspiciously like: *him, him, mine, mine.*

All that mattered was him.

His skin glittered gold, and he had a sultry smile in place as he moved. He arched his neck, one hand sliding down his front as he fell to the floor on his knees. His hips thrust up toward the sky, matching the beat of the song. He rolled, crawled, ran his tongue over his lips as he turned those dark eyes to the audience.

Fuck, he was transcendent. Beautiful. Like something from another world. Another planet. Jamie couldn't decide whether or not he wanted to watch Tyler dance forever or shut him away where no one but Jamie could see him like this.

On his hands and knees, Tyler took off his hat and placed it on the head of a woman in the front row. When he winked down at her, she squealed.

Now his hair was loose and wild around his head, shining with the beginnings of sweat as Tyler kept working the stage. He got to his feet, teasing the strap holding the overalls in place. The crowd cheered. A flutter of bills were thrown onto the stage.

Do it, Jamie wanted to shout. *Show me, dammit. Show me.*

Tyler gripped the fabric, gave the audience a wicked smile, and then *yanked*. The overalls ripped open, and Tyler tossed them aside as he stayed still, like he was giving the audience the opportunity to feast on his body.

And, fuck, it *was* a feast.

A black lace jock strap hung low on his hips, the only thing covering him other than the work-boots on his feet. Jamie wanted to take him all in, to really see every little detail of his body, to commit every tattoo and dip and shadow to memory.

But then he started moving again, and Jamie couldn't breathe. He just couldn't compute this man being *his*. This was what he wanted, and Jamie was there to get him.

Jamie had been to strip clubs before. He'd been on hockey teams his whole life. He'd been to clubs catering to straight men and clubs catering to the queer community. He'd survived a few lap dances, although he hadn't particularly enjoyed them.

He knew he couldn't march up to the stage and throw Tyler over his shoulder without interfering with the set. He'd get thrown out, and knowing how hard Tyler worked to support himself and Rowan, he'd probably get dumped before they even had the chance to try.

Tyler had invited him here for a reason. He was sharing this part of himself with Jamie, and Jamie knew it was a big deal. That this was an extension of truth and trust.

What Jamie wanted didn't matter. Not here. Not right now.

The song ended with Tyler kneeling at the edge of the stage, hands behind his head, as his bare chest rose and fell with heavy breaths. His hair hung in sweaty strands around his face. The people in the front row reached up to slide bills into the waistband of the jock, and before he knew what he was doing, Jamie was out of his seat.

He approached the stage slowly, staying back until the crowd around Tyler cleared. When he saw an opening, he moved forward, forcing himself to breathe.

Tyler's body went still when he saw Jamie, his mouth ticking up into a smile. "Oh, hey," he said, a hint of uncertainty in his voice, like he was bracing himself for disappointment.

Jamie needed to fix that. He couldn't have Tyler doubting

them–doubting *him*–already. "You were stunning up there," he said, holding Tyler's gaze.

Tyler's head tilted to the side, and Jamie could see the shimmer of makeup on his brow and cheeks. "Are you okay? With this?"

"It doesn't really matter, does it?" Jamie glanced around, a small smile on his face as he saw the blatant envy on the faces of some of the patrons. An older man in a suit did nothing to hide the deeply carved scowl on his face. Ignoring him, Jamie turned back to Tyler. "I'm here for you, and if this is a part of who you are, then I'm in."

"Fuck, I wish I didn't have to work right now," Tyler said, softly, his eyes full of longing.

Jamie wanted to touch him. Wanted to strip away the distance between them and press their bodies together. "I can wait."

"I have a break in an hour."

"I'll be here."

Jamie had moved to the bar and was slowly sipping a glass of ice water, trying to keep his shit together.

He'd tried and failed not to stare at Tyler as he worked the club floor in nothing but the tiniest pair of jean shorts he'd ever seen, with the lace waistband peeking out the top.

What the hell was he supposed to do when the man he wanted so badly trailed his fingers over the shoulders of strangers? When he circled his hips on someone's lap?

When he flashed that sinful, flirty smile at someone else?

Jamie knew it was Tyler's job. What he was doing here was work just like Jamie playing hockey was work.

"You're still here," Tyler came up to him, offering Jamie a tired smile. He'd put a big, cropped t-shirt on and still wore the denim shorts. "I've got half an hour if you want to talk?"

Jamie nodded, unable to get his mouth to form words when Tyler was so close to him.

"Come on, then."

Jamie willed his legs to move, following Tyler down a black-painted corridor and into a cluttered office.

"What is this?" Jamie asked, glancing around.

"The accountant's office." Tyler leaned back against the desk, crossing one of his legs over the other. Jamie noticed he wore his black Doc Martens. "They're not in on weekends."

Jamie licked his lips, and the buzzing in his hands telling him to *just fucking do something* reached an overwhelming volume. To save himself the embarrassment of grabbing a fistful of the denim covering Tyler's ass, he reached up behind his head and grabbed two handfuls of his hair, tugging hard.

Tyler's head tilted to the side. "Are you okay?"

CHAPTER 14
TYLER
NOT WHEN YOU'RE MINE

Jamie looked like he was about to crawl out of his skin.

He stood on the other side of the office, pacing back and forth in front of the door with his big hands yanking at his hair, his broad shoulders tight under his sweatshirt.

After their conversation that night in his living room, Tyler had barely slept.

Every part of him questioned Jamie's offer, his logical mind poking hole after hole in the idea of them being able to have a functional relationship. Someone would get hurt, or one of them would feel neglected. It was inevitable. There was no fucking way it could work, not with the reality of their lives and responsibilities.

The little moments they'd already shared had been amazing–Tyler wasn't so jaded that he could pretend otherwise. Jamie was a focused, intense man, and when his attention was directed at him, Tyler felt alive.

Maybe that could be enough. Maybe it was okay to go into a relationship knowing it would end. Maybe they could try, and piece together some happiness along the way.

Tyler had gotten ready for his shift at the club, just like he always did–a close shave on his face, his skincare routine, and a light base of his preferred makeup.

He didn't usually pick up afternoon shifts at The Blue Barn, but with the holidays so close, he'd said yes when one had opened up. Dotty and Sandra were thrilled to hang with Rowan, and had texted him a photo of the three of them making banana bread together.

He'd pulled into the parking lot of the club, turned his engine off, and sat staring out the front windshield, rubbing the heel of his hand absently over his sternum.

For the first time since becoming a dad, Tyler felt the absence of another person in his life, and with it, the longing to find someone to fill that space.

And for the first time, he knew exactly who he wanted to fill it.

It had been a gamble inviting Jamie here. But if they were going to give a relationship an honest try, he wanted Jamie to see him dance, and needed him to understand that this was a part of his life.

Now that Jamie was there, standing in front of him, Tyler wasn't sure he'd made the right call. Jamie had said he was fine, that he wanted in, but had he changed his mind? He'd watched Tyler work the room, grinding on laps, shaking his ass in the faces of strangers.

If this job was a dealbreaker, it was better to know now. "Are you okay?" Tyler asked.

Jamie exhaled heavily, bracing his hands on his hips. His cheeks were flushed, and he looked at Tyler like he was barely keeping himself together. "I–*fuck*, Tyler. Do you have any idea how good you look right now?"

There was no point in lying. He smirked. "Yeah."

"Of course you do," Jamie said, his voice rough and ragged. "I…I want to touch you. So fucking bad."

Tyler felt a flare of heat in his chest. He gripped the desk tighter. "You do?"

A desperate laugh fell from Jamie's mouth. "Are you kidding? Your legs? Those shorts? That fucking jock?"

"Some of the dancers wear old school white jocks, but I've always preferred lace," Tyler admitted. He liked to play with fashion, mixing big sweaters and utilitarian fabrics with delicate lace and feminine blouses and skirts. Nothing compared to the feeling of silk or satin against his bare skin.

Tyler's skin was hot, his nipples sensitive from the silver bars brushing against the loose fabric of his t-shirt, and his cock already hard and pressing against the lace jock he wore under his shorts.

"You are…" Jamie said, taking a step closer to him, his hands gesturing up and down Tyler's body. "You were fucking beautiful on that stage. I can't–the way you dance, Tyler. I've never wanted someone so badly in my life"

"Then touch me, Jamie."

Jamie froze, his body going unnaturally still. "Do you really mean that," he whispered.

"If you don't, then I'll find someone else," Tyler said, shrugging his shoulders and hoping his face projected teasing indifference.

That got Jamie moving again. "No, no, no." His head shook as he advanced, each step slow and calculated. "That's not going to work for me."

Well, fuck. That possessiveness was sure as hell working for Tyler. "Oh yeah?"

"No." Jamie loomed close now, his broad chest filling Tyler's vision. "You said you were in, Tyler. And if you're in, then no one else is going to touch you. Not when you're mine."

When he looked up, all Tyler saw were mossy eyes and that full, wide mouth that he wanted. He wanted, he wanted, *he wanted.* "Are we really doing this?" Tyler asked, needing to hear Jamie say it, just one more time.

Jamie's hand found the side of Tyler's neck, sliding up until it cupped his jaw. The rough pad of his thumb brushed over his cheek, sending a shiver of pleasure across his skin. One of Jamie's brows arched, his mouth curving up in a smile. "I'm in if you are."

Tyler barely had time to nod before Jamie kissed him.

It was almost rough, the way their mouths met. Tyler let out a soft, broken moan as Jamie's tongue slid against his, curling and demanding. He felt the kiss in his whole body, and he felt silly for waiting, for holding himself back when he could have had *this*.

Yes. A million times yes.

It was a hungry, desperate kiss. There was no pretense, as though all the talking in circles they'd done over the past weeks had eroded any remaining patience Jamie might have had. Tyler met him, equally starved.

Tyler clung to the front of Jamie's sweatshirt, pressing himself against the large, warm body in front of him. Their hips met, only an accidental brush, and Tyler gasped against Jamie's mouth and tried to move closer.

Jamie ripped away with a growl. Tyler stared up at him, at his wet, swollen lips and wild eyes.

"Fuck, do you see how hard I am just *seeing* you like this?" Jamie's voice came out rough and clumsy. Tyler watched, mouth open, as Jamie's un-bandaged hand closed around the bulge pressing against the front of his pants. "Just look at you, Tyler. Fuck, you want to be touched so bad, don't you?" Jamie's grip tightened around himself, and Tyler's knees threatened to buckle as heat surged low in his belly.

It was too easy to imagine that hand on him. Touching him, covering him, surrounding him completely. Tyler knew Jamie's touch could be his undoing.

"If you want it, then tell me," Jamie's voice was closer now. Tyler hadn't realized he'd closed his eyes, and when he forced them open, Jamie's face was hovering in front of his. Up close, he could see the freckles on his nose and the dirty blonde of his lashes. He could see the rough layer of blonde stubble on his cheeks. "If you need it, let me give it to you," Jamie went on, his voice dropping into a lower register as he leaned in closer, running the tip of his nose across Tyler's cheek. "Let me touch you like you're mine. I'll be patient. Sweet, if you need it. But you have to tell me it's what you want, or else I'm going to walk out that door."

Oh, he was good. He was too fucking good. "Please," Tyler whispered, his hips canting forward of their own will. "I need it so bad, so fucking bad, I don't know if I can–"

"I've got you," Jamie reassured. "You're mine now."

Jamie brushed a calloused thumb over Tyler's chest, catching on one of his piercings. Tyler arched toward the touch, and a whimper fell from Tyler's parted lips as he was overwhelmed by a sense of relief.

Relief at being touched.

Relief that it was *Jamie* who was touching him.

Their mouths met again, and Tyler's attention was torn between the dueling sensations of Jamie's lips on his, and Jamie's hand on his exposed skin.

Jamie's touch trailed down, over Tyler's upper thigh, down, down until he reached the hem of Tyler's shorts. His fingers paused, toying with the frayed fabric there for a moment before dropping to caress Tyler's bare thigh.

A shiver went through him.

"We don't have time to do everything I want to do to you." Jamie drew back, his forehead resting against Tyler's, his breaths growing shorter and sharper against Tyler's cheek. "I think I'll take care of you nice and quick. Take the edge off so you can go back to work."

"O-okay," Tyler gasped.

"Good." Jamie lowered his head and brushed his lips over the base of Tyler's throat.

Tyler had stopped breathing, each moment of prolonged waiting heightening the anticipation. Jamie's touch on his thigh so close to where he wanted it to be.

He hadn't let himself want in a while–not like this. Not the kind of wanting that reached inside his chest and held him, gripped him tightly like a closed fist.

Jamie's hand on his thigh trailed up. He flicked open the button of Tyler's shorts and tugged down the zipper. Large knuckles dragged across the lace that held Tyler's cock.

Tyler let out a sharp hiss, and his head fell back.

Oh, he was fucked.

Jamie teased, he fondled–fingers light and playful as he explored Tyler's body. His mouth was decisive on Tyler's neck, kissing, licking, barely-there scrapes of teeth that left Tyler craving a bite. The tickle of Jamie's mustache left him desperate, his skin tingling.

Jamie's big hand encircled Tyler's cock, squeezing gently, and Tyler couldn't help but rock his hips into the touch, chasing the friction.

"I love the lace." Jamie breathed the words against Tyler's ear. "It's the first time I've–" his words cut off with a groan. "I don't know if I'll ever be able to imagine a cock any other way."

"Oh," the word escaped–a whine and a whisper. "Fuck, Jamie, I'm…"

The fabric around his waist strained and squeezed as Jamie shoved his shorts down and yanked the jock strap out of the way, finally freeing his cock.

Jamie's hand wrapped around him, working his cock with a confidence that had Tyler hurtling toward his release. Tyler barely had time to touch himself, and it had been years since he'd had someone else's hands on him. And now, here was Jamie, taking him apart with nothing but a fucking handjob. Bracing his hands on the desk behind him, he met Jamie's hands thrust for thrust. His breaths were hot in his chest, pleasure curling in his core, tightening.

Too soon, he was there. "I'm gonna–"

Jamie didn't slow, maintaining the same pace with his hand as he crowded his body even closer to Tyler's.

Tyler came hard, almost doubling over as the orgasm pulsed

through him. As he lost himself in the euphoria, the pleasure that was good, *so* fucking good, Tyler couldn't think of anything but *this* and *here* and *now*. It was over too quickly, and the pleasure faded to a bone-deep satisfaction that left Tyler struggling to stay upright.

Jamie's hand was still gently stroking his sensitive cock. "Enough," Tyler whispered, blinking his eyes back into focus.

Jamie filled his vision. A damp blond curl hung down on his forehead, his face was flushed, his mouth parted and eyes still ravenous. Glancing down, Tyler's eyes widened.

The front of Jamie's black joggers were covered in Tyler's release, streaks of white dripping over the hard bulge of his cock pressing against the damp fabric.

Tyler's tongue slid across his lower lip. "Show me," he said softly, staring at the bulge in Jamie's joggers.

Jamie groaned as he pulled himself from his pants. He was proportional to the rest of his body, solid and uncut, and Tyler wanted to bury his face in the thick blonde hair that surrounded the base of his cock.

Jamie gripped himself, and Tyler couldn't look away as his fist started gliding up and down his shaft.

It was a beautiful thing, watching a man come undone.

Jamie's stomach muscles tightened, a low, vulnerable cry ripping from his chest as he came. He did his best to catch his release, cupping a hand under the flushed head of his cock, but drops of white slipped between his fingers.

Tyler reached for him, hesitating before he touched Jamie's cum-covered skin. "May I?" His mouth watered, already imagining the taste.

Jamie, eyes heavy, nodded. "Got tested last week," he grunted. "I'm in the clear."

That was all Tyler needed to hear. He wrapped a hand around Jamie's forearm, and brought his hand up to his mouth.

Tyler groaned, the taste of Jamie's cum tangy on his tongue. Tyler licked up his wrist, tracing each drip up Jamie's hand until he'd cleaned the release from his skin. Curling his tongue around two of his thick fingers, Tyler sucked them into his mouth. His lips closed around them, feeling the pressure on the back of his tongue. Then, because he could, he swallowed.

Jamie's eyes fluttered shut. "Tyler," he moaned.

Eventually, he let Jamie's fingers fall from his lips. Jamie tucked himself back into his pants, and Tyler did the same, grateful that Jamie had managed to save him from the discomfort of dealing with wet and sticky underwear.

"I don't know how we're going to save your pants," Tyler said, gesturing to Jamie's crotch.

Jamie shrugged, looking completely relaxed and unfazed. "I'll figure it out."

Tyler zipped up his shorts and then looked back at Jamie. "So."

"So," Jamie echoed.

"We're doing this? We're going to try?"

Jamie moved in closer and cupped the side of his neck. "I'm ready."

Tyler leaned into his touch. "Rowan is always going to come first," he said, needing Jamie to *really* hear him. "He's always going to be my priority."

"I know." Jamie smiled softly down at him. "All I'm asking is to come third."

It took a moment for Tyler to understand what he was saying, but when he did he frowned, confused. "Third? Who's second?"

"You, Tyler. *You* come second."

Tyler pressed his lips together, suddenly overwhelmed. Who was this man? He struggled to believe this was the same guy who'd knocked himself out trying to fight a snowman.

He'd met Jamie at his worst, drunk and stumbling in the night.

Now, he was the man who had taught Rowan to skate, who had waited on the couch while Tyler put Rowan to bed, and who kissed Tyler like it meant something real.

Tyler pushed Jamie's hair back from his damp forehead. "Do

you think a boyfriend who sometimes wears dresses would be too much for hockey fans?"

Jamie shook his head.

"A stripper boyfriend?"

"I don't give a shit." Jamie's voice came out low. "I'm proud to be with you, exactly as you are."

"Good thing we don't have to worry about that," Tyler said.

The amused grin Jamie gave him was all teeth and dimples as he walked around the desk. He lowered himself into the chair, and patted his thighs with both hands. "Get your ass over here."

Tyler obliged, his legs still unsteady.

Jamie tugged off his hoodie, draping it over the mess on his lap before pulling Tyler down, scooting his body back against his chest. Wrapping an arm around Tyler's middle, Jamie quickly navigated to his camera, holding his phone out in front of them.

"What are you doing?" Tyler asked, breathless.

"Taking a picture of my beautiful boyfriend." Jamie murmured against Tyler's neck, his mustache leaving Tyler's skin tingling in its wake. "You feel good on me, baby."

Baby. Fuck.

Tyler felt his skin flush as he shifted, standing and turning to straddle Jamie's lap. "Baby?"

Jamie looked up at him with unguarded wanting. "Is that okay?"

"More than okay," Tyler whispered, and then threaded his fingers through Jamie's hair and leaned forward, kissing the tip of Jamie's nose. "Now take your picture, Jamie."

Tyler's gaze roved freely over Jamie's face, cataloguing each feature. Jamie must have taken the picture at some point. His fingers trailed down Tyler's spine.

Tyler gave Jamie's nose one more kiss. "I really need to get back to work now," he said, wishing he could stay in the cramped office with his legs splayed over Jamie's lap.

"Wait," Jamie commanded. "One more for the road," he said and then he kissed him.

Tyler melted into the kiss, letting his limbs go slack because he knew he was safe in Jamie's arms. Jamie had him–tongue curling around his, hands sturdy on his waist, lips firm and wet and *there*.

Slowly, Jamie drew back, letting out a low, contented hum. "Better now," he murmured.

Tyler climbed off reluctantly, giving Jamie space as he tied his sweatshirt around his waist, the long part hanging over the stained crotch of his pants.

Tyler let out a loud laugh. "You look ridiculous."

Jamie shot him an unimpressed look. "And whose fault is that?"

"Yours. It's definitely yours."

Jamie bit back a smile as he walked to the door, holding it open for Tyler and placing a hand on his lower back as he passed by.

They walked down the hallway in silence. Tyler wasn't entirely sure what to say. It had been so long since he'd been in a relationship, and he felt out of practice. "Thanks for coming by," he said.

Rather than answering, Jamie gathered him close and kissed the top of his head. "Of course. When I have the time, I'll always be happy to give it to you."

When they walked out into the club, Tyler steered them around the back edge of the room, hoping to escape the notice of the patrons.

He'd forgotten about Handsy Dan.

The older man clocked them immediately. Tyler watched him out of the corner of his eye, and for the first time he wished he were bigger than Jamie, that his body was large enough to shield *him* from Dan's penetrating stare.

Tyler put a bit of distance between them, like that would somehow negate the fact that they'd very clearly walked out of the back hallway together.

Fuck.

Jamie's hand on his back distracted him, his solid, warm presence reminding Tyler that there was a man right there beside him who cared for him and wanted him and called him his.

That was what mattered.

Jamie paused at the door, waving as he left Tyler standing at the bar.

Tyler waved back, and then immediately felt embarrassed. Jamie smiled, and then he was gone.

"Oh. My. God."

Tyler glared at the bartender, Tessa, who was doing a terrible job holding in her laughter. "Shut it."

"You just got it on in the back office with that hot as fuck man. You legendary slut."

"I don't know what you're talking about," Tyler said, turning away, but he couldn't keep the smile from his face. "And the hot as fuck man? That's my boyfriend."

CHAPTER 15
JAMIE
WHAT'S DATING?

TYLER

How was PT?

JAMIE

Good. Cleared for full practice tomorrow.

Yes! Rowan says: Yay Jamie!

So sweet. Are you working on Sunday?

I've got the early morning shift at the coffee shop and get off around 10am. Why?

Team Christmas party at my house. I'd love for you both to be there.

What time?

Want to come over for lunch and then hang out while I get things set up? I borrowed a Pack n' Play from Mitchy so Rowan will have a place to nap. Even got one of those salt lamps in the guest room so he can have some light.

That would be amazing. One thing, though.

What is it?

Would you be okay with waiting to tell Rowan about us? At least for a little while?

Of course. I'm happy to follow your lead.

So does that mean no touching?

No obvious touching.

So...hugs?

We can hug.

🙂

Jamie.

What?

It's honestly suspicious.

What is?

How nice you are.

🙂 Can't wait to see you.

The hired cleaning service was just finishing in the living room when Jamie heard a knock on the front door.

"Coming!" He shouted, his sock-covered feet sliding on the wood floor. He pulled the door open and his face broke into a smile at the sight of Tyler and Rowan bundled up for the cold weather.

"Look at you guys," he said, not giving a shit that he was

probably grinning like a fool as he beckoned them in and closed the door behind them.

Tyler was wearing his mustard-yellow coat, and his pale purple beanie was pulled low on his head. Rowan was beside him in a red and white striped stocking cap that looked handmade. Tyler almost seemed shy as he moved toward Jamie, like he wasn't sure what he was supposed to do.

While a part of Jamie hated holding himself back from touching Tyler the way he wanted to, he understood. Their relationship was brand new. They needed to test the waters between them, to see if the promise of chemistry meant what he hoped it would.

But *fuck,* he wanted to hold Tyler close. He wanted to press his mouth to Tyler's chilled lips and kiss him until he was warm.

Instead, Jamie brushed a thumb over Tyler's bare knuckles, flushed red from the cold. "Hi," he said softly, feeling like something in him settled just knowing the two of them were safe and warm in his home.

"Look, Papa! A tree!" Rowan tried to wriggle out of Tyler's grip, pointing to the Christmas tree standing in the corner of the living room. Jamie made a point to get a real tree every year, and had several large plastic totes full of carefully wrapped ornaments he had been waiting to put up.

Jamie hadn't planned to leave the holiday decorating to the last minute, but he'd been feeling off ever since his injury. It was a struggle to find his rhythm when he was so used to his life being ruled by the team schedule. Despite a fairly full slate of rehab and on-ice conditioning, there were still long stretches of his days when he felt adrift and painfully aware of how lonely he was.

Onni and Ollie had offered to help him decorate the tree earlier, but the thought of Rowan and Tyler helping him had made him smile, so he decided to wait.

"Slow down," Tyler said to Rowan, laughing quietly. "Let's get these layers off and then you can go check it out."

Jamie's chest warmed when he saw Rowan wearing his jersey. "He insisted," Tyler said with a shrug, coming to stand next to Jamie as Rowan ran over to the tree.

Loud footsteps pounded up the basement stairs, and then Onni and Oliver were rounding the corner into the kitchen. They looked ridiculous in matching Muskie holiday sweaters that displayed a rhinestone-covered fish wrapped in Christmas lights.

"Hey! Tyler, right?" Oliver came over to offer his hand. "Great to see you again. You're dating Sully? Score, man. He's old, but he's a looker. Oh snap! It's your kiddo! What's up, little man? Isn't this tree rad? We got to help Sully pick it out, and they had hot apple cider at the tree place."

"Papa, what's dating?"

Oliver raised a hand to cover his mouth. "Was I not supposed to–shit," he whispered. "I mean, shart. Shat. Shoot."

Beside him, Onni buried his face in his hands, muttering something that sounded like, "What am I going to do with you?"

Tyler looked up at Jamie. Jamie held his gaze, hoping his eyes said: *Do whatever feels right for you and I'll be here with you. I'm not going anywhere.*

He watched Tyler's lips part as he let out a breath. "Kiddo," he said, kneeling down so he was eye-level with Rowan. "You know how Jamie is our friend, right?"

Rowan nodded.

"So, Jamie and I are...*Really* good friends. I think he could be someone special in my life." Tyler's brown eyes found Jamie's. "In *our* life."

Jamie thought his heart was going to beat out of his chest. He watched Rowan, who nodded along seriously as he listened to Tyler's explanation.

"Are you and Jamie like Mimi and Pop Pop?"

"Well," Tyler began. "Maybe someday. But for now, we are getting to know each other better, and we call that dating."

Rowan looked up at Jamie then, his blue eyes bright. "Jamie, are you going to hug my papa and give him kisses if you're dating?"

Jamie smiled. "If he wants them, then yes."

"Good." Rowan nodded, a serious look on his face. "I like dating. Papa needs hugs and kisses."

"This is the sweetest thing I've ever seen," Ollie whispered, grinning with his palms pressed to his cheeks.

Now that Rowan's questions about dating had been answered, he scampered over to the living room, singing to himself. Oliver jogged behind before dropping to his hands and knees on the carpet, talking a million miles a minute with Rowan about... *Apples*?

"It is good he has another kid to play with now." Onni walked more slowly, his fair blonde hair still damp from a shower. "Maybe he will take nap later and give me a break."

"You love him," Jamie retorted.

Onni snorted. "Yes, he is good. Good for me and good for team. Inconvenient at times, but good."

"Rowan, have you ever played mini sticks?" Oliver asked from over in the living room. "No? Onni! We have to teach him how to play!" Oliver sprinted past them, likely going downstairs to grab the necessary equipment.

Onni looked torn for a brief second before turning to Tyler and Jamie, a grave expression on his face. "I must go. I will make sure kids are safe."

Jamie chuckled as the two NHL players got down on the floor with a set of mini sticks and started explaining the rules of the game. Rowan was entranced, his big eyes darting between the two young men.

"If my living room turns into a non-stop hockey game, I'm blaming you." Tyler turned, wrapping his arms around Jamie's middle. The pink and blue striped sweater he was wearing was soft, and Jamie's fingers brushed back and forth over the loose stitching covering his back.

"So, that happened," Jamie said, smiling down at him.

Tyler shook his head fondly. "Yeah, it did."

"You okay?"

Tyler leaned his cheek on Jamie's chest. "Better than okay."

"Can I get you something to drink? Some tea? Some coffee? I looked up a video on how to make matcha, and, I've gotta be honest with you, that was too much for me to figure out, but there's delivery if you really–"

His words were cut off when Tyler pressed his palm over Jamie's mouth. "Jamie. I'm here, in your house, because I want to be here. You don't need to convince me to stay."

Jamie nipped at one of Tyler's fingers, then kissed it. "But I like taking care of people."

"Fine," Tyler said, tone teasing. "How about a cup of herbal tea?"

"Coming right up."

Jamie's heart was full, almost painfully so, as he filled the kettle while Tyler hopped up on the counter. He glanced back at this man–his *boyfriend*–admiring his slender legs and the spread wings of the moth embracing the base of his neck. The way his features softened as he watched Jamie move around the kitchen.

Nothing made him happier than seeing Tyler and Rowan comfortable in his home.

Maybe this would actually work. Maybe Tyler was different from the men he'd dated before. Maybe their busy lives could match up, and Jamie could be a place of comfort, of connection and pleasure, where Tyler and Rowan were welcome whenever there was time. Maybe Tyler was better equipped to handle Jamie's long absences and devotion to the team, because he had obligations of his own.

Maybe they could build something just for them.

They hung the ornaments on the tree while a playlist of greatest Christmas hits played. Rowan's attention span quickly waned, but he occupied himself with a plastic nativity scene while

Jamie, Tyler, and the rookies finished up. Tyler, who'd seemed almost subdued when they'd first met, now badgered him for the backstory of every one of his childhood ornaments.

He loved how easy it was to make Tyler smile. He loved that he now knew Tyler kept little sparkly clips in his pocket for when his hair got in his eyes. He loved the gentle way Tyler spoke to his son.

Tyler moved through Jamie's house like it was already familiar, and Jamie kept having to check himself to make sure he wasn't smiling *too* much.

Later, Onni and Oliver made grilled cheese sandwiches for lunch while Jamie heated up tomato soup, and soon they were all gathered around the table. Rowan sat happily on a booster seat between the two rookies, who he'd declared were his "most favorite buddies," and Tyler scooted his chair close enough to Jamie's that their thighs could press together under the table.

When they were finished, Jamie left the rookies to do the dishes, and led Tyler and Rowan upstairs to the guest room. Rowan clambered up onto the bed, leaping and rolling over the pillows, while Jamie showed Tyler the Pack n' Play, salt lamp, and an outlet where he could plug in the baby monitor.

The grateful smile Tyler gave him meant everything. It meant fucking *everything*. And then Rowan sat tucked against Jamie's side as he read *Corduroy*, the story about the bear in a department store who was missing a button and went on an adventure through the store to find it. He read the last line and closed the book.

"I think it's your rest time, bud," Jamie said, reaching a hand up to fluff Rowan's curls.

Rowan nodded in response. "I'm a tired kitty today."

Jamie left them, whispering in Tyler's ear that he was going to be in the basement getting a quick workout in. The door closed behind him with a click, and he felt like the little, empty corners of his life were finally filling in.

Tyler found him half an hour later.

Jamie saw him in the mirrored wall of his basement gym, leaning against the doorway watching him run, his arms crossed over his chest. Jamie slowed the treadmill down to a walk, immediately feeling the rush of heat down his legs where sweat trailed through his fuzzy blonde hair. He'd changed earlier into a pair of shorts, knowing he'd be sweating buckets.

Tyler's tongue traced his lower lip as his gaze dropped to Jamie's shorts. Jamie kept walking, eyes fixed on Tyler as he watched his boyfriend's eyes trail over his legs. It felt so fucking good to be watched like that. To be watched, and to be *wanted.*

Jamie's attention never strayed from Tyler's face as he turned off the treadmill and removed his soaked t-shirt, tossing it over his shoulder.

Tyler's mouth twitched into a smirk. "I like the view from over here."

Jamie grinned, jumping off the treadmill and crossing the room. "Hey." He stopped in front of Tyler, trying to catch his breath.

Tyler looked up at him, an almost wicked glint in his eyes, and snagged the elastic waist of Jamie's shorts between his fingers. His knuckles brushed the hair trailing down from Jamie's bellybutton, and Jamie hissed, a sharp surge of arousal threatening to make his knees buckle.

"Upstairs. Now." Jamie grabbed Tyler's hand, practically dragging him out of the gym and up the stairs.

Jamie started laughing, and then Tyler was laughing, and they tried to be quiet, but Tyler kept making adorable snorting sounds and Jamie couldn't hold it together. Finally, they stumbled into Jamie's room, the door clicking shut behind them. Jamie leaned back against the wall, his breaths heavy as he watched Tyler take the baby monitor from his pocket and set it on top of the dresser.

Their laughter faded as they looked at each other.

"Can I get you naked, baby?" Tyler was already nodding as Jamie approached him. Jamie groaned, because *fuck,* he'd been dying for this moment.

Tyler went straight to Jamie's bare chest, mouthing at one of his hairy pecs. Jamie tried to pull Tyler's sweater off, but couldn't get his limbs to cooperate when there was a hot, eager mouth licking the sweat from his skin.

Somehow, he managed to get Tyler's upper half naked. He needed more time, but settled for making a promise to himself that he'd spend hours in the future getting to know each and every tattoo covering his boyfriend's skin, and the twin silver bars that pierced his nipples. Right now, he needed to peel off those fucking jeans.

Tyler's tongue flicked against Jamie's nipple and Jamie gasped, pleasure shooting over the surface of his skin and gathering below his belly. His hands fumbled with the button of Tyler's jeans as Tyler's fingers slipped under the waistband of Jamie's shorts.

Within moments they were both naked. Sweat still dampened Jamie's skin, but Tyler didn't seem to mind. *I can fucking work with that,* Jamie thought as he felt his cock brush against the smooth skin of Tyler's stomach.

Jamie stepped back, needing to get a better look at his boyfriend's body.

It wasn't the first time he'd had his hands on Tyler's hips, brushed his thumb over his throat, held his hard cock in his hand. But to see all of him now, without anything between them, to see the lean muscle of his legs and the square set of his hips, to see the thatch of dark hair at the base of his cock, the flared head almost purple and already glistening with precum.

To see the piercings in his nipples right there where he could reach them.

To see all of Tyler was overwhelming. *Beautiful*. He was so, so beautiful.

He could feel Tyler's eyes on him, too. He vaguely wondered

what the smaller man thought of him: his bulky, hairy body, and his average-sized, uncut cock.

Jamie wondered, but he didn't worry. There was nothing to worry about when Tyler looked at him like maybe, he found Jamie beautiful, too.

"Come here," Jamie said, backing up until his thighs hit the edge of the bed and then sitting down.

Tyler followed, moving with the grace of a cat until he stood between Jamie's thighs.

Before Jamie could tell Tyler to get his ass up in his lap, his boyfriend lowered himself to his knees and practically dove into the crease of Jamie's crotch, nuzzling and licking his skin.

"Why does your sweat taste so good?" Tyler asked, his voice muffled by blonde pubic hair. "It feels fucking filthy to like it, but it's–*fuck*, Jamie, it's so *good*."

Jamie ran his fingers through Tyler's hair, tugging gently once he reached the back of his head. "I like to hear that," he said, staring down at the man between his thighs. "Tell me what you like. What you want in bed."

Tyler licked a long line from Jamie's inner thigh up to his hip, brown eyes locked on his. "Everything." He nipped at Jamie's skin. "I want you, above me. I don't…I haven't always trusted someone enough to ask for it, but I like being told what to do."

"Fuck," Jamie said, his hard cock twitching where it lay against hist stomach, hard and neglected. "I fucking *love* the sound of that."

"You do?" Tyler hummed, dipping his head to nudge at Jamie's sack with his nose.

"Mmhm. I prefer to be in charge–*dammit,* baby," he cut off. He couldn't think, couldn't do *anything* as Tyler sucked one of his balls into his hot, wet mouth. "See, that's so fucking good when you do that." He tightened his grip on Tyler's hair. "Just like that. Fuck, you're distracting me. I'm vers, too."

Tyler grinned, the skin around his mouth shiny with spit. "Good."

"Condoms?"

"Only if you want," Tyler replied. "There hasn't been anyone else since I tested, and I never stopped taking PrEP."

"If you," Jamie hissed as Tyler scraped his teeth over the skin of his inner thigh. "If you're okay with it, then no condoms. I'm on PrEP, too, and *fuck,* Tyler. I want to feel you. Nothing between us."

Tyler made a sweet little whimpering sound. Jamie felt himself smile. He wanted to hear Tyler make that sound again. "You like that?"

"Mmhm."

Jamie's hips bucked, the need for Tyler winning out over his control.

Tyler cocked an eyebrow at him. "Now can I suck you?"

"Yes," Jamie said, his voice a pleased purr. "Get to work, baby."

Tyler started at the tip, briefly flicking his tongue over the loose skin of Jamie's foreskin before wrapping one of his tattooed hands around Jamie's cock. He slid his hand down, exposing the head, and Jamie thought he was going to *fucking lose it* when Tyler wrapped his lips around his crown and *sucked.*

"Baby, *yes,*" Jamie didn't try to hold back the words falling from his mouth. "Just like that, *fuck*…" He needed Tyler to hear him, wanted him to hear just how *fucking good* he was.

Just when the pleasure started tightening in the base of his spine, Tyler would withdraw, switching his attention to Jamie's full sack. Tyler continued working him over, sucking him down and then pulling back, occasionally looking up at him with that teasing smirk that made Jamie feel fucking *wild.*

"To the shower," Jamie gasped. He knew they needed to be mindful of the time, but he wanted to savor every single moment of being with Tyler. Tyler grabbed the baby monitor and followed Jamie, turning up the volume and then setting it beside the sink before walking into Jamie's open arms.

They kissed lazily while the water warmed up, Jamie's large

en-suite filling with steam as he got lost in Tyler's tongue and wandering touches.

Jamie led Tyler in, making sure he got under the direct flow of the water first. He ran his hands over tattooed skin, up Tyler's arms and down his chest, pausing to tweak his nipples before circling his cock and giving it a few easy strokes. He lowered his mouth to Tyler's ear. "Can I eat your ass?"

"Fuck," Tyler gasped, shuddering against him.

"Not an answer."

"Yes. Please, yes."

"Good, baby. Put your hands on the wall and stick your ass out so I can see you."

As soon as Tyler's hands were braced against the wall, Jamie lowered himself to the floor.

"That's it. You're being so good for me." His mouth watered as he spread Tyler's cheeks, revealing a pink hole surrounded by fine, dark hairs. *Yes, please, yes*–his thoughts echoing Tyler's words as his tongue ran over the puckered skin.

Time melted away as Jamie's tongue sunk into Tyler's hole. It was one of his favorite things: taking a man apart this way, tasting their musk and feeling the clench and release of their muscles around him.

Tyler rocked backward on his tongue and Jamie felt his cock throb between his legs. He needed more. Needed his cock on Tyler. Not in him yet–he wouldn't be rushed when he sunk into Tyler's body for the first time.

Jamie could have stayed on his knees for hours, but he knew they didn't have time for him to indulge. Standing, he turned Tyler around, loving the way his body went lax under his touch, fully surrendering to him.

Grabbing the bottle of lube from the shelf in the shower, Jamie filled his palm before lining up their cocks. His hand couldn't quite wrap around them both, but it was enough to hold them pressed together while he stroked over their slick shafts.

Tyler's eyes were blown wide, his inky lashes damp as water

trailed down his face. He looked *beautiful*, and Jamie couldn't believe Tyler was his. Tyler must have felt the same desperation, because he started to thrust, his cock dragging against Jamie's within the vice of his fist.

"Fuck, that's so good," Jamie praised, staring down at their bodies, at his own hairy chest against pale, decorated skin. It all felt sweeter, knowing who Tyler was. Knowing he kept his heart locked up tight, reserved only for those who'd earned it.

Jamie was going to fucking *earn it*. "I'm almost there," he gritted out between clenched teeth, the heat that was curling low in his gut tightening. "I'm going to mark you, baby. Remind you that you're *mine*."

"Jamie—" Tyler threw his head back with a gasp.

Jamie snarled, giving in to the chase, his fist flying over their cocks without restraint. Tyler was slick and hot against him, and he was *there*.

Right fucking there.

Jamie came with a shout, his body going rigid as his cock pulsed, shooting thick stripes over Tyler's stomach. The pleasure was too much, leaving Jamie's ears ringing and his vision blurring. Somehow, he kept his hand moving, even as the touch grew overwhelming.

Tyler came with a shudder, his hips bucking as his come spilled over both their cocks. Jamie kept sliding his hand over him until the last drip of white leaked from Tyler's flushed, red tip.

Beautiful. So damn beautiful.

Carefully, Jamie gathered Tyler into his arms, maneuvering them under the warm spray. He started to wash Tyler, wiping his body down with gentle caresses. His boyfriend nuzzled into his chest, his fingertips tracing softly along Jamie's back.

"How was that?" Jamie whispered into Tyler's wet hair.

Tyler tilted his head back, resting his chin against Jamie's chest. "Perfect," he said, with a cheeky little smile.

Jamie let out a deep breath. "As much as I'd love to stay here forever, I've got a party to host, and everyone will be here soon."

He turned the water off and grabbed a towel, handing it to Tyler before he got his own. "Feel free to relax while I get ready."

"No, I want to help." Tyler toweled off his dark hair and then shook his head, sending little droplets of water flying through the air. "We're a team, right?"

"Yeah, baby. We fucking are."

CHAPTER 16
TYLER
HE'S IN.

There hadn't been a single second of quiet since the first of the Muskies players showed up at Jamie's house for the team holiday party.

Booming laughs, shouts, shrieks, and laughter of children filled every corner of Jamie's home, and Tyler understood, then, why a man like Jamie lived in such a large place.

Jamie had introduced Tyler to his teammates, their partners, and kids, only removing his big hand from Tyler's back to give everyone a hug. Tyler had been surprised to learn a few members of the Muskies staff were queer, and had loved seeing how openly they were welcomed into the fold.

A lean, dark-haired man wearing a vibrant green Grinch sweater rushed at Jamie, wrapping his arms around Jamie's body in a bear hug. "We missed you, big guy," he said, voice muffled against the front of Jamie's sweater.

"Get off," Jamie groaned, but Tyler saw that he couldn't hold back a smile. "Oi!" Jamie called out toward the living room full of people. "Someone come get Matty!"

"He is not my problem!" Elias Svensson, a Swedish defenseman, held up his hands where he sat on the couch. "I am too old for rookies."

"Shut it, Svenny," Carter called out from across the room, grinning to reveal his missing front tooth. He had a hint of a Boston accent. "You don't get to claim you're old until you start doing yoga at the hotel with the vets."

Bailey Cox, one of the other young players, scowled from where he was sitting with his girlfriend, Juliet. "Hey! It isn't just for the old guys, Carts. I've been going and I swear it's helping my stamina."

That got a loud chorus of laughs and crude jokes from the young guys, followed immediately by the quiet reminder that there were *actual* kids in the room from the older guys on the team.

Tyler had given up trying to keep track of the rest of the players' names, but thankfully Jamie had been whispering reminders in his ear throughout the afternoon.

The main topic of the party was the upcoming Winter Classic, a highly-publicized game played outdoors in a football stadium or ballpark. This year, the Muskies were hosting, and a rink was already being built at Camp Randall Stadium, where the University of Wisconsin's football team played.

Jamie had mentioned the game briefly before, but Tyler hadn't realized what a big deal it was. Apparently, the league hosted only one per year, and spent months promoting and advertising the event. It was scheduled for the day after New Years, and there would be a flurry of media events around the game that the players were expected to attend.

Listening as the players ribbed their captain about the silliness of his injury–shouting at him to "watch the hand, Sully," whenever he picked up a plate or got someone a drink–made Tyler smile.

It was obvious his teammates missed him and loved him. Tyler understood what Jamie's commitment was to the team, why they came first: Jamie had been chosen to lead them. They looked to him for guidance, and in turn, he took care of them.

They were ready for Jamie to be back.

When it was time to eat, the parents with young kids went through the buffet line first. The spread was classic holiday fare–a turkey, a spiral ham, a few different types of stuffing, more casseroles than Tyler had ever seen in his life, and enough desserts to fill Jamie's entire kitchen island.

Another defenseman, John Moore, had a newborn baby strapped to his chest in a soft wrap like the one Tyler used to use with Rowan. Tyler watched as players came by, whispering encouragement to John as he stood at the edge of the room and swayed the baby to sleep.

Tyler hadn't been sure how Rowan was going to do with such a large group of people. At first, he'd clung to Tyler's hand, staying close amid the chaos. But soon enough, Henri and Jack had arrived, and Rowan had been coaxed into playing with them. Tyler made sure never to go too far away, but he relaxed, realizing he wasn't worried about his son.

He trusted that Rowan was safe around these people.

"Tyler!" Layla walked up to Tyler and gave him a hug. "It's so good to see you."

"Hi." Tyler felt a little lightheaded, a giddy kind of joy that sent him reeling. "Great to see you, too."

"Come sit with me." She grabbed him by the hand, pulling him over to an empty pair of stools by the kitchen bar. They still had a clear view of the kids, who were building something elaborate with colorful magnet tiles.

Once they were sitting, Layla's expression turned conspiratorial. She wore her hair up in a bun, and a red and white knit sweater hung off of one of her shoulders. "So. You and Sully." She held up her hand, her expression apologetic. "Sorry, you don't have to tell me anything. I'm just excited. He's always been so closed off about dating, especially during the season."

Tyler pressed his lips together, considering what he wanted to share. What they had was new, wasn't it? Was there a reason to keep it a secret?

More importantly, would Jamie mind him talking about their relationship?

But then he remembered how Jamie had introduced him to his teammates, how he hadn't hesitated when he'd said: *This is Tyler, my boyfriend, and his son, Rowan.*

He also remembered the picture Jamie had put up of the two of them on his social media, with Tyler in his lap, kissing his nose. The caption below, which had said: "*Life, lately*", followed by a black heart emoji.

"We're going to try," Tyler said, unable to keep himself from smiling.

Layla let out a loud whoop, raising her hands above her head. When half the people in the room turned to look at them, she waved them off with a loud, "None of your business!" She turned back toward Tyler with a smile. "How did it happen?"

"Well, we sort of kept running into each other, and he kept showing up and doing thoughtful things. Once we started saying what we wanted out loud, it didn't take us too long to realize we might be a good fit." He ducked his head. "Or, it didn't take Jamie long. It took me a while. I just..." Tyler sighed, looking at Layla and hoping she'd understand. "I didn't think I had time for someone else."

"I get it. When there's a kid in your life, it's easy to put your needs on the back-burner. Their needs are immediate, while we can survive for a while without much more than an occasional meal and a few hours of sleep. But eventually, everyone needs somebody. Maybe not romantically, maybe not even physically, but it's okay to need people."

Tyler nodded. "I get that. Doesn't mean I like it, but I get it."

They both laughed, and Tyler realized Layla really *did* get it. It was such a relief to not have to explain himself, to not have to try to put into words what it was like to feel torn in two, suspended between what *you* want and what is best for your kid.

"For what it's worth," Layla said, "Sully loves kids. He's always been like an uncle to ours. That man has so much love bottled up inside of him. He can be tightly wound, but I think he's just been waiting for the right person to stick with him. And when they do, I think he's going to love the hell out of them."

Tyler smiled fondly, trying to quiet the little kernel of fear in his chest. It was too easy to allow himself to imagine that he could be the one to stick with Jamie, the one who wouldn't leave. The one who understood how much of his heart belonged to hockey, and who could accept what remained.

"I hope we're enough for him." The admission slipped out.

Layla shook her head. "None of that shit," she said, looking Tyler in the eye. "Anyone would be lucky to have you and Rowan in their life. Sully wouldn't be dating you if he wasn't invested. That man doesn't do spontaneous things. So, if Sully says he's in, he's in."

Tyler felt himself relax. "Thanks," he said, and then turned in his seat to check on the kids. "Shit. Rowan's gotta pee."

Layla followed his gaze and burst into laughter. "Oh, yep. That's a pee dance if I've ever seen one."

As the afternoon faded into evening, Tyler felt himself getting more and more tired. Jamie found him sitting on the floor with Rowan curled up on his lap, listening to Arturi Alexeyev, one of the Russian players, telling a group of kids the story of Ded Moroz, a character from Russian folklore. Tyler had completely lost the plot of the story, but Rowan and the rest of the kids were totally captivated.

Jamie's arms wrapped around him, and Tyler felt the tickle of his mustache against his cheek as Jamie kissed him. "Wanted to let you know it's almost seven," Jamie whispered. "I would love to have you guys for a sleepover, but this crew will be here for a while."

Tyler looked up at him. Jamie's cheeks were flushed, and his hair had escaped the swept-back style he'd tamed it into after their earlier shower.

"Thank you," Tyler whispered back.

It was a "thank you" for checking the time, for always

thinking of Rowan. It was a "thank you" for how patient he had been while Tyler worked up the courage to say *yes* to Jamie. It was a "thank you" for everything.

Jamie hummed, and pressed a chaste kiss to Tyler's lips. He settled in beside them as Arturi finished the story, and then helped Tyler gather up their things. Tyler tugged on his boots and coat before kneeling down and helping a sleepy, yawning Rowan into his jacket.

"Thanks for coming to my house, buddy," Jamie said to Rowan. "You're welcome to come over any time, got it?"

Rowan nodded. "You're my most favorite best friend."

Jamie's eyes went soft. Tyler's heart flopped in his chest.

Jamie looked down at Tyler, and there was *so much* there in his eyes, like he knew what it meant when a kid chose you. When you were granted an important place in their world.

When a kid decided you were *theirs*.

"Thanks, Rowan," Jamie said, opening his arms. "Hug?"

Rowan rushed into his embrace, and Tyler put a hand over his mouth. His eyes burned, but he blinked before any tears could escape.

Jamie walked them to their car, Rowan in his arms. Tyler started the engine while Jamie put Rowan in his carseat, and then stepped aside so Tyler could buckle him in.

They moved together like they'd done this before. Like loading the car was a routine part of their life. Closing the car door, Tyler turned to Jamie.

"Thank you," Tyler said, his voice breaking.

"Hey," Jamie said, moving toward him, and then Tyler was surrounded by a puffy coat and warmth and the unassuming smell of *Jamie* as he pressed gentle kisses to Tyler's forehead. "What's going on?"

"I'm just so happy, Jamie. Do you know how scary that is?"

He felt Jamie nod against the top of his head. "Yeah. I know."

"Rowan loves you," Tyler went on. "My kid, he…He *loves* you.

I never thought I'd have someone, and never imagined there could be someone who wanted both of us."

"You're a package deal," Jamie said, softly.

"We are."

Jamie leaned in and kissed Tyler's nose, then his cheek, then his chin. There was a quiet, fond smile on his face. "You need to get Rowan home, and I need to make sure the rookies haven't set my house on fire."

Tyler laughed quietly, wiping his eyes. "Good luck with them."

"I'll be fine."

"Text me?"

"Of course." After one more kiss, Tyler climbed into the car. He watched Jamie walk back to the brightly lit house, his body a looming shadow in the night.

"Papa!"

Tyler looked at Rowan in the rearview mirror as he put the car in gear. "What's up, kiddo?"

His hands clapped together, his face split open in a grin. "You gave Jamie a mouth kiss!"

Tyler smiled. "Yeah, I did."

CHAPTER 17
JAMIE
GOOD TASTE. NICE HAIR.

Jamie jogged down the hallway in the Muskies practice arena. He'd already changed into his compression base layers and his team hoodie, and had spent about an hour doing PT for his hand before going through his usual warm-up.

His body was warm, muscles limber and ready.

Jamie opened the door to the locker room and inhaled. A smile stretched across his face at the sharp smell of sweat and the steady rumble of voices. Somebody had put on some electronic metal music–probably Esa. *The Finns all loved that shit.*

"Cap!" Matty looked up from where he was strapping on his shin pads. "Guys, look! Look! Sully's back!"

The whole room erupted in cheers. Jamie felt his cheeks heat as he made the rounds, clapping backs and bumping fists. He'd just seen them all at the Christmas party, but still, it was different to be back at the rink.

Jamie took his usual spot between Mitchy and Coop, and muscle memory took over. His hands worked of their own accord, strapping on his pads before slapping them to check their tightness and positioning. Around him, guys worked on gearing up and taping their sticks.

"You're coming with us on the road, right?" Cooper asked.

Jamie nodded. "It'll be good to play before the Winter Classic. Hopefully get my legs under me and work out any kinks."

"Thank fuck," Mitch said from his other side. "I need you back as my plane buddy. Pauly took your seat, and all he talks about is Roman history."

"We could learn a lot from studying their infantry formations!" Paul Roy shouted from his stall on the far wall.

"Can someone please explain to me what Roman infantry has to do with hockey?"

Pauly shook his head. "You just aren't ready to think outside the box."

"Thinking outside the box? What is this, a multi-level marketing scheme?" Mitch shot back.

Matt Lee poked his head into the locker room. "Wait, what do you guys think about me selling essential oils? My sister does it and makes bank."

The response was loud and unified: "No!"

"I like your boyfriend."

Jamie glanced over at Emīls, whose face flushed pink, like maybe he hadn't meant to say something out loud. "Sorry," the younger Swede continued. "I talked to him about music at your party and he is very nice. Good taste. Nice hair."

"Great hair," Onni chimed in, nodding. He was already in his pads, staring out at the room from his stall with solemn stoicism. "Much too cool for you."

"What the hell, Onni?" Jamie looked over at the rookie goalie, indignant. "You live for free in my basement, you'd think you'd be nicer to me!"

Onni shrugged. "I am nice. I also tell truth."

The guys around him laughed, and Jamie felt like he was finally releasing a breath he'd been holding. He was back with the boys, where he belonged.

The team made their way to the ice where they were joined by the coaches. Jamie skated in aimless circles, testing his edges and reminding his body of the weight of his gear, the feel of his stick in his hand.

The drills were second nature. He started slow, gradually working his body up to full speed and effort. Sweat beaded under his helmet, and he went by the bench to grab a drink before he lined up against Carter to work on corner puck battles.

On the whistle, they skated hard to the corner. Jamie's body hit the boards and he turned, trying to get his stick in position to win the puck.

Carter was huge, taller and broader than Jamie, and he used every advantage he had to push Jamie out of position. Jamie worked his skate in, trying to kick the puck toward his stick.

"You wish, old man," Carter growled, but there was humor in his voice.

"Spoke too soon," Jamie shot back, right as he dug his stick in and scooped the puck out.

Carter groaned. "I hate how good you are."

Jamie threw his hands up and laughed. "I'm on your team, man!"

They circled up to review their face-off sets, taking a knee around the whiteboard Coach Hollister had wheeled out onto the ice.

"Some knees are not made for kneeling," Ollie muttered under his breath beside him.

Jamie nudged him in the shoulder. "Focus up. You've had some good chances to score off the face-off, especially if you get position in front of the net."

Ollie turned his attention to their coach, and Jamie smiled.

He was so fucking back.

Practice had ended, but Jamie wasn't done. After his time off, he needed the extra minutes on the ice, the extra reps with the puck.

He could push himself today, and still have plenty of time to recover before he was back on the ice.

It was their last practice before their Christmas break–the whole league took off for three days, and then after the holiday the team would be hitting the road for two quick away games–Dallas and Chicago–before coming home for the Winter Classic.

Jamie made his way around the rink, gathering all the pucks in the center of the ice. Grabbing one on his stick, he practiced his stickhandling through the pucks, doing his best not to hit any of them. He wove his way back and forth, building speed as he began to feel more comfortable. His hand had felt good throughout practice, and even now any lingering discomfort was barely noticeable.

He heard someone fall in behind him, but he ignored them. After he came out the other side, he turned and saw Ollie, Bailey, Matty, Victor, Emīls, and Carter had all gathered around the center circle.

Jamie felt a wave of pride. "Go on then," he said, pointing his stick to a few loose pucks at the edges. "Grab a puck and follow along." He looked down the ice, and saw Anders and Onni still running drills in the crease. "Maybe we can rope in a goalie to stick around."

After stickhandling, Jamie had them skate the full length of the ice and take shots against Onni, who'd been thrilled to get the extra reps in net.

"Might as well wear a sign telling Onni where you're going to shoot!" Jamie shouted at Matty, who'd telegraphed his shot, making it an easy save for the rookie goalie.

When it was Jamie's turn, he challenged himself to push faster, to pick up his feet. He managed a hard fake on Onni, but the young goalie still managed to snatch the puck from the air. "Now, *that* was pretty," Jamie said, tapping Onni on the pads with his stick as he skated by. "You earned that one."

Eventually, the guys' play started to get sloppy, and Jamie knew it was time to wrap it up. They gathered the pucks, and

Jamie made sure to compliment everyone who'd stuck around, tapping pads and gloves as they walked toward the locker room.

"Sully!"

Jamie glanced over, finding Coach Hollister sitting alone in the stands. "Hey, Coach."

"Got a minute?"

Jamie nodded. Coach met him in the hallway, wearing his usual head-to-toe Muskies sweats. He looked out at the ice, his hands in his pockets with a pensive frown on his face.

Jamie waited, catching his breath. He'd been around Coach long enough to know he would talk when he was ready.

"They haven't done that while you've been gone," he said, nodding his chin toward the ice. "Sometimes Onni would stay, but the rest of them?" He looked at Jamie. "You inspire them."

Jamie exhaled. "I'm trying," he said. "I know I haven't been as good as Sharpie this year, but I'm trying to lead them."

"The truth is, Sully–and I don't want you to take this the wrong way–a lot of them are better than you. On paper, at least a third of the guys on this team have more skill than you've ever had. But you have something intangible. You're our second line center because you take what talent and skill you do have, and you match it with hard work. Real, gritty, hard work and determination. These guys see that. You show them the things that matter beyond the skills, beyond the shit you can get good at alone in your garage. You model work ethic. The willingness to keep striving. You teach them to not settle for "good enough." To have integrity. You show them what it really means to be a pro. What it means to be a good teammate and a leader."

Jamie opened his mouth to protest, but Coach cut him off. "That doesn't mean do more, Sully. You already do enough. Keep showing up and doing the things you've always done. Do your job on the ice, and everything else will fall into place. Just you being here makes the whole team better."

Shifting his stick from one hand to the other, Jamie tried

tugging at his hair but his helmet was in the way, and his bulky glove kept him from getting a good grip. *Dammit.*

"Thanks, Coach," he managed. "I…I think I needed to hear that."

Coach Hollister nodded, clapping him on the shoulder pad. "Nothing wrong with needing a reminder every now and then." He raised his graying brows at Jamie. "I don't want to see any more of that garbage you were doing on the ice at the beginning of the year, got it?"

Jamie snorted. "Got it."

"Now get your ass out of here. I want to go home."

"Yes, Coach."

Jamie plodded down the quiet hall toward the locker room.

After he cleaned up, he'd head home, and finish the last of the gift wrapping. Early Christmas morning, he'd drive up to see his dad and step-mom. Every year they made waffles and opened presents at their house before a big lunch with extended family. Jamie didn't get to see his dad very much during the season, and looked forward to Christmas with their family every year.

This year, though, Jamie caught himself wondering when he'd be back in Madison. Maybe, if he got back early enough, he'd get to spend some time that evening with Tyler and Rowan.

As he walked into the locker room and joined the guys stripping off their gear, he had an idea. He looked around until he found who he was looking for. "Oi, Cheerios!"

Ollie and Onni looked up at the same time from where they were sitting side by side in their base layers. It was almost creepy, the way they moved in perfect unison.

"Mind helping me with something tomorrow?"

Oliver tilted his head, sweaty brown hair flopping onto his forehead. "Will there be snacks?"

Jamie rolled his eyes, huffing out a laugh. "Yes. I'll make sure to provide snacks."

CHAPTER 18
TYLER
BEST SURPRISE EVER

Tyler loved Christmas morning.

Bing Crosby's Christmas album played on a small bluetooth speaker, and the whole house smelled like the cinnamon and apples he'd sautéed in butter. Rowan had torn through the wrapped presents under the tree, and was fully immersed in playing with the set of wooden farm animals that Tyler's mom had mailed them. They were still in their pajamas, and had no plans to change anytime soon.

The scraggly tree they'd gotten on sale was set up in the corner, rainbow lights glowing beside strands of popcorn and cranberries they'd made a few days ago.

Dotty and Sandra had come upstairs earlier with a French toast casserole and half of a glazed ham. They'd also brought presents for both of them: a pair of butterfly wings for Rowan that strapped onto his back, and a beautiful matcha bowl and a whisk for Tyler. Tyler and Rowan had worked together on the crochet-hooked potholders they'd made for their downstairs neighbors, picking Muskies colors for Dotty and a combination of pinks and purples for Sandra.

The women had left a while ago to volunteer at the local soup kitchen, a Christmas day tradition they'd shared for as long as they'd been together. Someday, when Rowan was a little older, Tyler hoped to join them.

His mom had called, and, after the *Merry Christmas*'s and *We miss you*'s, his mom had, once again, brought up moving back home. Tyler had wished, for a moment, that she and his dad could acknowledge the magic he'd created for himself and Rowan this year. That they could see him doing exactly what he'd set out to do: providing for himself and Rowan on his own.

Tyler's phone buzzed on the couch beside him. He picked it up, and smiled as soon as he saw who the message was from.

JAMIE

Merry Christmas! When you get a chance, go look outside 🙂

Putting his phone in his pocket, Tyler grabbed their jackets. "Kiddo," he said, shoving his feet into his snow boots. "I think there's something outside."

That got Rowan's attention. His head shot up. "Reindeer?"

Tyler laughed. "Maybe. Let's get your boots on and check it out."

They climbed down the stairs and out the door, Tyler following right behind Rowan.

"Papa, look!"

There, in the middle of the front yard, was a snowman. It was imperfect, as the best snowmen should always be–the bottom ball a bit lopsided, and one of the stick arms significantly longer than the other.

But it had a long carrot nose and two round, black, button eyes, and wore a now-familiar hockey jersey with the white C embroidered on the chest.

Rowan ran down to get a closer look, laughing and jumping as he chattered about how amazing the snowman was. Tyler's whole body felt warm as he watched, content in the knowledge that his son was happy, that he'd pulled off Christmas on their own.

Only, he wasn't on his own. Not this year. Dotty and Sandra

had played a part in their day, and now, here was a snowman–*a fucking snowman*–made by the man who'd crashed into their life with a broken hand and a flimsy right hook. Jamie was a part of it now. A part of the life Tyler was building for himself, and for Rowan.

"Papa, there's something on the steps!"

Tyler looked down, and sure enough, there was a red gift bag tied with a green ribbon. He picked it up and looked at the tag. *For Tyler,* it read.

He pulled apart the tissue paper, and when he saw what was inside he inhaled sharply, his hands trembling as he held the gift closer.

It was a small notebook, bound in soft leather. As Tyler carefully opened the cover, several pieces of paper fell out of the pages inside. He picked them up.

The first: an annual pass to the Children's Museum.

The second was a printed photo of Tyler and Rowan. It was artfully blurry, but it was clearly them.

A hand covered half of Tyler's face, doing a poor job of concealing the curve of a smile. His eyes were closed, deep laugh lines extending from their corners, like he'd been captured mid-laugh. He looked joyful. Rowan was right beside him, his cheek pressed against Tyler's face and a big grin showing off his teeth.

Jamie must have taken the picture at the Children's Museum. Instantly, it became Tyler's favorite picture of them.

One last paper fell out–a handwritten note.

Merry Christmas, Tyler.
Maybe you can write some words here, when the time is right.
XX
Jamie

His emotions tangled together. There was a sense of being

overwhelmed battling with gratitude, and a feeling of happiness that felt powerful enough to warm his body in the cold. Jamie must have remembered that day in the coffee shop, when Tyler had opened up to him about how much he missed writing poetry.

Tyler grabbed his phone from his pocket. He wanted to call Jamie, wanted to hear his voice in his ear, but he hesitated. He didn't want to bother Jamie while he was with his family. He didn't want to interrupt his life.

Maybe there would be time to talk later. Tyler pressed his lips together as he typed out a message.

TYLER:

Thank you, Jamie. Rowan loves his gift. As do I.

When his phone rang a moment later, Tyler answered. "Hi," he said, already smiling.

"You saw it?" Jamie asked, his voice warm and rich in Tyler's ear. He could hear the soft sound of conversation in the background. "Rowan found his snowman?"

Tyler watched Rowan, who was now running in circles around the snowman shouting gleefully about "Putting the puck!" and "Goalie interference!"

"Can you hear him?" Tyler asked. "He loves it."

"Yes!" Jamie let out a low laugh. "I'm so glad he likes it."

Tyler sat down on the front steps, resting his elbows on his knees. "How early did you get up to do this?"

"It wasn't too bad. I made the rookies help me."

"Jamie!" Tyler's voice rose, indignant. "You made them help you on Christmas?"

Jamie laughed again, and Tyler let his eyes close for just a moment, savoring the sound. "They wanted to help," he protested. "And I had snacks."

"Are all hockey players food-motivated?"

"Yes."

Tyler couldn't stop smiling. "Are you having a good visit with your dad?"

"Yeah. I..." Jamie stopped and cleared his throat. "I told them about you."

"Really?"

"Everyone's excited to meet you. You know, someday. Whenever you're ready, or if you're ever ready, or–"

"Jamie."

"Yeah?"

"I'd love to meet them." It was probably too soon to talk about things like meeting parents and looking into the future, but Tyler couldn't pretend that he wasn't ready for all of it. It didn't scare him, anymore, how much Jamie had come to mean to them in such a short amount of time. Rowan came running over, his cheeks flushed and eyes bright. "Kiddo, do you want to say hi to Jamie?"

He put the phone on speaker. "Jamie!" Rowan shouted. "This is the most bestest snowman!"

"I'm glad you like it, buddy." Jamie replied. "Depending on what time I get back, would you guys be up for a visit later?"

Rowan turned his pleading eyes to Tyler. "Please, Papa? Can we please see Jamie?"

"We'd love that." Tyler couldn't imagine a better way to end their first Christmas in Madison.

Tyler pulled into Jamie's driveway and parked behind Layla's minivan. The whole Jackson family was there, the kids bundled in snow suits next to a pile of plastic sleds. Mitch was already standing at Jamie's garage, punching in the code to open the large bay.

Tyler hadn't been sure what to do for Jamie for Christmas. After spending hours trying to think back on everything he'd learned about Jamie, he landed on something Jamie had told him the day he'd come to the Children's Museum.

He got Rowan out of his carseat and into his snow gear.

"Thanks for making this happen," Tyler said, giving Layla a hug. "I know it's Christmas and all."

Layla smiled. "Are you kidding me? The kids love Sully's back hill. This is the perfect way to work off all the sugar they ate this morning with my folks."

"Can you guys help me carry this?" Mitch stood in the garage next to a large pile of gear. "In all of my years knowing Sully, I've never actually set this up." He looked over at Tyler. "Do you know what you're doing?"

"Not a clue." Tyler shrugged. "That's what the internet is for."

Mitch threw his hands in the air as Layla burst out laughing. "Sully's lucky to have you," Mitch said, smiling.

They found a tracked sled in Jamie's garage, and stacked bags and boxes of gear labeled "ICE FISHING SHIT." Somehow, they managed to drag the pile of gear down the hill to the edge of the frozen lake. Tyler had found a local website that updated the ice conditions for the lakes around Madison, and was confident the ice was thick enough to safely walk on. Judging by the other huts visible across the lake, he assumed they would be fine.

Mitch stayed with the kids while Tyler and Layla dragged the sled out onto the ice.

"I think we're supposed to wear skates for this part," Layla said, already gasping for air as she tried to stay upright on the ice.

Tyler laughed. "This was such a bad idea," he said, trying to catch his breath. "Neither of us know anything about setting up an ice fishing hut."

"But that's what the internet is for, Ty!"

Tyler couldn't stop laughing. They slipped and slid across the ice until they decided that they were far enough from the shore to set up.

They managed the tent without instructions. It was similar to most modern camping tents, with collapsable poles. Once the tent was up, they dragged the other bags and boxes inside. One case held a huge contraption that resembled some kind of corkscrew as long as Tyler's leg, while another box had a propane heater. A long case held fishing poles, and a folding camp chair.

Huddled over Tyler's phone, they watched videos of people using the corkscrew to drill through the ice. Apparently, what Jamie had was a hand auger, which seemed relatively straightforward to use.

"Do you want to do it?" He asked Layla, looking alternately at her and the long auger that sat on the ice between them.

"Nope," she said, shooting him a cheeky grin. "This is a grand Christmas gesture for your man. You get to aug."

Tyler snorted. "That's not a real word." He picked up the tool, careful to hold it out and away from his body. The two angled blades at the bottom looked really fucking sharp. "Okay. I can do this."

"I will be here to cheer you on and run for help if you get hurt."

Tyler stuck his tongue out at Layla. "I can't figure out if you're a good friend or a terrible one." He made sure the auger was straight and upright, and then, slowly, with one hand holding the top, he began to crank the handle.

It took him a second to figure out how to hold it steady, but then a quiet churning sound filled the small tent as the auger cut into the ice. A minute later, it dropped through, sending a pile of shaved ice bursting out of the opening. Tyler pulled out the tool as Layla cheered, sweeping the ice chips away from the hole.

"I can't believe that worked," Tyler said, looking up at Layla.

She clapped. "I'm honestly impressed."

"Okay." Tyler stood up, wiping the ice from his gloves. "I'm going to leave everything else for Jamie to set up." He checked the time on his phone. "He should be home from his dad's place in twenty minutes."

They organized the remaining gear as best as they could, and then hustled back across the ice to Jamie's yard. The kids were red-nosed and happily sliding down the gentle slope of the hill, with Mitch dragging them up to the top over and over again.

"Thank you again for helping me," Tyler said, leaning his shoulder against Layla.

She smiled, leaning back into him. "This is what friends do. We show up for each other."

Tyler felt his throat tighten with emotion. There was no way Layla could have known what those simple words meant to him. How much it meant to hear someone call him a friend.

"Can we have dinner again soon?" Tyler asked, trying not to sound too hopeful. "I can come over early and help cook?"

"Of course," Layla said, like it wasn't a big deal to her. "I'd love that." She cupped her hands around her mouth. "Come on, kids! Time to head home!"

The kids mobbed them, and there was a flurry of goodbyes and promises to see each other soon as they loaded up into their van.

Tyler led Rowan into the house through Jamie's garage. Mitch had reassured him that Jamie would be thrilled to see them, and had encouraged them to go right in and make themselves at home.

Tyler got their snow gear off and found the blocks Jamie kept stashed in his hall closet. They settled into the living room, Rowan happily playing on the floor while Tyler got them both water from the kitchen.

There was a knock on the door, and Tyler ran over to get it, his wool socks sliding against the wood floor.

He paid the delivery driver cash and carried the bag back to the kitchen, setting it on the counter before joining Rowan on the floor.

"Hello?" The door shut loudly behind Jamie as he walked into the kitchen from the garage. *Fuck,* he looked good. He wore a green and red argyle sweater with dark wool trousers that hugged his thighs. When Jamie saw them, his face split into a huge smile, and any doubt in Tyler's mind about sneaking into his boyfriend's house was washed away. "Hey! What are you two doing here?"

Rowan jumped up and ran over to Jamie, bouncing up and

down. "We did a surprise for you, Jamie! A Christmas surprise! Because it's Christmas today!"

Jamie's eyes widened. "Really?"

Tyler walked over to Jamie, wrapping his arms around him. "Merry Christmas," he said, going up on his toes with a silent request.

Jamie kissed him softly. "I'm so happy you're here," he said against Tyler's lips. "Best surprise ever."

Tyler sank back down to his heels and looked at Rowan. "Should we show Jamie his Christmas surprise?"

Rowan nodded eagerly.

"Okay," Tyler started, reaching for the bag on the counter. "There was a little hiccup in step one of your surprise, because Culver's is closed on Christmas. I hope Chinese food is alright—I got you General Tso's chicken and egg drop soup."

Jamie bent over the bag and inhaled. "Mmmmm," he said. "Smells perfect. Did you get some for you guys, too?"

"Yeah," Tyler went on. "And there's a case of Spotted Cow in the fridge."

"Really? You got me a Cow case?"

"And, for the main event, you'll probably want to throw another layer on."

A few minutes later, they were all layered up for the cold afternoon again. Rowan walked between them, holding tightly to both of their hands. When they reached the edge of the lake, Jamie let out a warm laugh. "You didn't," he said, glancing between the distant ice fishing hut and Tyler. "Did you set up my hut?"

Tyler grinned, satisfaction curling in him at the happiness on Jamie's face. "I used the auger and everything."

Jamie leaned over and kissed him hard. When he drew back, his eyes were bright, the green taking on an almost-blue hue under the pale sky. "I can't believe you did this."

"Papa says you're his favorite friend," Rowan said, looking up at them. "And we should do nice things for our favorite people."

Jamie's eyes softened. "Your Papa is a smart guy," he said,

before rubbing his palms together. "How about I teach you boys how to ice fish?"

"Yes!" Rowan clapped his mittens together. "Are there snacks?"

"Let's eat the food your Papa got us, and then we can go out to the hut and get cozy." Jamie reached down and scooped Rowan into his arms. "Did you know I have a special heater in the ice hut?"

Later, Rowan sat curled up on Tyler's lap, his eyes drifting shut. The light was fading in the small hut, which was surprisingly warm given how small the heater was. Soft country music filled the air, and Jamie sat across from them with the wooden handle of the fishing pole tucked under one thigh.

He watched them with a small smile on his face.

"What?" Tyler asked.

Jamie just shrugged. "It feels good to have you here."

"It feels good to be here," Tyler echoed. "I want to keep making time for you. For us."

"Me too." Jamie reached out with his boot and nudged Tyler's shin. "It's been amazing spending all this time together. Moments like this are going to be rare once I go back into the lineup. I'll be busy again."

"Are you excited to play?"

Jamie nodded. "Yeah. I've missed it." Tyler watched him closely, noticing the slip in his smile. "I'm nervous. It sounds ridiculous, but–"

"Not ridiculous," Tyler cut in.

"It is, a little bit. I've been playing hockey for so long, and I was out longer than this when I pulled my groin eight years ago."

"So what feels different now?"

Jamie's lips parted in a sigh. "I'm the captain now," he started. "It means more. What I do out there…It's always mattered, but now I've got to be better. At the beginning of the season I was trying to do too many things out there on the ice. I can see that now. But I can't help but worry that I'm–that what I bring to the team isn't enough."

Tyler watched Jamie's eyes. He saw the fear right there on the surface, even as the light was fading in the little tent. "We both know I don't know shit about hockey," Tyler said, grinning when he got a smile from Jamie. "But I'm getting to know you, and I've met your team, and I think if you asked any of them they'd say that you are the only captain they want. You're a leader, Jamie, and you're going to figure it all out. I know it."

"I really want to kiss you right now," Jamie said, giving him a fond smile.

A quiet laugh escaped him. "Sorry, Cap. I've got my hands full."

Quiet settled between them. Rowan shifted in Tyler's lap, burrowing his warm face against Tyler's neck. Jamie watched them, his expression soft and fond and everything Tyler had ever hoped for.

"I'm going to be gone a lot," Jamie said, breaking the silence. Tyler could hear the apology in his voice. "But I'll give you as much time as I can."

Tyler wrapped his arms tighter around Rowan. "I'll be here. I knew who you were when I said yes to dating you, Jamie. I know what you mean to your team and to this town. I'm with you every step of the way."

CHAPTER 19
JAMIE
THE GREAT CANADIAN SLUMBERJACK

Daniel: Welcome back, I'm Daniel Cummings, joined by my colleague, Tabitha Dunkirk. Tabitha, have you managed to get any barbecue yet?

Tabitha: I was able to sneak out after the morning skate to visit one of my favorite spots. You know how I like a good rack of ribs every time we travel to Dallas.

Daniel: Boy howdy do I ever. A word to the wise: never stand between my cohost and a plate full of baby back ribs.

Tabitha: Dan, I don't think the fans tune in to hear your stories. Let's get back to the game.

Daniel: Alright, Tabitha. You win this round. What are we looking at this evening?

Tabitha: Tonight, the Muskies are rejoined by their captain, Jamie Sullivan, who has been out for four and a half weeks with a hand injury that he sustained in an on-ice fight back in November. He practiced with the team just before the winter break and he's out on the ice for warm-ups here in Dallas. All eyes are on the captain to see what he will do in his return. What should we expect from his first game back?

Daniel: All the reports we've gotten over the past few weeks have been positive, and at this point there's no reason to expect anything but the best from Sullivan. Leading up to his injury, we had seen a drop in his productivity on the ice, but I'd say that the optimism about Sullivan's return is by no means misplaced.

Tabitha: The Muskies stand in third place in the Central Division, with Dallas hot on their heels. Two points tonight could go a long way toward securing a playoff spot for the spring.

Daniel: The Muskies also have the Winter Classic to think about. To face Minnesota, who currently leads the division, is a huge opportunity for the Muskies, and especially Jamie Sullivan, to show the league and fans of the game what their team is made of.

Tabitha: I know we'll all be watching the captain closely tonight. We'll be right back for puck-drop and live game coverage.

Jamie squirted water into his mouth, glancing up at the clock.

"Kolshnevich is slow getting back on the wing." Beside him on the bench, Cooper Bell pointed to the Dallas player on the ice, raising his voice over the roar of the arena. "Next time we're out there with him, you push up the middle and I'll feed it to you."

"You're faster," Jamie shot back, eyes never leaving the ice. "I'll carry it up the middle, draw in Dwyer, and that'll leave you one-on-one with Kolshnevich. That's a matchup you'll win every time."

Cooper nodded. "Got it, Sully."

Jamie tapped his stick against the boards when the third line came in for a change and the first line climbed over the boards. "Ollie, your positioning is good in front of the net," he called down the bench as Oliver reached for a water bottle. "Stick with it. The rebounds will be there."

The younger player shot him a salute and picked up an iPad to review his shift.

Jamie took a deep breath. *Fuck,* it felt good to be back. From the bench, the rink smelled like ice and sweat, the shouts of the crowd muted as he watched the players streaking up and down the ice.

He'd missed this. He'd missed the game and the team and the immediacy of his job. Everything else faded away but the game, the team. The *now*.

They were up 2-1 with five minutes left in the third. Jamie was starting to feel the burn in his legs–no amount of conditioning could fully prepare a body for the demands of a live game. But his hand felt good, his body felt ready, and his mind was focused.

For the first time all year, he was playing *his* game. Not Sharpie's game, but the kind of play that had earned him a spot on the second line for the past five years. He focused on the things he did best–defending Dallas' top line, and keeping their star forward without a point for the period. On their end of the ice, he worked the puck from the top and then from behind the net, using his sharp eye to find passing lanes to Coop and Esa.

He was working his ass off, but he wasn't trying to do more than his role required. He wasn't trying to be someone else.

Just be Sully.

As his line was called and he hopped back over the boards and onto the ice, he'd never loved hockey more.

"Great work, boys!" Jamie, still in his shoulder pads and skates, made the rounds, tapping shoulders and slapping helmets as the guys started shedding their gear in the locker room. "Bergy, unreal save there in the third. You were amazing out there."

Anders Berglund gave Jamie a rare smile. "Is good you are back, Sully. We missed you."

Jamie squeezed his shoulder. It meant a lot to hear those words from their veteran goalie, who tended to be more of the stoic type.

"Cap, we thought you had that clapper from the circle off the draw," Matt Lee tossed his jersey into the laundry cart. "That would've been epic."

Jamie shrugged. "Ollie was right there for the rebound. It all worked out."

They'd finished the game 4-1, with two late goals locking in their victory. Dallas' star player, Kevin Smith, who Jamie had matched up with, hadn't gotten a single point. Jamie was riding high, his smile so big his cheeks hurt.

"Next practice, can we work on tips?" Ollie was still breathing hard, half of his gear still strapped on, when he sat down next to Jamie's stall. "You're right. I'm getting the chances in front. That rebound off your shot…I see it now."

Jamie nodded, tapping the rookie on the knee. "You got it, kid."

"I will help," Onni said from his stall, as he removed the last pieces of his dry gear. He hadn't played tonight, but still sat on the sidelines, ready to go in as the backup if the team needed him. "I need more practice with rebound control. We will get better. Together."

The two rookies shared a long look and a nod that Jamie didn't even attempt to understand.

"Count me in for training with the Cap," Liam Olsson shouted from across the room. "I need to learn how he does that silky neutral zone footwork."

Jamie felt a pleased, and slightly embarrassed flush climb up the back of his neck.

Maybe I can do this, he thought.

Coach Hollister came into the room. He clapped Jamie on the back, offering him a crooked smile. "It's good to have you back, Sully. What you did out there tonight? *That* is the player we named Captain of this team. Keep it up and we just might surprise everyone this year."

Jamie thanked his coach before stripping off the rest of his pads. There would be just enough time to run home, clean, and then pack, before heading to the team plane. They were flying to Chicago that night, and would have a day of practice before their game the following day.

It was good to be back.

When Jamie got to his hotel room in Chicago late that night, he stripped down to his briefs, brushed his teeth, and collapsed onto the bed with his phone in his hand.

It was late, but he wanted to hear Tyler's voice. If he was already sleeping, his phone would be off and Jamie would leave him a message.

He fucking *missed* him.

The phone rang twice before Tyler picked up. "Hey," he said.

Immediately, Jamie heard loud cries in the background. "You guys okay?"

"Um," Tyler started, and Jamie hated how ragged and defeated that one word sounded. "Kiddo, I know. We already had some cheese and apples, and now it's time to find your rest."

"Noooo!" Rowan's small voice wailed, more strained than Jamie had ever heard it. "Sleep is not cominggggg!"

Jamie wished he was there. He wished he could pick Rowan up in his arms and share some of the load.

"Jamie, I've got to go," Tyler said quietly.

"Wait," Jamie sat up in his bed. "Baby, can I try something?"

Tyler paused, and Rowan's cries grew louder. "Sure."

"Put me on speaker." After a pause, Jamie said, "Hey, buddy."

There was a little sniffle and the cries quieted. "Jamie?"

"Can I sing you a song?"

Again, it was quiet.

"He's nodding," Tyler said, and Jamie could hear the hint of amusement in his voice.

Jamie cleared his throat. He wasn't much of a singer, but he'd sung this particular Okee Dokee Brothers song to Mitch's kids and it had seemed to calm them down.

> "As the northern lights come out
> And the forest goes to bed
> The Great Canadian Slumberjack

Starts singin' 'bove your head
From the pines of the big woods
Spreadin' sawdust and sand
With an ax and with a saw
To the dreamers of the northern land
Singin' see what ya saw
And saw what you see
Saw the logs of Slumbertown
Without cuttin' down a tree."

He forgot the rest of the words, so he sang the same part again and again until his throat started to ache. He got to the last line, and trailed off into silence. He felt a little bit silly, then, singing into his phone alone in his hotel room.

"Jamie," Tyler's voice whispered through the phone.

Jamie matched his tone. "Yeah?"

"He's asleep."

Jamie grinned. "Really?"

"Really."

Jamie laid back down, curling onto his side with the phone held tightly against his cheek. "Tough night?"

"Fucking terrible."

"I'm sorry."

"It's okay. Sometimes it's like this." Jamie heard his soft exhale. "Am I allowed to say that I miss you?"

"Yeah, baby. I miss you, too."

"Tell me about the game."

He told Tyler how it felt to be back in the locker room, how something in him settled as he slipped on his game jersey. He talked about how some of the guys lost their shit around the Dallas ice crew, who were almost exclusively beautiful women doused in perfume.

After Tyler yawned for the second time, Jamie cut himself off. "Go to bed," he said softly.

"I like hearing you talk about hockey."

Jamie snorted. "You say that now."

"I mean it," Tyler said, and then yawned again. "Okay. I'm fading. G'night, Jamie."

"Goodnight."

Long after Jamie hung up, he lay there with his phone in his hand, smiling at the lights of Chicago blurred by the rain on his hotel room window.

By the time they pulled out the close win against Chicago, Jamie was ready to be home. He was thrilled to be back with the team, relieved to return to the rhythm that guided his life, but now there was someone waiting for him in Madison.

They had a quick post-game meal at the arena before their flight back to Madison. It was a short flight from Chicago, and Jamie was still wired from the game as he boarded the plane, staring out the window at the bright lights of the city as they took off.

Mitchy settled into the same row, tossing the pillow with a black silk case he took on every road trip onto the empty seat between them. "Battleship?"

Jamie nodded.

They set up their mini Battleship boards with the practiced efficiency of two people who had spent the last six years playing the same game on the team plane together. Some guys played cards, some guys watched movies, and others slept.

Jamie and Mitch liked to play Battleship.

They shot the shit like they usually did, but Jamie was distracted. It would be a little after midnight when they landed, and he knew he should go home and get some sleep. He could already tell his body was going to be sore tomorrow.

That would be the responsible thing to do.

He knew Tyler was working at the club tonight, and he was scheduled to get off around one.

Maybe Jamie could go surprise him. Maybe after they could go home and crawl into bed together, find the kind of bone-deep rest that came from being wrapped around someone close, someone safe. Someone who felt a hell of a lot like home.

"Sully, your move."

Jamie exhaled, and focused on his board.

He was going to go see his boyfriend when he got home.

It was crowded at The Blue Barn. Jamie paid the cover and slipped in the back, finding an empty table. His body was sore, protesting as he lowered himself onto the uncomfortable chair, but it was worth it if he got to see Tyler.

He pulled his baseball cap low. It wasn't that he was embarrassed to be seen there. He just didn't want to draw attention to himself, not when he was at Tyler's place of work.

A dancer with the build of a wrestler was onstage, dressed in something skintight and sequined, with a matching cowboy hat. Jamie watched him for a moment with a detached appreciation. The man was attractive, sure, but Jamie didn't have eyes for anyone but his boyfriend.

There was a large crowd, mostly sitting in groups around the low, round tables surrounding the stage. In the back corner of the room, an older man with harsh, angular features in an ill-fitting suit stared at something over Jamie's shoulder.

He turned just in time to see Tyler walking out from behind the bar.

Mine, mine, mine.

Jamie recognized the uniform, the denim shorts and boots, the glitter brushed over his tattooed skin, giving the illusion of a burnished brass statue. His hair curled around his shoulders, his lips glistened, and Jamie wanted to *lick* him and then nuzzle his head into the side of his neck.

It had barely been any time at all since he left on the road trip, but he'd missed him.

When Tyler's eyes snagged on him, a slow smile spread across his face. He moved through the tables, shooting the obligatory sultry looks at the patrons he passed, before running the last few yards to Jamie.

Jamie wanted to stand up, wanted to lift Tyler into his arms and spin him around like they were the leads in a holiday rom-com, but he didn't want to overstep. He still didn't fully understand the conventions of Tyler's work, and the last thing he wanted was to get Tyler in trouble.

"What are you doing here?" Tyler asked, his voice bright and almost breathless as he stood above Jamie.

"Hi," Jamie said, pretty sure he was smiling like a fool. He pressed his palms to his thighs in an effort to keep himself from touching his boyfriend, from wrapping him up in his arms and never letting go.

Tyler wore a fond expression as he brushed a thumb across Jamie's cheek. Jamie sighed, leaning into the touch.

"Can I hug you?" Jamie mumbled, his brain a little hazy.

"Probably not a good idea," Tyler said softly. "Can't have these folks getting any ideas."

Jamie opened his eyes, nodding in understanding. "I'm just really fucking happy to see you. I didn't want to wait."

"And I'm happy you're here." Tyler dropped his hand back to his side. "You played great tonight."

Jamie felt his chest puff like he was a fucking rooster or something. "You watched?"

Tyler nodded. "I mean, we didn't *watch*, but we listened to the play-by-play while we ate dinner."

"That's–I…" Jamie began. His chest felt tight, full to the point of overflowing. "Thank you for following the game."

Tyler's smile spread over his whole face. "Want a dance, big guy?"

Jamie considered the offer. He wanted that, someday. He

wanted to *feel* Tyler dance, to see him move his body in a practiced flow designed to turn him on. But he didn't want an audience. He wanted to touch Tyler, to show him with his hands and mouth and words how much he cared, how grateful he was to Tyler for sharing the gift of his body with him.

"Not here," Jamie said, and lifted his fingers to briefly graze across Tyler's belly button. He watched the muscles contract, the little shiver passing through his boyfriend's body, and smiled. "Someday, when it's just you and me."

Tyler's eyes darkened. "Fifteen minutes and then I'm done."

"I'll be here."

"Will you come stay at my place tonight?"

"Please."

Tyler gave him one more lingering look, and then turned and made his way back to the bar.

Fuck, he's beautiful. Jamie shook his head, still a little baffled at how he'd ended up with this perfect man. He watched Tyler's hips sway, his tattoos shifting like ripples on the surface of the water as he walked toward the bar.

CHAPTER 20
TYLER
DONE FOR THE NIGHT

Tyler couldn't stop smiling as he leaned against the bar, trying to catch Tessa's attention for a quick drink of water.

Jamie was there. His burly, hockey-playing boyfriend had come to see *him*, at work, in the middle of the night. Despite looking perfectly put together in a navy peacoat over a deep green sweater and gray slacks, he could tell Jamie was exhausted. His green eyes had taken on a sleepy haze that made Tyler want to wrap him up in a blanket like a burrito and put him to bed.

He'd broken a cardinal family rule earlier, and had kept his phone at the table while he and Rowan ate an early supper before he went to work. Jamie had shown him how to get live play-by-play game stats and a local radio broadcast from the hockey league website. Rowan had asked a million questions, but they'd listened to the game together.

Tyler figured they could break the rules for Jamie.

They'd both cheered, their cheeks full of rice and beans, when Ollie scored off of Jamie's rebound. Rowan had been fussy, complaining about a sore tummy through most of the afternoon, but the game had provided a good distraction.

Afterwards he'd put Rowan to bed, handed the baby monitor off to Dotty, and then left for the club.

There was a good crowd tonight. Tyler didn't know what it was about the holidays that brought people to the strip club in droves. Maybe it was the Christmas bonuses or prolonged time around family.

Whatever it was, Tyler couldn't complain. He already had a nice wad of cash stashed in his locker, and was counting down the final minutes of his shift before he could get the fuck out of there and go home with his boyfriend.

He'd managed to avoid Handsy Dan sitting in the back corner, in the same starched suit he always wore. *Fucking asshole.* There had been another white rose and envelope of cash at his station when he'd shown up. Tyler dropped the envelope with Tessa at the bar, knowing she'd return it to Handsy Dan, and threw the flower in the trash.

It was easy enough to ignore him. Tyler had enough going on in his life without humoring a deluded man who thought he could wave money at him in exchange for sexual favors.

For now, dancing was working for him. He could handle a day of being exhausted when he earned more in one night at the club than he had delivering groceries. If Dotty and Sandra kept extending their generosity with Rowan, Tyler thought it might all work out.

He was raising Rowan, and supporting them financially. They had found a home that was *perfect* for them, and were making friends with kids, like Layla and Mitch. And Jamie. Tyler still couldn't believe he had Jamie.

"Troy."

Tyler stiffened. He hadn't seen Handsy Dan get up from his seat. Tyler braced his elbows on the sticky wood, and noticed Tessa watching them carefully from her post behind the bar. One of her pierced brows cocked in a question. He shook his head and turned to the man beside him. "Hello."

"You've been neglecting your duties," Dan slurred, his cheeks and nose ruddy from the rum and cokes he drank. "Last time I checked, your job was to work the whole room, boy. That includes me."

Tyler rolled his eyes. "I'm heading up," he said, pointing to the back hall that led to the dressing room. Handsy Dan had said shit like this before, and Tyler knew the only thing to do was disengage. "See you around."

"Hold on, now." Dan blocked his path, and Tyler ran into his chest, stumbling a bit before regaining his footing.

A few things happened all at once. Tyler heard Tessa's firm "Hands off," barked out from behind him. A large, muscular body slid between him and Handsy Dan, sending the older man shuffling back with a muttered curse.

"How about you take a step back?"

Jamie's voice was low, devoid of any of the warmth Tyler had come to associate with him. Tyler could feel how tightly Jamie held himself, his muscles taut and ready.

"Who the hell are–" Handsy Dan let out a wheezing chuckle. "Oh, this is too good. There he is. Jamie Sullivan, big bad hockey player. Thought I saw you sniffing around here the other day." Dan craned his neck to the side, sneering at Tyler from around Jamie's broad shoulders. "So this is the kind of man that's good enough for you, huh, Troy? A man needs professional athlete money to touch you?"

"Dan, you're done for the night," Tessa said loudly. "Jordy and Damien are coming over right now."

Tyler felt a sliver of relief that their bouncers were going to intervene.

"Don't look at him," Jamie went on. "Look at me."

"It's his job to be looked at," Handsy Dan retorted. "Sluts like him love the attention."

When Dan lunged forward, reaching for Tyler like he wanted to grab him, Jamie reacted, throwing his hands up to shield Tyler from the unwanted touch. Jamie's broad back blocked Tyler's view, but he heard a shout, and the next thing he knew, Handsy Dan was falling backwards.

Jordy and Damien ran up, glancing uncertainly from the man on the ground to Jamie, before seemingly coming to the same conclusion. Each grabbed one of Jamie's shoulders.

"Wait!" Tyler shouted, indignant, trying to pry their hands from Jamie's body. "He was trying to keep Dan from touching me! He didn't do anything!"

"Shit," he heard Tessa mutter behind him. Tyler spun around.

Tessa pointed to where at least five phones were raised, their bright white lights aimed at Jamie. Everyone in the club was watching them.

"Fuck," Tyler whispered. "It was self defense," he said to Tessa, his voice taking on a pleading edge. "That's what the videos will show. If they watch them, they'll see!"

Tessa nodded, her expression grim. Tyler looked over his shoulder, and saw that their boss, Eddie, had emerged from his office in the back. *Fuck*. Tyler tried to push his way into the group gathered around Jamie.

"Call the fucking cops, Eddie," Handsy Dan picked himself up off the ground, wiping a hand over his mouth. Tyler's stomach dropped when he saw that Dan had somehow split his lip, the blood bright against his pale lips. He pointed a shaking finger at Jamie. "The guy's a professional athlete, for fuck's sake!"

Tyler looked at Jamie then, still held by the two bouncers. He didn't move, his expression carefully neutral with the exception of his eyes, which stared right at Tyler with so much care and anguish and panic that Tyler felt his breath catch in his chest.

Turning to Eddie, Tyler squared his shoulders. "It was self defense," Tyler said, trying to project his voice over the music that still blared out of the club's sound system. "Dan tried to grab me, and Jamie was keeping me safe."

Eddie took off his glasses and rubbed the bridge of his nose, looking like he'd rather be anywhere else in the world. "Tessa, what'd you see?"

Tessa straightened behind the bar. "Tyler's right, sir. Dan was out of line. *Again*."

Eddie turned to glare at Dan. "What am I going to see if I pull the tapes?"

"Eddie–"

"None of that bullshit, Dan. I know we go way back. Fuck, I let you get away with a lot more than I should around here. The way I see it, if you want to press charges against this guy, you go for it. You'll never set foot in my club again, but you can try to get your payout. If you want to stick around here? You drop this, recognize a lost cause when it smacks you in the face, and go home."

Handsy Dan's jaw worked, looking around the room. "You're a real fucking asshole, Eddie," he spat, before turning and storming out of the club.

Sighing, Eddie waved at Jordy and Damien, who immediately let go of Jamie. Eddie turned to Tyler, his expression more annoyed than anything else. "Is this going to be a problem?" He asked, gesturing to Jamie.

Tyler looked over at his boyfriend, who still stood frozen in place, a blank, stoney expression on his face. "No."

"Get out of here, then. You're done for the night."

Tyler found Jamie already in his bed, stripped down to his boxer briefs and sprawled out on his back, holding his phone above his face.

"Go to bed," Tyler whispered, setting down the monitor he'd grabbed from beside a sleeping Dotty downstairs on the couch. He'd apologize to her tomorrow for the late night.

Jamie's eyes were fixed on his phone, a deep furrow between his brows.

"What is it?" Tyler asked, flopping down on the pillow next to him.

Jamie just held out his phone in response.

The first thing Tyler noticed was how big Jamie looked in the photograph. He loomed over the rest of them, and with his arms outstretched and a snarl twisting his mouth, he looked–

"Fuck."

Beside him, Jamie grunted in agreement.

"People have to know–"

"It's the internet, Tyler. People don't care about what's real. A story about an aggressive hockey player assaulting somebody in a strip club is convenient, so that's what they go with." His voice was heavy with defeat and resignation.

Tyler tossed the phone aside and leaned over to catch Jamie's gaze. "Hey."

Jamie's eyes were downcast, and he worried his lower lip with his teeth. His hand had disappeared behind his head, fingers twirling and tugging at his hair.

"Jamie," Tyler tried again, spreading his hands over Jamie's furry chest.

Finally, Jamie looked up. "I'm so sorry."

"For what?"

"They're saying fucking terrible, awful things about you. About your work and your character and–" He sucked in a sharp breath. "None of this would be happening if it wasn't for me, and I...I fucking *hate* to think that I've made your life worse."

"What are you–*Jamie,*" Tyler placed his hands on Jamie's cheeks, pressing his fingertips into the blonde stubble. "What the hell are you talking about? Tonight was–"

"I shouldn't have–"

"Jamie! Can you shut up for one second?"

Jamie blinked up at him.

"Everything about my life has gotten better with you in it." Leaning down, Tyler brushed a kiss to Jamie's eyebrow. "I don't care if the world knows I'm a stripper. I'm not ashamed." He kissed the tip of Jamie's nose. "So, don't worry about me, Captain." Jamie's cheeks tinged pink, and Tyler brushed his thumbs across his flushed skin. "I can't imagine they're saying good things about you, either."

Jamie winced, then nodded.

"So, what do we need to do?"

"I'll text Sharon. She's the head of PR for the Muskies. We can go to her office together, and ask her to help us make a plan." Jamie cradled Tyler's face in his big hands. "I need you to know that I don't give a shit what anyone online says about you. If your job makes them uncomfortable, that's their own fucking problem."

Tyler had to fight to keep his eyes from welling up. "I," he began. "Thank you. For saying that."

Jamie yawned. "I'm so tired," he said, his words stretched as he yawned again.

Tyler ran his fingers through Jamie's hair. "Get comfy, big guy."

Jamie nodded. "Come here."

Their bodies found each other under Tyler's pile of quilts. Jamie's skin was hot, and Tyler didn't hesitate to press himself close, trying to steal as much warmth as possible.

"We'll figure this out," Tyler murmured against Jamie's neck. "I promise. We'll get through this."

It took Jamie a minute to respond. When he did, his voice was a soft breath against Tyler's hair. "Okay, baby."

CHAPTER 21
JAMIE
COOKIES WILL HELP

The water was hot on Jamie's back as he scrubbed the sweat from his body. He'd gotten in an extra workout after their team meeting that morning, before the official practice and film session happening later that afternoon.

The meeting, which had been divided between reviewing the schedule for the Winter Classic with the team admin, and talking game strategy for their matchup against Minnesota, had left little room for interaction with his teammates. Beyond a few claps on the back and nods from the guys, Jamie hadn't been able to bring himself to linger. He wasn't ready to answer their inevitable questions.

He'd worked his ass off to get back to playing good hockey, only to fuck up less than a week into his return. And even worse, he'd probably messed things up for the only man who might actually stick around.

It had been a relief to lose himself in training, in the burn of his muscles. He'd pushed himself on the bike until he was sweating, and moved through agility exercises in the gym. One of the trainers had worked on a tight spot in his hamstring, and the dull, throbbing pain had allowed him to escape his thoughts. At least for a little while.

Tyler was due at the arena in ten minutes so they could meet with Sharon and come up with a plan for how to handle the pictures and subsequent articles that had come out overnight.

The photos were…Well, they were damning. Jamie looked like a brute. His relative size, looming over that fucking *creep* falling backwards, painted a condemning picture.

The articles themselves were mixed. Those who shared the videos–which showed the man named Dan reaching for Tyler first–portrayed Jamie as a valiant lover coming to his boyfriend's defense. The others were more of what he'd expected: questions about his sobriety, criticism of him being in a strip club, and the assumption that, based on his fight earlier in the season, Jamie had been the instigator of the whole thing.

What he hated, what had his blood fucking *boiling*, were the things people had written and commented about Tyler. Jamie couldn't believe the fucking audacity of people. He knew there was a stigma about strippers. In the past, he'd heard comparisons of someone's partner to a stripper thrown around other locker rooms or on the ice as an insult.

Jamie toweled off. He wished he could wrap Tyler and Rowan up and hide them away in his house. He wished he could provide them with everything they needed to live a happy, peaceful life. He had more than enough to support himself–and he'd always wanted a family.

But would Tyler even want that? Setting his pride and independence aside, would Tyler even consider going all in with Jamie after the clusterfuck last night? Tyler had enough on his plate already. And now, because of Jamie, he was thrust into the public eye, facing a deluge of unwanted criticism.

Tyler was doing it on his own, carrying all of his responsibilities with a grace and poise that Jamie aspired to bring to his captaincy. Tyler was making ends meet, providing for his little family, one Jamie felt honored to play some tiny, peripheral role in.

He'd just slipped into jeans and a team quarter-zip when

Mitch appeared, dressed down for their team meeting. "Stop avoiding me."

Jamie winced, sitting down in his stall to put on his shoes. "Sorry," he muttered.

Mitch sat beside him. "Are you going to meet with Sharon now?"

Jamie nodded.

"How's Tyler?"

"Acting like everything is fine."

"And you?"

"Fine."

Mitch snorted. "Bullshit."

Jamie glared at his hands in his lap. *Fucking Mitch.* "I'm embarrassed," he admitted. "I don't regret what I did, because, Mitchy, the way this guy was treating Tyler was fucking horrifying, and I had to do *something*."

"I can only imagine, man."

"I hate that people think I'm like that, though. Like I'm the kind of man who is out in the world starting fights with strangers."

"You know the team doesn't think that, right?"

"And the fans?"

Mitch went quiet, giving the question serious thought before responding. "They're going to see you out on the ice, and they're going to remember who you are, Sully. That's all you can control. You're a good guy. We all know that. And in the meantime, the team has your back."

"Thanks, man." Jamie slumped forward, resting his elbows on his knees.

Mitch put a hand on his back. "Make sure Tyler knows you don't care about this crap. Even when people seem unfazed, all this bullshit can get to them."

Jamie nodded, shooting his friend a grateful smile. "Do you think it's going to be okay?" He asked, not trying to hide just how fucking terrified he was that everything was going to fall apart.

That just when he had everything he'd ever wanted, it was going to slip through his fingers.

Mitch nodded. "You got this. Both of you."

"It's going to be okay," Tyler said.

His hand was warm, the soft skin of his palm pressed against Jamie's callouses. Tyler stood next to him, wrapped in his yellow coat and lavender beanie, as they took the elevator up to the team offices.

He still couldn't quite believe that Tyler was there beside him. It was too easy to imagine a world where they'd never met, or a world where Tyler refused to take a chance on him after their disastrous first meeting.

Everything had changed since then. Jamie was back in the lineup, back with the guys, back on the ice where he belonged. He'd found his game again. He had a man in his life.

Only now he couldn't quiet the voice in his head that said he'd fucked it all up.

The elevator doors slid open, and Jamie squeezed Tyler's hand. "Thank you for being here with me," he managed.

Tyler nudged his shoulder with his head, and Jamie was reminded of how his mom had first described Tyler: *a black cat covered in tattoos.*

Fuck, Jamie didn't want to lose him.

A minute later, he and Tyler sat across from Sharon, who'd greeted Tyler with the same detached politeness she used with all the Muskies players.

"So. Thank you both for coming in." She looked up from her computer with a grim expression on her face.

"Thanks for taking the time," Jamie said, shifting in his seat.

Sharon surveyed them, and then steepled her fingers on the desk in front of her.

"For now, the team has declined any requests for comments,"

she started. "The man in the video is not pressing charges, and given that the footage in its entirety seems to exonerate you, I don't think we'll have any issues with law enforcement."

That's a small fucking relief.

"My job is to represent the Muskies organization and the players. While I have empathy for you in this situation, Tyler, I need to be clear on what my priorities are moving forward." Jamie opened his mouth to protest, but she went on. "While there is still a certain amount of buzz claiming Jamie as the aggressor, those arguments are going to lose steam as the full video continues to circulate online. What fans are fixating on now is why their captain, newly returned from injury and on the cusp of an important game for the team and the community, is spending his free time hanging out in strip clubs and getting into fights."

Jamie clenched his jaw, indignant. "I'm not–"

"My professional advice is that you immediately put some distance between yourselves. Jamie, you deflect any questions about your relationship with Tyler. People are quick to judge, and in this case, the online response has been overwhelmingly negative."

Jamie was already shaking his head.

"The Winter Classic is in a few days," she continued. "*That* is the organization's focus. We'll release a brief statement explaining that you came to a strangers' defense, and then redirect their focus to you at practice, looking like yourself on the ice. Show the fans you're back and better than ever. Show them you aren't distracted by this situation. Not only does that help the organization, but it helps Tyler. If he's no longer connected to you, he can return to a life without this kind of public scrutiny and criticism."

"You want me to–" Jamie began, sweat pricking on his skin. He turned to Tyler. "Unless you want–"

"No." Tyler sat forward in his seat. "Jamie is my partner," he said, his intense gaze fixed on Sharon. "I have no interest pretending otherwise."

Jamie wasn't sure if he wanted to cry or kiss Tyler. He chest felt crowded with relief and hope but he was also in fucking disbelief. Jamie was supposed to be the one fighting for Tyler, and instead his boyfriend was fighting for him.

Sharon looked between the two of them. She sighed, her eyes closing. "Nothing about this job can be easy, can it," she muttered, before focusing back on Jamie and Tyler. "In that case, I'd suggest Tyler not attend the Winter Classic in any formal capacity. He could still go to the game, still join the team families in the suite if he wants, but not participate in the family skate or wear whatever coordinated outfit the WAGs have planned. Keep him out of photos. Keep him away from you."

Jamie felt Tyler stiffen beside him.

"Tyler," Jamie said, turning to look at his boyfriend. "I want you guys to be there, but–"

"But what? Don't tell me you're embarrassed by–"

"No–*god*, Tyler, it's not that."

"If having us there will be a distraction to you and your team, then we'll sit this one out, okay? I know how much this game means to you." Tyler slid his fingers between Jamie's where his hand gripped his knee. Jamie felt his muscles relax, his body softening as he let Tyler's hand–smaller, softer–cradle his. "I'm in this for the long haul. There will be more games and more chances for us to celebrate how incredible you are."

Jamie was already protesting. "Everyone on this team gets to have a moment with their family out there on the ice!" His voice was too loud–he knew that, but it didn't fucking matter, because the thought of getting out on that ice without Tyler by his side, without seeing Rowan's toothy grin behind a helmet? The thought of doing it without them made him sick. "Yes, this game means everything to me, but so do *you*. I want to see the people I care about wearing my name proudly. I want to share it all with you." He looked right into Tyler's eyes then, finding comfort in his unwavering gaze. "But I won't sacrifice you and Rowan's well-being just because I selfishly want you out there."

Tyler looked at him, lips slightly parted, seeming to search his face for something. The ring in his nose caught the light, drawing Jamie's attention to his mouth. *Fuck, he'd forgotten to kiss him that morning. What kind of idiot would forget to kiss a mouth like that?*

He'd never make that mistake again.

Across from them, Sharon stood, reaching for a to-go thermos with the Muskies logo on the side. "I'm going to grab a coffee. You two take a minute."

"Tell me what you're thinking," Tyler asked the moment the door closed behind Sharon.

"What people are saying about you, I just…" Jamie pressed his lips together. He wished his mind was sharper, wished that he was as good with words as Tyler was. "I don't think they're going to stop, and what if this shit follows you and Rowan because of me? All I wanted was to see you and I wasn't thinking about what could go wrong. It was selfish, and *fuck*, Tyler, I'm so sorry."

"Let me decide what's too much," Tyler said. "Taking care of Rowan, worrying about us? That's *my* job."

Jamie heard a distinct buzz from Tyler's pocket, but they both ignored it. He looked at Tyler, hit by a sharp pang of longing that started in his throat and dropped down into his chest. "I want to worry about you, too," Jamie whispered, his voice breaking at the end.

"Jamie," Tyler started, but his phone vibrated again. "Dammit, hang on." He fished it out of his coat and answered. "Hey, Sandra."

Jamie watched Tyler closely, and saw the exact moment his face tightened with worry. "I'll be right there," Tyler said quickly. "Thank you. Tell him I'm coming." He was halfway to the door when he hung up. He glanced back at Jamie, apologetic. "Rowan's sick."

"Oh, shit. Of course, go. Let me know if you need anything, okay?"

Tyler nodded, dazed, and then, without looking back, he was gone.

"Is everything alright?" Sharon walked back into the office with her coffee, shooting Jamie a confused look.

"His son is sick," Jamie said, feeling the frustration of the day catching up with him.

"I hope he's alright," she said, sitting down behind her desk. "What decision did the two of you make about the Winter Classic? Whatever you decide to do, the team will want to be prepared."

"We didn't." He paused. "He wants to be there."

And Jamie wanted them to be there, too. Tyler *and* Rowan. *Fuck*, he wanted it so badly.

He knew it was the selfish part of himself, the voice he had made a habit of ignoring. It was the part of him that he pushed down when he was with the team, when he was considering the needs of the guys around him first.

The team came first. Always.

Now, though, he'd tasted what it was like to have a partner. Tyler by his side at the Christmas party, Rowan trusting him enough to reach for his hand–it was the future Jamie had always wanted for himself.

He wanted that moment, out there on the ice–that *family* moment, with Tyler and Rowan by his side, proudly wearing his name.

He just couldn't figure out how to have that *and* shield Tyler and Rowan from the harsh judgement of the world.

"For what it's worth, that man seems to care about you."

Jamie buried his head in his hands, making no effort to hold back a frustrated groan.

"Are you okay?"

Jamie looked at Sharon, who was watching him helplessly. He was past the point of pretending he wasn't upset. He coughed to try to ease the tightness in his throat but what came out was a wet, wretched noise that sounded like he was crumbling from the inside out. "No, I'm not."

She looked even more uncomfortable. "Is there…Can I do anything for you?"

"No." To his horror, Jamie felt his eyes burn with unshed tears. He rubbed his eyes in a furtive attempt to stop the tears before they started.

Of course, it didn't work.

Sharon fidgeted behind her desk. "I have cookies?"

Jamie sniffed, still rubbing at his eyes. *Get your shit together, Jamie*. "What kind?"

She opened a drawer. "Chocolate chip or Vanilla Wafers."

"Vanilla, please." He paused. "If you're offering, that is."

She frowned at him. "Will cookies help you stop crying?"

Jamie laughed, which unleashed another wave of tears down his cheeks. "Cookies will help."

CHAPTER 22
TYLER
WE'RE NOT ALONE IN THIS

"Let it out, kiddo," Tyler murmured, rubbing Rowan's sweat-soaked back as he unloaded the contents of his stomach into the toilet.

Rowan whimpered. "Papa, it hurts."

Tyler hated it when Rowan was sick. He hated watching his kid suffer, knowing there was nothing he could do but sit by Rowan's side as he worked his way through it. Tyler had tried to give him some ginger tea, but it had come right back up.

He wiped Rowan's mouth with a wet cloth before he climbed back into Tyler's lap, curling up into a tight ball, crying softly against Tyler's chest. They'd been camped out on the floor of the bathroom for the past few hours, alternating between reading books and throwing up.

Dotty and Sandra had wanted to stay and help, but they'd already committed to driving to the Twin Cities to be with Dotty's mother for New Year's before coming back to Madison for the Winter Classic.

He and Rowan were in it alone.

But it wasn't really just the two of them. Not anymore.

They had Jamie.

Tyler remembered Jamie mentioning he had practice that afternoon, followed by a team-only event in the evening, and another practice at the outdoor rink tomorrow, and then…Tyler couldn't remember what else Jamie had on his schedule, only that almost every hour of the days leading up to the Winter Classic game was full.

This was Jamie's life. Hockey defined Jamie–it was as much a part of him as fatherhood was to Tyler. From what Jamie had told him, his previous partners hadn't been able to reconcile with the fact that Jamie always put his team first. They had wanted him to put them first, always wanting *more*–more time, more attention. More.

Tyler wanted to be different. He didn't want more than Jamie was able to give.

But right now, he just wanted to call his boyfriend. He wanted to tell Jamie how tired he was, how much it hurt to see Rowan like this. He wanted to hear Jamie's low voice in his ear, reassuring him that he was a good, competent father. That Rowan was going to be okay.

His phone vibrated on the floor beside him and he sighed as he picked it up. "Hi, Mom."

"Hi, honey. Are you doing okay?"

"I'm okay." He rolled his neck, trying to ease the tension in his shoulders.

Rowan shifted against him. "Papa, my tummy," he whimpered. Tyler made a soft, soothing sound and pressed a kiss to his damp curls.

"Is Rowan alright?" His mom must have heard Rowan's voice.

"It's just a stomach bug."

"Honey, please think about coming home. If you were here, I could–"

"We're okay. I promise, we're okay."

It was quiet for a moment.

"Tyler, we…We're worried about you."

Closing his eyes, Tyler tipped his head back until it *thunked* against the bathroom wall. He forced himself to take a deep breath, releasing it through his nose. "Did you see the pictures?"

"We did. It's awful, the things they're saying about you."

Tyler couldn't argue with her. He'd caved and read some of the comments online. Some nosy internet sleuth with nothing better to do had put two and two together, finding Tyler's blurry face in the background of a picture from the team Christmas party at Jamie's house. Even though Rowan's face was hidden, it was clear Tyler was holding a child. From there, the comments went wild: Tyler was a gold-digger, or he was somehow blackmailing the Muskies captain into sleeping with him, or, the worst of them, where people claimed it should be illegal for strippers to have children. That he was somehow incapable as a father.

Tyler waited, knowing his mom wasn't done.

"Are you sure being in Madison is worth it? I don't know what you have going on with this Jamie fellow, but having your name in tabloids? Is this really what you want?" He heard her sigh. "I just wish you'd come home, Tyler. I wish you'd let us help."

"I'm right where I want to be," he said, but his voice sounded weak in his own ears.

"You wouldn't have to dance if you were back here," she pressed. "You know we don't judge you for it, but those late nights away from Rowan? I just don't understand–"

"I need to go, Mom."

"Tyler," she began.

"Love you. Say hi to dad for me."

He heard her sigh. "I love you too."

He hung up, tossing the phone on the floor.

Tyler forced himself to take a slow breath–in, hold, and then out. The strain of holding himself together for Rowan while projecting confidence he didn't feel to his mom was almost too much.

Of course, it was tempting to throw in the towel on their life in Madison. If he was back in Vermont, he had no doubt his mom would be right there on the bathroom floor beside him. His dad would be warming up homemade chicken stock or running to the store for ginger ale.

So many things about their life would be easier.

And yet, Vermont wasn't home anymore.

At some point, returning to Madison had become so much more than a stubborn display fueled by his own need to prove something. Tyler's job at The Daily Grind had become routine. Rowan had come to love Dotty and Sandra like family. An accidental run-in with a professional hockey player had given them a community.

Madison had become their home.

Rowan's cries had quieted, his breathing slowing. He'd fallen asleep curled up in Tyler's lap. Tyler grabbed his phone.

"Tyler!" Kids' voices were loud in the background when Layla answered the phone. "How are you? I saw the articles. What a bunch of crap."

Tyler made out Henri's voice shouting, "Mom, crap is a bad word!"

"Yes, I know, sweetie. But sometimes people do mean things and it's okay for Mom to use a bad word. Really, Tyler, are you guys okay?"

Tyler smiled, even as his eyes welled up with tears. "Rowan's got a stomach bug," he managed, his voice cracking. "Sorry. A lot going on right now, you know?"

"Oh, babe," Layla said. "That's so much. How can I help?"

"No no, you've got your hands full with the kids." Tyler sniffed, running a free hand over his eyes. "I just needed to talk to a friend."

"I'm so glad you called. You never need a reason to call me, okay? Raising kids in this world is hard. It's so, so hard. Even when you have all the resources, it's still hard. You're a part of this family now, and we take care of each other. Do you have what you need? Tell me what's going on with Rowan and we'll get you taken care of. You're not alone in this, Tyler."

Tyler was really crying now. He wiped tears from his cheeks as he explained Rowan's symptoms, and within minutes, Layla had asked for his address and had ended the call with a promise that everything would be taken care of.

He let out a shuddering exhale, tightening his arms around Rowan.

We're not alone in this.

The next few hours passed in a blur. Rowan woke up and allowed Tyler to move him into the bath. He gave him a quick wash and changed him into clean jammies before carrying him to the living room.

They cuddled up under a quilt on the couch with a pile of books. It had been a while since Rowan had last thrown up, but Tyler wanted to be certain before he tried to get Rowan to eat anything else.

When Rowan said he wanted to draw, Tyler climbed onto the floor beside him, a pile of colorful crayons laid out beside an old brown paper grocery bag. He cut it in half to expose the blank paper on the inside.

Tyler let his mind wander for just a quick, brief moment. He thought about Jamie standing up for him at the club, the misconstrued photos and articles, the gravity of the Winter Classic, and again, about Jamie. What he had with Jamie was still so new, but the past twenty-four hours had solidified Tyler's belief in what they had together.

He loved the way Jamie had stood up for him and Rowan. Tyler never would have put "protective instincts" on a list of desirable qualities before, but now that he'd seen Jamie's commitment to taking care of them? It made him feel cared for and safe and like maybe he *didn't* have to do it all by himself.

He wasn't going to let some bullshit that people were saying on the internet keep him from showing up for Jamie. *Their* Jamie.

We just got him, and he belongs to us. Maybe, maybe, *we can belong to him, too.*

He remembered what Jamie had said in Sharon's office: *I want to see the people I care about wearing my name proudly.*

Rowan's soft humming pulled him from his thoughts. Tyler leaned over, looking down at the swirls of blue, orange, green, and gray on the paper. "What are you working on, kiddo?"

"This is the day we met Jamie."

"Oh yeah?"

Rowan nodded solemnly. "Mmhm. It was gray out, but he was big and tall and serious, and now we know him and he's our friend and you give him mouth kisses sometimes."

Tyler didn't know what to say. Toddler words were remarkable like that–simple combinations, no beating around the bush.

Honest. Raw.

Rowan resumed his drawing. Tyler leaned back against the couch, reaching for his phone. His fingers itched and there was a warm humming head as he navigated to his social media profile.

There were still so many things Tyler didn't know. He couldn't predict the future. He still wasn't sure how he was going to build a life that felt financially stable. He didn't know how long they'd be able to rely on Dotty and Sandra.

He didn't know how to shield Rowan from a future where strangers publicly criticized Tyler's job.

But they were going to go to that fucking hockey game.

It only took him a minute to find the right picture. It was the snowman Jamie had made them on Christmas morning, Muskies jersey and all, illuminated in the dim light of the gray morning.

He quickly typed: *Always cheering our captain on.*

There was a knock on the door right as he hit the button to post it.

Tyler jogged down the narrow stairs and opened the door, finding a pile of grocery bags and Tupperware. A woman he recognized from the Christmas party stood there in a stylish winter coat, her sleek black hair tied up in a ponytail. "Hi!" Her voice was cheerful. "Tyler, right?"

He nodded.

"I'm Lily, Cooper's wife. Layla called me and told me your son has a stomach bug? I'm a pediatric nurse and always offer to help when a kid gets sick." She pointed to the pile of bags and containers. "Mila made bone broth, Marlowe packed some fresh ginger tea Finn made yesterday, and Kirsten made a grocery run for saltines and ginger ale." She held up her hands and shrugged. "Let me know if this is too much. We just want to help."

Tyler opened his mouth, and then closed it. "I…Thank you. I don't know what to say."

Lily smiled. "What's your son's name?"

"Rowan."

"That's right! Apparently, Sully talks about him with the boys all the time." She raised a dark brow, her almond-shaped eyes kind. "Really, if you just want a hand carrying things in, I'm happy to do that."

Tyler stepped aside, reaching for one of the bags. "Please, I won't say no if you're offering."

When they walked into the apartment, Rowan peeked up from the couch, his hair sticking up from his head and his eyes still heavy.

"Hey Row, this is Lily." Rowan waved. "Think we can tell her about your tummy?"

Lily was kind, obviously a pro at working with little kids, and soon she had Rowan laughing and bundled in blankets on the couch. She helped Tyler warm up some broth while Rowan started sipping ginger ale.

"I still can't believe you came over to my house," Tyler said half an hour later. Rowan had fallen asleep on his lap again after having a small bowl of broth, and Tyler had made some herbal tea for himself and Lily.

"Being with a professional athlete isn't easy. They're gone all the time, and especially once people have families, it's a lot for one person to juggle. This is just how the team is. The guys have each other on the ice, and we have each other off of it."

"It's all I've ever wanted," Tyler admitted, running a hand over Rowan's hair. "A community. For me *and* for him."

"You're a superstar," Lily said, smiling at him. "Being a single parent is amazing. What you do for Rowan, *everything* you do," she said, and Tyler could tell she was referring to the articles online, "is amazing. We all see it, and we're here for you."

Tyler felt his eyes welling up, and groaned, looking up at the ceiling. "I've cried more today than I have in the last year," he said, letting out a quiet, wet laugh. "Sorry."

She waved off his apology. "You're fine. We cry a lot around here."

"Thank you again," he said. "For everything."

Lily insisted on running a load of laundry and doing the dishes, in spite of Tyler's protests. She bustled around the kitchen, and then sent Tyler to take a shower while she kept an eye on Rowan.

She made sure Tyler had her number in case Rowan got worse, and then gave him a hug. "Hope the night goes okay," she said at the front door. "And please, call if you need anything."

"Will do," Tyler said, overwhelmed with gratitude.

"Will we see you at the Classic?"

Tyler smiled. "I want to be there. Jamie's stressed about the media and everything, but I can't imagine missing it."

Lily scoffed, waving a hand. "The media and fans will always have something to say. All you can do is decide whose opinion really matters to you. It's obvious Sully doesn't care what people think about your work. From talking to Cooper, I know the other players don't care either. They love Sully and want to see him happy. None of the other WAGs care." She shrugged. "Don't miss the game because of what a bunch of strangers on the internet are saying. The people who matter want you there."

After exchanging a hug at the door, Tyler waved goodbye as her silver Lexus pulled out of the driveway.

Rowan was finally asleep. He'd eaten a few saltine crackers and some more broth. He was obviously hungry, but Tyler had him take it slow.

Tyler was curled up on the beanbag chair in Rowan's room when his phone buzzed.

JAMIE

How's Rowan?

Coop told me Lily came over to help.

I'm so sorry I can't be there.

Tyler's mouth curved into a fond smile as he typed a response.

TYLER

He's feeling better! Exhausted, but keeping down some broth and crackers.

Oof. Poor guy. Glad he's doing better.

Are we okay?

So much about the situation was shitty, but were *they* okay? Would Tyler and Jamie and the relationship they were trying to build together survive this?

We are, Jamie. I'm still in if you are.

I'm in.

I know and trust that you will do whatever feels right for you and Rowan, but I need you to hear me when I say I want you at the game. I know it hasn't been very long, and so much is still new, but I think you could be the best thing that's ever happened to me.

Tyler glanced across the room to where Rowan's face was lit

by the golden-pink glow of the salt lamp. He was deeply asleep, his chest rising and falling under the quilt.

Carefully, Tyler crept out of the room.

The game was still two days away, but now there was Rowan's stomach to think about.

In his closet, two custom-made puffy jackets–one child-sized and one adult-sized, were tucked away, the fabric pristine and untouched. Orange stitching on green letters across the breast wrote out "Sullivan," and the number three was embroidered on the arms.

When Layla had asked for their measurements for the team-issued family jackets, Tyler had wavered. He hadn't known then if he and Jamie had that kind of staying power, or if Jamie would want him and Rowan showing up with him to team events in any sort of formal capacity.

The two jackets were there, waiting, a visual announcement to the world that they were with Jamie. He and Rowan were the captain's chosen few. His *other* team. The team he came to visit after a roadtrip. The team he went with to the Children's Museum, who got the gift of his soft smile and warmth.

The sheets were cold when he crawled into bed. Tyler grabbed his phone, typed out a quick response to Jamie, and then tossed it face down on the floor beside his bed.

TYLER

We're with you, Captain.

CHAPTER 23
JAMIE
THE MUSKIES FAMILY

"Alright, cut."

"Where to next?" Jamie lifted his chin as one of the network assistants unclipped the mic from the collar of his team-issued jacket. They'd been given brand new team gear with the Winter Classic logo, and the players had specific instructions detailing what they were expected to be wearing at each event leading up to the game.

Beside him, Mitch wiped his forehead. "Aren't you the one with the schedule memorized?"

Jamie shook his head, pushing to his feet and pulling out his phone to check their schedule. *Lunch. Thank god.* He was ravenous.

He and Mitch had just finished filming some silly content videos intended for social media. For as long as they'd been on the same team, the media had highlighted his and Mitch's friendship. Today, they'd taken a best friend quiz about each other, writing their answers on little white boards.

Of course he knew Mitch's favorite candy was Swedish Fish, even though they were, objectively, disgusting.

It was the kind of stuff people loved, and the league made sure to flood the fans with behind-the-scenes videos leading up to their big events.

Outside of the playoffs, the Winter Classic was one of the biggest events of the year. The league usually picked rivalry matchups, and tended to select two teams within a relatively close distance in an effort to get fans to travel to the event. This year's game, between the Muskies and the Minnesota Moose, was a perfect example. The two franchises had a long history of vying for the top spot in the Central Division.

The team had gone to Camp Randall Stadium first thing that morning. The rink had been constructed in the middle of the football field, complete with boards, high plexiglass walls, and team benches. The rest of the grass was covered in white plastic that was stamped with massive logos for the league, Madison, and Minnesota.

After a few photos were snapped of them exploring the stadium, the team had left to check out the locker room they'd use, and changed into their gear. It took the team a while to familiarize themselves with the new location–hockey players were such creatures of habit that even something small like the section of wall where they threw a medicine ball to warm up could impact their focus.

Finally, they'd made it out onto the ice. It was freezing, the wind sharp against their faces.

Jamie barely noticed the cold. He felt an excited energy buzzing throughout his body. The atmosphere was completely different–from the distance of the stands to the lighting and the feeling of the fresh air against his skin.

Tomorrow they were going to play an outdoor game in front of their fans. This was their chance to give them a show.

Jamie wasn't worried about the game. He trusted his team and their preparation. They were fucking ready.

But there were still the articles and photos from the club to worry about.

There had been a palpable layer of discomfort in every room

he walked into that morning. He'd felt the long looks from the rink staff and production assistants. Sharon had taken him aside earlier, and had told him that the team was refraining from making an official statement about the photos until after the game, and that Jamie should do the same.

So far, he'd done what was asked of him.

"Sully, we've got you on in five with Harrison Lytel," Sharon called out from across the conference room where they were finishing up their lunch.

"Got it!" He scraped up the last of the pasta sauce from his plate with a piece of grilled chicken. Popping it into his mouth, he chewed as he walked his dishes over to a bin. "Food was great," he called out to the black-clad employees lining the wall. "Thanks."

The interview was set up in a large player's lounge. Harrison Lytel was a well-respected reporter in professional hockey, and an ex-player himself, who'd spent years earning the trust of players and teams alike with his honest and fair reporting.

"Good to see you, Sully," Harrison said, shaking his hand as Jamie joined him on one of the two leather chairs set up under bright studio lights. Multiple cameras were positioned in front of them.

"Good to see you too, Harrison."

After a production assistant clipped a mic to his shirt and someone with a makeup brush dabbed some powder onto Jamie's forehead, the woman behind the camera counted them down from five, pointing at Harrison to cue him.

"We're live from Camp Randall Stadium on the eve of the Winter Classic," Harrison said, looking into the camera. "I'm Harrison Lytel, joined by Jamie Sullivan, captain of the Muskies." He turned to address Jamie. "Jamie. First off, I know I speak for the whole league when I say we've loved seeing you back on the ice. How is your hand feeling after your first few games back?"

Jamie gave the other man a practiced smile. "Our medical staff have been amazing, and thanks to their help, I'm back to one hundred percent." He held up his hand, flexing his fingers. "You'll see me doing some extra stretching and PT before the game, but I'm ready to play."

"That's great news. I want to ask you about the first half of the season. Everyone in the league knows and admires the career of the Muskies' previous captain, Aaron Sharpe. What has stepping into this role been like for you?"

"Anyone who has watched the Muskies play over the years knows what kind of impact Sharpie had on this organization, on and off the ice. Beyond being a goal scorer, Sharpie was the kind of leader we all looked up to." Jamie paused, wetting his lips. He'd practiced this, affirming to himself that he didn't *need* to be like Sharpie to be a good leader. That he possessed qualities that made him a good captain, even if he didn't score as much as Sharpie had. "I'm not the same kind of player Sharpie was, and it has taken me some time to understand that I have something valuable to offer my teammates, even if it looks different from my predecessor."

Harrison nodded. "Talk to me about that. What would you say you bring to the Muskies?"

"Work ethic, to start," Jamie said without hesitating. "I didn't make it this far by being the best skill guy or the fastest skater on the ice. My career has been built on two-way defense, being committed to the forecheck, and matching up against the best goal-scorers in the league. I got away from the fundamentals at the start of the season, but now I'm back. I'm back to playing my game now."

A genuine smile spread across Harrison's face. "I'm sure Muskies fans are thrilled to hear that. On a lighter note, I called my old buddy Sharpie before coming over here this morning."

Jamie groaned and let out a rueful chuckle. "Oh, no."

Harrison laughed. "He told me to ask you about your sweet tooth."

"Of course he did," Jamie said, shaking his head.

"Can you give us your top five local spots for getting something sweet around Madison?"

Jamie listed off a few of his favorite local bakeries, and made sure to mention The Daily Grind, specifically their mocha with the seasonal topping.

It was obvious the interview was coming to a close, but there was something else he wanted to say.

"Harrison, do you mind if I bring something up?"

If Harrison was surprised, he hid it well. Gesturing to the camera, he sat back. "Go right ahead."

Leaning forward, Jamie ran a hand over his mustache.

He could have kept his mouth shut. It was what was expected of him. But Jamie couldn't stand the thought that there were people out there in the world looking at the pictures, reading the articles and coming to the wrong conclusions about him or Tyler. Jamie couldn't handle anyone thinking that Tyler was dispensable, that he was anything less than *everything* to Jamie.

"By now, I'm sure most people have seen the photos and articles online," Jamie began, looking into the camera, "of an altercation involving myself and another individual at a club." He rolled his shoulders, trying to ease some of the tension in his head. "It was not my intention to harm anyone. I know hockey is a physical sport, and there is a time and a place on the ice for fighting. I want to be clear: I do not condone fighting outside of the hockey rink. I was trying to deescalate a situation where a stranger was trying to hurt someone important to me." His hands flexed on his legs, smoothing them over his thighs. "I've seen what's being said online about myself and the man I'm proud to call my partner, and I just have one thing to say in response: He means the world to me, and he is a part of the Muskies family."

Jamie sat back in the chair, suddenly aware of the silence in the room. His face was hot and his heartbeat hammered in his ears.

Harrison gave him an appraising nod. "Thank you, Jamie, for shedding some light on this situation." To the cameras, the older man added: "In the time we live in, we in the media have an increased responsibility to decide which stories are the ones worth being told."

Jamie sat there, dazed and a little bit numb. He was swept up in a wave of relief and adrenaline, and he could feel sweat trailing down his back.

"Any last words for the Muskies fans out there?"

He cleared his throat, trying to bring his mind back to hockey. "We've got an amazing group of guys in the room who are putting in the work and bringing their best every day. And as their captain, I'm going to get out there and leave everything I have on the ice tomorrow and bring home a win for our fans."

"We appreciate you taking the time to sit down with us. I'm looking forward to seeing what you do out there tomorrow."

"Thank you."

"We're out!" The producer behind the camera called out. The same rush of people came forward, unclipping the mic and moving lights out of the way. Sharon hovered by the door, tapping away on her tablet, an unreadable expression on her face.

Jamie was still in a bit of a daze as Harrison pulled him to the corner of the room and handed him a bottle of water. "You alright?"

Jamie took the water gratefully, unscrewing the cap and guzzling half of it. "Fine. Might have given the team another headache to deal with, but I needed to say something."

Harrison nodded. "It was great. From where I'm standing, I think you did the right thing."

"Thanks." Jamie looked over at Sharon again. "I probably need to go face the music."

Laughing, Harrison shook Jamie's hand. "Good luck out there, Sully."

Jamie returned the handshake, and walked over to Sharon. She gestured to the door. They walked silently down the hallway side by side, back in the direction of the Muskies locker room.

At least thirty seconds passed, and Jamie was about to crawl out of his skin. "Well?"

Beside him, Sharon snorted, obviously amused.

"Aren't you going to say something? About what I said back there?"

"No."

Jamie threw his hands up. "No?"

Sharon stopped short of the locker room door, and turned to face him. "No, Jamie. There's nothing more to say. You defended a single parent back there. You stood up for him and for his son. It was a beautiful display of your character and integrity. Myself and the team will stand by you, and your partner."

"I…" Jamie began. He let out a breath. "Thank you."

She nodded. "Now get in there and do your captain thing. The show is just getting started."

"Listen up, boys! Sully's got something to say!" Mitchy shouted. Around them, players fell quiet. Someone turned off the music.

Jamie stood up in front of his stall. He was already in his pads and skates, ready to go out on the ice for a short practice before their families joined them.

"I just want to thank all of you guys for showing up and working your bags off this year," Jamie said, raising his voice to fill the room. "And I want to thank you for trusting me. I know I've sucked this year–" He waved away the loud protests, shaking his head. "No, really, boys, I've been brutal out there." The room broke out into chuckles at that. "I was trying to do more than my job. Trying to play like someone I'm not. But now, I'm back, and I'm fucking ready. We've got a great chance here to show our fans and the league what we're about. Minnesota is coming into this game thinking they're going to catch us on our heels. But fuck that!"

"Fuck that!" The guys echoed.

"Finish getting geared up and let's go enjoy this moment. When you're out there, take a second and breathe it in. You've all earned your place out on that ice. And after practice, when the families join us, make sure to thank them for all that they do for us. Never forget about the people off the ice. We play for them, too."

The room erupted with cheers and hollers. Jamie was jostled from both sides with claps on his shoulder pads, and in that moment, he'd never felt more a part of them–a part of his team.

Jamie let Matty smear eyeblack across his cheeks, and laughed when Ollie managed to get the dark paint on his own nose.

Jamie was walking back from the bathroom when he noticed Carter handing out little slips of paper to all the guys.

"What's that?" Jamie asked.

"Some of the guys and I were talking," he started, and there was no sign of the cocky glint in his eyes that Jamie was used to seeing. "And we're going to put on a coat drive tomorrow at the game. Ask people to bring in any extra gear, and then after we'll donate them to kids who need them." Carter looked around the room at the team. "Things were rough for me growing up. It was just me and my ma and I'll never forget all the ways she supported us. I just…I know I'm new, but I wanted to do something good."

"That's amazing, Carts," Jamie said, and pulled the taller man into a hug.

Carter's cheeks were pink when Jamie pulled away.

"Is your mom going to make it to the game?"

Carter grinned, revealing his missing tooth. "Yeah. Can't wait to see her out there."

"That's awesome, man. Introduce me, will ya?"

Matty catcalled from the other side of the room. "Sully, you trying to make a move on Carts' mom?"

"I'm happily taken, asshole," Jamie shouted back. "Happy, and gay!"

Five minutes later, he and Mitch stood side by side in front of the long bank of mirrors above the sinks.

"We look fucking good," Mitch said, grinning at their reflections.

Their practice uniforms were a handsome dark green with orange and cream accents. The C was right where it always was, embroidered on his chest, Mitch's A placed in the same spot. They both wore the beanies they'd been given, striped in the team colors with an orange pom on the top.

"We really do," Jamie agreed. He combed his fingers through his mustache.

"Leave it alone." Mitch slapped his hand away. "It looks good."

Jamie grumbled, but dropped his hand. Their shoulders brushed, Jamie just a bit taller than his best friend. His thoughts suddenly turned to his messy-haired and beautiful boyfriend and his son. Just imagining them out there on the ice was enough to make his breath catch in his chest. *Dammit,* he wanted them there. "Do you think they're going to come?"

Mitch nodded. "They'll be here."

After they'd finished their light practice, everyone's attention turned to the people who had gathered just beyond the rink. Guys sped over to grab their kids and partners and ushered them out onto the ice. It was tradition for the WAGs to make some sort of matching jacket for them all to wear for the family skate. Jamie knew Layla had helped design them. This year they were puffy down jackets with the player names stitched on the breast and the Muskie logo on the back.

They looked fucking *amazing*.

Henri was, to no one's surprise, the first of the Muskies kids to hit the ice. In her cream colored jacket with *Jackson* stitched on the back and box braids streaming behind her, she whipped circles around the outdoor rink, hollering at the top of her lungs.

Jamie watched as Mitch tried to catch up with her, laughing as he skated over to the bench to grab a drink from his water bottle.

What if Tyler had decided to sit this one out? What if it was all too much?

He wouldn't blame him–no, Jamie couldn't blame a man who didn't want to put himself in front of a crowd after all of the articles, after everything people had said online. He'd understand if Tyler kept Rowan home.

But Jamie hoped. He really fucking hoped.

"Jamie!"

Maybe, sometimes, hoping was enough. Because there, hovering at the edge of the rink, were the two people Jamie wanted to see most in the world. A little blue-eyed boy with a stuffed sloth in tow and his beautiful father, both smiling and waving at him.

Jamie skated over to them as fast as he could, his cheeks aching because he couldn't stop fucking *smiling*. By the time he'd dodged and weaved through everyone on the ice, Tyler was already skating slowly toward him with Rowan in his arms.

They looked perfect with their matching mullets and their jackets with Jamie's last name stitched on the breast. *Right here, with me, just where they're supposed to be.*

"You're here," Jamie said, relief making his voice waver. He was about to fucking cry, right there, and he didn't fucking care, because they had come. They were fucking *there*. "I'm so, so happy you came."

Tyler skated right into his arms. Jamie inhaled, letting everything around him fade but the cold plastic of Rowan's helmet against his shoulder and the soft tickle of Tyler's hair against his chin. He tightened his grip on them, and then pressed a kiss to Rowan's helmet.

"What do you think of all this, buddy?"

Rowan's grin was huge behind the cage. "It's big like you!" He squinted his eyes, his nose scrunching up. "You have something on your face, Jamie."

Jamie laughed. "We put special paint on our faces to help with the glare on the ice."

"I want some."

Tyler looked up from where his face had been tucked against Jamie's chest. "Hey, big guy," he said, an almost-sleepy, rumpled smile on his face. "I heard what you said. In the interview."

"Yeah?" Jamie cleared his throat, suddenly self-conscious. "Did I overstep?"

"No," Tyler said, shaking his head. "What you said was–" he sniffed, looking over Jamie's shoulder, and Jamie saw tears gathering in the corners of his eyes. "What you said was perfect, Jamie. I'm so proud to be here, with you, wearing your name."

"Baby," Jamie breathed, doing his best to gently brush a finger over Tyler's cheek with his bulky gloves. "If you start crying I swear I'm going to fu–forking go down with you."

Tyler let out a wet laugh. "I just want to say thank you. For saying something when you didn't have to." He ran his tongue over his bottom lip hesitantly "*You*, Jamie, are worth all of it."

Jamie leaned down, pressing a kiss to the wet trail on Tyler's cold cheek. "Number three, remember?" He looked over at Rowan, who was watching them with a pleased grin on his face. "What are you smiling at?" Jamie asked him.

Rowan giggled, and reached for him. Jamie scooped him from Tyler's arms, holding him on his hip. Rowan squirmed, and then held Bunny up in front of his face. "Bunny says you and papa should love each other and kiss noses."

Jamie vaguely registered Tyler's sputtering reaction, but he looked right at Rowan when he responded. "That's the plan, kiddo. Come on, I want to see if you remember those mushy banana knees."

It took a moment for Jamie to get Rowan back and settled on the ice, and there were giggles and laughter as he skated with the young boy between his legs. Tyler skated beside them, cheering Rowan on.

Rowan wasn't Jamie's. Not really. Not yet.

But it really did feel like Rowan and Tyler belonged right there beside him on the ice, wearing his name on their jackets. They were Muskies now. They were part of the team. They were family.

And maybe, someday, at the end of a roadtrip, rather than driving to the apartment above his moms' house or swinging by The Daily Grind, he'd open the door of his too-large home and hear laughter and the whistling of the tea pot. Maybe there would be a yellow coat with duct tape across the bottom and a lavender beanie hanging by the front door. Maybe there would be blocks spread across the living room floor.

Maybe someday, they would be his family.

Jamie was all in.

Day by day, making time.

CHAPTER 24
TYLER
THE POETRY ALL ALONG

THE MUSKIES ON THE EVE OF THE WINTER CLASSIC

Reported by Arush Lakhani

This afternoon, at Camp Randall Stadium, the Madison Muskies held a brief practice, and tomorrow, they will host the Winter Classic. After months of preparation, the time has come for the Muskies to face off against the Minnesota Moose in front of their hometown fans.

But first, the players enjoyed a family skate with their loved ones, a time-honored tradition to share this moment in a player's career with the people who matter most to them.

"I'm from the area," said defenseman John Moore, who had his infant daughter strapped to his chest in a baby carrier. "Going to Badgers games in this stadium is a huge part of life growing up in Madison. It's an amazing opportunity to get to play here, and to give our fans this experience."

"I've never experienced anything like this," rookie Oliver Campbell said. "The whole city is buzzing and excited, and it's great that it's a conference game. We're ready to go out there and play hard."

When I asked the players about the recent events that led to speculative articles and comments about their captain, Jamie Sullivan, and his partner, I was met with a consistent message.

"We stand by Sully and Tyler," team veteran and alternate captain

Hugo Andersson told me. "He is a good captain. Takes care of everyone who is team [sic]."

"Sully is the best," said defenseman Elias Svensson. "The team missed him when he was injured. We are so very happy to have him back."

While tomorrow's main event will no doubt be the on-ice rivalry between Madison and Minnesota, the Muskies players have organized an accompanying charity drive in an effort to give back to those less fortunate in the Madison area

"We're hosting a coat drive," said forward Cooper Bell. "There will be donation bins set up both in and around the stadium. We hope anyone with extra children's winter wear will consider bringing them tomorrow. We will donate them to local organizations who make sure they end up with the kids who need them most."

When I got the chance to speak with Jamie Sullivan, he was standing hand in hand with his partner, Tyler Raymond, holding Tyler's young son in his arms. They were all smiles in their team jackets, matching the rest of the families.

"This is an amazing moment for the Muskies," Sullivan said. "And we are committed to making this a memorable game for the fans. As for me, I'm just trying to take it all in. Playing hockey professionally is a gift, and getting to share this moment with the people who matter to me is something I'll never take for granted."

"It's really good to have Sully back," said forward Matt Lee. "He's the kind of player who impacts everything around him on the ice. When he's out there, everyone plays better. We've missed that."

While the Muskies might be enjoying a skate under the stadium lights with their families tonight, their focus is on the game tomorrow.

When I spoke to goalie Anders Berglund, he mentioned something Sully had said to the team in the locker room. "Sully reminded us that we are a good team and well-positioned to make a deep playoff run. This is a meaningful game, and we plan to walk away with two points."

"Minnesota is going to underestimate us," Sullivan said. "And it's our job to capitalize on that."

For more details on the coat drive, visit the Muskies website and social media page.

"Don't you need to be doing something special the night before a game?" Tyler looked back over his shoulder as he seasoned a bowl of chicken thighs marinating in yogurt. "Aren't superstitions a hockey player thing?"

Across Tyler's small kitchen, Jamie shrugged. He'd shown up twenty minutes ago in faded sweatpants and a Muskies hoodie, hair still damp from a shower after their last media obligation of the day.

"As long as I eat a big, well-balanced meal and get some good sleep, I'm fine." He smiled, his gaze dipping down Tyler's body and then back up to hover over his mouth. "I don't see why I can't do that here."

Tyler looked at his hands. "You don't have to, if it–"

Hands gripped his hips and the rasp of facial hair brushed against his neck. Tyler's breath caught in his throat. "I'm here because I want to be here," Jamie said, voice low. "I want to make time for you. For us." He paused. "*All* of us."

For a moment, Tyler sank back into Jamie's warm, steady body.

"Now tell me what the hell you're doing to this chicken."

With Jamie still wrapped around him, Tyler explained his seasoning choices. Rowan played happily across the room, narrating some sort of game with his wooden animals, while Tyler and Jamie finished preparing the meal.

Soon they were sitting together at the small table, and Tyler could imagine that *this* was what their life together would look like. Jamie jumped right into helping Rowan blow on bites of chicken, roasted cauliflower, and rice, and not a minute later Rowan had crawled onto his lap, and was alternating between shoving chicken into his own mouth and offering Jamie little pieces.

Tyler's heart melted when Jamie didn't hesitate to take the offered bites, humming softly in appreciation as he chewed.

"The chicken is amazing," Jamie said, nudging Tyler's thigh with his knee under the table. "Next time I have a break will you come over to my place and make some with me? I know you are busy, and now I'm asking you to help me cook, but it's just so tasty, and spending time with you–"

"Jamie." Tyler reached out and brushed his thumb over Jamie's chin. All he wanted to do was touch him, to ease the worry he saw creeping onto Jamie's face. "I'd love to come over. I know Rowan would, too. Making time goes both ways, you know? I want to make time for you, too."

"Jamie?" Rowan asked, his hand covered in sticky grains of rice. No matter how many times Tyler confirmed that his son *did* actually know how to use a spoon, Rowan ended up using his hands to eat. "Are you scared about your game?"

Jamie shook his head. "Nope. I'm just excited."

"I drew you a picture."

Jamie looked at Tyler, and he would have laughed at the look on his boyfriend's face if it hadn't been for the sincere vulnerability there in his green eyes. Tyler offered him an encouraging smile. "Really?" Jamie asked, looking back at Rowan.

"Papa, may I please leave the table to get Jamie's picture?"

"Yeah, kiddo. Thanks for asking."

Rowan pitter-pattered across the floor toward his room. He reappeared a second later, with a piece of a recycled paper grocery bag in his hands. With a grin on his face, he handed the paper to Jamie.

"Oh," Jamie said, his face softening as he looked at the picture. "I love this so much."

Rowan clapped his hands together. "Papa wrote the words, but I did all the colors."

Tyler watched Jamie's eyes trace over the upper corner of the page, where Tyler had scrawled out a few clumsy, imperfect words, words that couldn't come close to expressing everything he felt.

Jamie turned to Tyler, eyes full of emotion. "Tyler," he breathed. "You wrote me a poem."

"They're just words," Tyler said, a feeble attempt to brush off the awe in Jamie's voice.

"None of that. These words are too beautiful to be *just words*." Jamie looked back at Rowan. "This is the coolest picture ever, bud. Can I put this on my fridge?"

Rowan nodded, grinning.

A few hours ago, Tyler had been sprawled on his belly beside Rowan on the floor, beeswax crayons and markers scattered around them. Rowan had explained that he was drawing the three of them: himself, Papa, and Jamie, and that he was also adding Bunny because *he* was a part of the family too. The scratches of blue were the ice and the scribbles of yellow were bright lights, because they were happy together.

The figures were barely discernible, but that was the beauty of art created by children. They hadn't been broken by the demands of perfectionism yet. Rowan drew on the paper with all the confidence of a master, and Tyler swore he saw the truth in every line and squiggle.

It was brave, art like that. Not to Rowan, who was too young to have felt the constraints of expectations brought by the world, but to Tyler, it seemed like the greatest form of courage.

It was brave to live like that too, to live with hope and joy in the face of pessimism. To take a chance on love when it seemed so likely to fail.

Tyler had decided to be brave, too.

He'd grabbed one of the felt tipped markers and had begun to write. The marker was starting to dry out, the letters frayed and inconsistent, but it did the job.

What was left was the first poem he'd written in years.

Poetry used to come in the night–
Eyes wide, head still pounding
Glitter still clinging to my chest.
It would swell in my gut,
Tightening, winding up: a chokehold
Until it spilled from a wanting throat.

There was a symphony in my head,
A cacophony of warm, open tones
And all I had to do was pluck out the
Threads to weave a melody.

It is silent now.
The moon sunk below the oaks.
Eyes heavy, head empty of everything but
Sun and you.
There is nothing unseen,
My head swims with little joys
No symphony.
No notes.
Not a thread to be found in the night.

But in the day?
There we are. Eyes soft against the
Bright, glittering sky.

Maybe this was the poetry all along.

Rowan returned to his animals while Jamie and Tyler cleaned up the kitchen. Jamie hand-washed the dishes, while Tyler put leftovers away in recycled yogurt containers.

Jamie came up beside him, placing a hand on Tyler's back. "What are the chances you have something sweet?" Jamie nuzzled the side of his neck.

Tyler glanced up to see the sheepish hope on his boyfriend's face. Tyler rolled his eyes good-naturedly, and grabbed a little box of ginger snaps that he'd stashed in a cabinet.

Jamie thanked him and opened the box. He frowned. "You have a mouse problem," he said.

"What?"

Jamie held up one of the large cookies, which was missing a corner.

Tyler laughed. "Oh, that's me."

"You're a mouse?"

"No!" Tyler couldn't stop laughing now, giggles spilling from him with every breath. "I just eat a little nibble when I feel like it."

Jamie looked completely taken aback, staring open-mouthed at Tyler like he'd just revealed he routinely ran naked around Lake Minocqua in January. "You're telling me you have tasty treats in your house and you have the discipline to only take these tiny little bites? Who the hell are you?"

Tyler crossed over to him, going up on his toes to put his mouth right next to Jamie's ear. "It's called edging, big guy," he whispered. "Ever heard of delayed gratification?"

Something between a laugh and a groan rumbled from Jamie's throat. "You're crazy for this," he said, leaning down to give Tyler a hard, demanding kiss.

Tyler pulled away, running his tongue over his wet lips as he looked up at Jamie's kiss-softened mouth. "Later," he said, his words a promise.

Jamie grinned. "Later."

"I thought he was never going to go down," Tyler said, shutting the door of his room behind him.

Jamie smiled lazily from where he lay sprawled out on Tyler's bed. He pointed to the monitor, which was turned on and emitting the low, static *whir* of the sound machine. "I never knew there were so many verses in "Old MacDonald.""

"Oh, that one has infinite possibilities. Don't be fooled by the limitations of traditional pastoral fauna."

Jamie snorted. "Whatever the hell that means," he muttered fondly. "Get over here."

Tyler climbed onto the bed and into Jamie's open arms. Any remaining tension in his body melted away as he dropped into the curve of Jamie's arm, laying his head on Jamie's broad chest.

Jamie's arms tightened around him, and Tyler felt the ghost of fingertips trailing down his back. They dipped beneath his sweatshirt, finding bare skin before arriving at the waistband of his lace panties.

A low hum vibrated against Tyler's ear. "I want to see these," Jamie said.

Tyler grinned, rubbing his cheek against Jamie's chest hair. "Don't you need to sleep?"

Jamie shifted, rolling them so he hovered above Tyler. His grin was wicked, playful, and Tyler realized then how burdened Jamie had seemed when he first met him.

Now Jamie looked confident. Certain. Jamie leaned in close and ran his nose up Tyler's neck, kissing his throat right on his tattoo of the luna moth.

"I'll sleep eventually," Jamie whispered.

"Tell me what you need tonight," Tyler asked, squirming as Jamie continued to kiss his way along his jaw.

"I'd really, *really* like to fuck you."

Tyler let out a whine, his cock swelling against the lace containing him. "Please," he breathed.

Jamie hummed. "But next time?" He ran his tongue over the shell of Tyler's ear, sending a shiver of pleasure down his spine. "After tomorrow's game?"

"Yeah?"

Jamie dropped his hips then, dragging his bulge over Tyler's hips. Tyler gasped as Jamie lined his cock up perfectly against his, pressing them together. "Tomorrow I'm going to need your cock inside me."

"Fuck," Tyler said, his voice already wrecked. He imagined parting Jamie's cheeks and tasting him, slicking his hole with his tongue before sinking into his body.

Tyler tugged at the waistband of Jamie's sweats, but the man above him didn't budge. Tyler let out a frustrated growl. "Get naked and get up here."

Jamie laughed, standing only long enough to strip away his clothes. Tyler watched him hungrily, drinking in every inch of him. The blonde, fuzzy hair on his chest, stomach, and thick thighs. His cock hanging heavy, already flushed and hard.

"Why am I the only one who's naked?" Jamie asked, indignant.

Tyler laughed, and wriggled out of his pants. He went for his panties, but Jamie's hand on his wrist stopped him.

"Leave them on." Jamie brushed a knuckle over the lace, and Tyler choked out a soft cry.

Tyler ripped his shirt off and lay back. Jamie stood above him. "Where do you want me?"

Tyler smirked and crooked his finger. Jamie climbed onto the bed, his muscles perfectly on display. When he stopped above Tyler's hips, Tyler shook his head. "Closer."

Jamie arched a brow, but complied. He hovered above Tyler's chest, his dick hanging hard and leaking between them.

"Now turn around."

Tyler sighed as Jamie's ass filled his vision. He ran his hands over him, feeling the light fuzz of hair covering his skin. He squeezed, grinning at the flex of muscle under his palms.

"Sit down," he commanded.

Above him, Jamie chuckled. "I'll crush you."

"No you won't." Tyler smacked his hip.

"I prefer my men breathing!"

Tyler made a sound of protest, but he couldn't help but smile. It was easy to do this with Jamie. It was new, thrilling and exciting, but there was something easy about it. Safe. "I won't break, Jamie."

The moment Jamie's weight settled on his face, Tyler dove in with his tongue. Jamie was right, in a way–Tyler could barely breathe with his face buried in Jamie's ass, but it was enough. Just enough for him to take in his soapy musk and the ghost of sweat.

Jamie's hole was tight against his tongue, but Tyler wasn't in a hurry. He dragged it up and down Jamie's crease, curling circles around the whorl of flesh, the taste of Jamie's skin only amplifying the pleasure that was already gathering low in his belly.

A groan ripped from Tyler's throat as a hot, wet tongue dragged across his lace-covered cock. He got lost in himself as Jamie mouthed the front of his lace panties, licking up and down, sucking on the head of his cock where it strained against the fabric.

Tyler tightened his grip on Jamie's hips, holding him firmly against him. He worked his tongue inside, thrusting and twisting, pressing his lips against the puckered skin of Jamie's hole. He felt Jamie's desperate, mumbled *Fuck* against his cock, and raised his hips, greedy for *more, more, more.*

"I swear I could come like this," Jamie said, his low, gravelly voice making Tyler's balls draw up against his body. "Your tongue doing whatever that fucking magic is back there, with the view of your pretty cock trapped in lace."

Tyler whimpered when Jamie's big hand gripped his sack with just enough pressure to send his heartbeat wild.

"But I want to feel you around me when I come tonight," Jamie went on. Tyler made a sound of protest when Jamie lifted himself up, but he didn't waste any time before he turned around and covered Tyler's mouth with his.

It was a filthy kiss, their tastes mingling. Jamie sucked on Tyler's tongue like he was chasing the traces of himself, and the desire and wanting that had been simmering in Tyler since they started reached a fever pitch.

He reached for the lube he kept in a wooden box beside his bed, pressing the bottle into Jamie's waiting hand. "Don't fuck around," Tyler said, sounding as desperate as he felt. "Just enough to get you inside."

Jamie nodded, and made quick work of pulling off Tyler's panties. Tyler let his head fall back on the bed as he heard the click of the lube bottle opening. Jamie's warm hand maneuvered his legs, and then he felt the cold brush of a wet finger against him.

He bore down the moment Jamie pushed. He was too far gone to want prolonged prep, not when Jamie's cock hung hard and dripping with precum between his thighs.

Jamie's finger slid in easily, and he didn't waste time adding a second and then a third. The moment Tyler felt his body relax, the moment the sting faded, he nodded. "Now, Jamie. Fucking now."

Jamie removed his fingers and Tyler's hole clenched around nothing, desperate to be filled again, as Jamie slicked himself with more lube. "Baby, you are so good, so fucking good. I'm going to take care of you, okay?"

Tyler was spread open, legs draped over Jamie's arms, when he finally thrust inside. Tyler sighed–*fucking sighed*–with the relief and pleasure of it, his body arching, seeking out more of Jamie.

He'd imagined this. Imagined Jamie's cock in him, imagined his big body hovering over him, filling every bit of his vision.

Somehow, it was better than he'd imagined. It was sweeter than the dreams, the pleasure deeper than he'd thought was possible.

"Baby," Jamie rasped, his voice shaky.

Jamie's pace quickened, and Tyler couldn't look away. It didn't matter that his erection flagged as the pressure of Jamie pushing into his body overwhelmed him. Something bigger that grew beyond physical pleasure, the way their bodies found a rhythm like they were made for each other.

Jamie's green eyes were fixed on him, piercing under his blonde brows, staring at Tyler like he wanted to ask: *Where have you been?*

Tyler was sure his own eyes, which met Jamie's gaze head on, responded: *I didn't know I was waiting for you.*

Their breaths grew harsh, stuttering, tripping over each other. The pleasure regained its footing, and Tyler's cock lay hard, flushed and throbbing against his stomach.

Jamie's hand wrapped around him, jerking him off with quick, precise pulls. "I'm almost there," Jamie grunted, his forehead furrowed as he stared, open-mouthed, at the place where his cock plunged into Tyler's body. "Can you get there too, baby?"

Tyler nodded furiously. He was *right* there, his pleasure in Jamie's hand. He chased it, a simultaneous reach and surrender for what was coming, sinking into the tightness, the build, until he was close, so fucking close.

"I'm–" Tyler gasped, and he forced himself to keep his eyes open, even as the wave tugged him under, ripping his orgasm through him with the unrelenting pull of an undertow. He didn't want to miss Jamie, even as his own cock shot cum all over his chest, smearing white across his tattoos.

He saw the moment Jamie came, the silent cry, his eyes drifting shut as his stomach clenched, hips stuttering as he finished. Tyler could feel him, Jamie's cock throbbing in him, and it was *everything*.

Jamie collapsed on top of him, and Tyler hissed as Jamie's softening cock slipped from his body. He let out a little whimper when Jamie kissed him, his fingers returning to gently thrust in and out of Tyler's tender hole.

Tyler was in a daze. Jamie pulled away, grinning down at him. "Hi," he whispered, crooking his fingers.

Tyler shuddered, his soft, sensitive cock twitching against his thigh. "Are you trying to kill me?"

Jamie's smile widened and he laughed, kissing Tyler again as he slipped his fingers from his body. "Want to shower?" He nodded down at the mess on both their abdomens.

They showered quickly, only sharing a few lingering kisses as they cleaned up. While Tyler wanted to sleep naked, they both agreed if Rowan were to wake up in the middle of the night, it would be better if they were clothed.

The light was out and Jamie lay curled around him, one of his hands resting on Tyler's hip. Tyler wondered if Jamie knew his thumb was absently brushing back and forth, back and forth against his skin.

He knew that nights like this were precious. Jamie wouldn't always be there. They'd have more nights apart than together, between both of their jobs and Jamie's travel.

But when he was there, he made it count.

When Jamie was there, they had all of him.

CHAPTER 25
JAMIE
LAVENDER BEANIE

The weather couldn't have been better for an outdoor game. Jamie stood in the tunnel at one end of Camp Randall Stadium, shifting his weight between his skates, tapping his stick against his shins, looking up at the vivid blue sky stretching above the stands. It was cold enough to keep the ice in good shape, but not so cold that it would impact their bodies.

Somewhere, in the suite with the WAGs and other family, Tyler and Rowan were with his mom and Dotty. His dad and step-mom had splurged on seats closer to the ice. His family, and now, for the first time, a man who'd chosen him, were all there to support him. A man who believed that what Jamie had to offer was enough. A man with a son who, he imagined, maybe someday could call his own.

The stadium already felt electric. There was a tangible excitement in the air, the stands crawling with orange and green as fans found their seats to watch the teams make their entrance

The guys around Jamie must have felt it too. Matty was jumping up and down, puffing out breaths, while Ollie was…Was he really dancing?

Even the vets had an antsy energy about them. Not all of them had been on the team when they won the cup, or when they had made their deep playoff runs a few years ago. There was something gained from playing under that kind of pressure. A trust in yourself and the team that was hard to explain.

But now, as they waited to walk out into the stadium, it was Jamie's job to try.

"Get over here, boys!" His voice echoed in the tunnel.

The guys jostled to form a loose circle around him, their bodies bumping together as they shifted to make space for Onni and Anders in their goalie gear. Once they were somewhat settled, Jamie took a moment to look around at all of them–Finn, Bailey, and Onni, who had the future of the franchise riding on their shoulders, the new trades like Carter and Emīls, and the old guard, Sergei, Hugo, Zach, and Mitchy, who'd spent their entire careers with the Muskies.

They had the chance to do something special out there today.

"There's a shit-ton of people out there," Jamie began. The guys chuckled. He felt a grin tugging at his mouth. "No, really. Not only do we get to go out there and play the sport we love, but we get to do it in front of people who love the game as much as we do." The guys nodded along with him. "But you know who I want to play for today? I want us to play a damn good hockey game for each other. I want to play my ass off because that's the way I say *thank you* to you guys for having my back." He pointed a glove at Anders. "I'm going to block some shots to say *thank you* for being the top goalie in the league." Mitchy whooped, and tapped Anders on the helmet. "I'm going to work my ass off on the forecheck so one of you fast kids–" he pointed between Esa and Cooper, his younger, faster linemates– "can pick off a pass and get us a goal." All the guys cheered now, and it was like the nervous energy had transformed into something targeted, a ravenous hunger to get out there on the ice and *play*. "Let's go out there and play hard, do the things we know work, and have each others' backs because we love each other, okay?"

"Let's go, Cap!"

A heavy arm wrapped around his shoulders as a hand clapped

him on the back. He wasn't sure who kissed his helmet or tapped their stick against his. All he knew was he was smothered in the guys, surrounded by *team,* and he knew they were ready.

The first goal was a fluke.

Jamie had been sliding across the crease, working to get position on the Minnesota D-man in front of the net, when a shot fired from Pauly from the top bounced off his ass and over the goalie's glove.

Jamie threw his hands into the air when the horn blared, skating hard for Pauly. It wasn't until his teammates jumped onto him that he realized *he* had been the one to score the goal.

"Dat ass, though!" Mitchy had shouted at him as he skated by the bench to high-five his teammates.

Five minutes into the first period and the Muskies were up 1-0, thanks to Jamie's ass goal. Minnesota wasn't making it easy on them, though–they'd earned the top spot in their division for a reason. Their first line center, Pavel Egorov, was a Russian player who was having a career high season in points, leading the league in even-strength goals.

Jamie's line was matched up against his. When Egorov was on the ice, it was Jamie's job to shut him down.

Egorov had only managed to get two shots on goal so far, so Jamie figured he was doing alright. His body felt good–his hand was strong, and his legs were just warming up, welcoming the burn.

Their lead didn't last long–a tripping call against Carter put Minnesota on the power play, and they got a quick goal.

"We've got this, boys," Jamie called down the bench before climbing over the boards.

He skated out to center ice, lining up for the face-off against Egorov. The Russian player grinned at him. "We heard you were bad now, Sullivan. This is not true."

Jamie let out a loud laugh, shaking his head as he popped his mouthguard out of the side of his mouth. "Sorry to disappoint," he replied.

The ref approached and dropped the puck.

Jamie won the face-off.

He was reminded of why he loved hockey as he slammed an unsuspecting Minnesota player against the boards, scooping up the loose puck and passing it up to Esa. Jamie sped down the ice, staying in position for a pass behind the play.

But Esa fed the puck to Elias in the middle, who hit Cooper backdoor for an easy goal.

Jamie shouted, his voice already going hoarse, and joined his teammates as they embraced Cooper. "Attaboy, Coop! Let's keep it going!"

When the horn signaled the end of the first period, the guys made the long trek to their locker room. Spirits were high, and everyone was focused on doing what they needed to keep their bodies fresh. Jamie had a banana and an electrolyte drink, and worked his way around the room.

The guys looked good out there. They were all playing at their best. He didn't need to do more than encourage them to keep it up. He avoided talking to Anders, settling for a stick tap to the goalies' pads. Jamie had played with him long enough to know he preferred to be left alone between periods.

The second period passed in a blur. The energy from the crowd kept them all buzzing, and when Jamie scored again on a breakaway, he thought he was going to collapse under the weight of Mitch jumping into his arms.

"I'm not even out here trying to score," he said, laughing as he pressed his helmet to his best friends'.

Sweat glistened on Mitch's forehead as he grinned at Jamie. "You're out here playing hockey, Sully. Sometimes playing hockey means shooting the damn puck."

He thought about what Mitch said as he skated by the bench for another round of high-fives. Earlier in the season, he'd been desperate to score, constantly thinking about how he was going to get the puck in the net.

Somewhere along the way, he'd forgotten the kind of play that had earned him his spot in the league. The kind of play that had earned him a captaincy.

Scoring chances came when Jamie played his game. When he played hard defense, when he did his job, scoring chances presented themselves. When he forechecked, giveaways happened.

"Hatty watch for the captain!" Ollie yelled from the bench, pointing his stick at Jamie.

Jamie rolled his eyes, but he couldn't stop smiling.

Getting two goals was one thing, but a hat trick?

He snorted, amused. *No fucking way was that going to happen.*

His main job was to keep Egorov contained. He'd gotten a few good chances this period, and Jamie was determined to keep him pointless.

With three minutes left in the third period, the Muskies led by one goal.

Minnesota was pounding them, rotating between their top two lines, playing with tangible desperation as they did whatever they could to score. Jamie had forgotten he was capable of sweating this much, and he could barely keep his visor clear with all the condensation from his heaving breaths.

Minnesota transitioned the puck, and Jamie skated back on defense. He saw the moment the goalie took off for the bench, shouting "Empty net, boys," as he picked up a forward, stretching his stick into the passing lane.

As soon as the extra skater joined them in their zone, Minnesota started working around the perimeter. They were patient, passing the puck, waiting for the Muskies to get out of position, hoping to draw them out until their defense inevitably broke down.

Jamie looked up at the clock. Two and a half minutes left.

Yeah, fuck that.

He trusted his teammates would have his back if he took a defensive gamble. If he played it right, it could win them the game.

The moment Egorov got the puck on his stick, Jamie skated at him hard. It wasn't the smart thing to do–it would have been easy for a guy to use Jamie's momentum against him and skate past him toward the net. But he managed to catch him off guard, and after only a few seconds of grappling, Jamie had the puck on his stick.

He skated hard down the ice, head on a swivel as he looked for a teammate to dish the puck to.

There was a flash of maroon in the corner of his eye–a Minnesota player coming at him.

He glanced around again, before looking ahead up the ice and–

The net was empty.

It was too easy, really. He slowed down just enough to drop the puck back on his stick. With an exhale, Jamie set his feet and took the shot from mid-ice.

He felt a desperate tap of the Minnesota players' stick against his skate, but it was too late.

The puck skittered over the ice. When the lamp lit and the horn sounded, the stadium erupted. The fans' cheers filled the early evening air, and Jamie was surrounded by a mob of screaming men, his teammates and brothers, who sounded happier for him than he was for himself.

Hats rained down on the ice, tossed by the fans over the glass. The players all skated to their benches to wait for the ice to be cleaned up, and Jamie leaned back against the boards, looking over the scattered hats on the ice.

This wasn't his first hat trick, but he knew, without a doubt, it would be the one he always remembered. With that in mind, he skated out before the rink attendants could shovel them all away. He passed Muskies hats in every color, a few red University of Wisconsin hats, and then he stopped.

There, half buried under a black snap-back, was a lavender beanie.

He skated over to it, bending down and picking it up. Before he could think better of it, he lifted the knit cotton to his nose and breathed in.

It was Tyler's.

He looked up, scanning the crowd. There was no chance of finding his boyfriend among the thousands of fans, but that didn't matter.

Jamie felt a wave of pride and joy all so tangled together there was no hope of separating them, and he was left breathless.

Tyler was there. He was there, and he was watching.

Jamie held the beanie to his chest, and reached a gloved hand up to his lips. He pressed a kiss to his fingers, and then lifted his hand to the crowd.

The fans' cheers grew louder. He smiled, turning and skating back to the bench. He handed the hat to one of the trainers. "Hang on to this one for me, please."

When the clock ran out, the team spilled out onto the ice, gathering around Bergy as the crowd roared around them. Jamie basked in it all–the cheers, the flushed, smiling faces of his teammates, and the certainty that they'd played the best hockey they could. After shaking hands with Minnesota, the Muskies gathered in the middle of the ice, sticks lifted in thanks to their fans.

There was a final wave of applause, and Jamie reminded himself to notice the little things–the bite of cold air on his sweat-soaked cheeks, the throbbing in his ribcage where he'd taken a hit. The devotion of the crowd. The smiles on his teammates' faces as they, too, soaked in this moment.

Finally they headed back to the locker room, exhausted and laughing, still buzzing from the win.

Guys started making plans for going out afterwards as they tore the tape from their pants and started stripping off their gear. Someone put on Beyoncé, and Jamie was bobbing his head to "Hold Up" as he unlaced his skates.

"You coming out tonight, Cap?" Cody asked from across the room.

Jamie thought about it. It would be good to celebrate with the team tonight. They'd done something incredible out there on the ice.

But tonight there was something he wanted more. Somewhere he'd rather be.

"I'll join you for one, but then I'm going to head home and see my boys," Jamie said. "You guys go out and have fun." He chuckled, shaking his head as he tossed his jersey into the laundry cart. "But make sure you watch out for snowmen."

Beside him, Mitch laughed. Jamie just smiled, ignoring the confused looks the rest of the guys gave him.

There was a particular energy that came in the wake of winning a big game. A hum in Jamie's bones, a rolling boil that needed an outlet, somewhere to go. It cut through the exhaustion and the aches in his muscles.

He climbed out of his truck, the garage door closed behind him. He'd joined the guys for a beer at Caps, but had made a quick exit.

He was ready to be home.

He dropped his bag to the floor. It was quiet.

"Jamie?"

Tyler was sitting on the couch, legs tucked up under him, with a blanket wrapped tightly around his body. When he saw Jamie, his face transformed into a bright, radiant smile that hit Jamie like a blow to the chest.

Then Tyler was on his feet, running on bare feet across the rug. He jumped up into Jamie's waiting arms, wrapping his arms and legs around his body like a koala. Jamie let out a laugh as he settled his hands under Tyler's ass.

Jamie felt a warm puff of breath against his neck, and buried his face into Tyler's hair.

"Hi," Jamie breathed.

A kiss ghosted the side of his neck. "You were amazing," Tyler said softly. "I mean, I knew you had to be good at hockey, but you are *really fucking good at hockey*."

Jamie laughed. "I'm so glad you were there."

"Remember that one time when you were drunk and sad and shouting about how you couldn't captain the Muskies for shit?"

"Is that really what I said?" Jamie let out a groan.

"Yep." Tyler exhaled, his laugh warm against Jamie's skin. "You were full of it."

"Gee, thanks."

"No, really. Every one of those guys was following your lead tonight. You looked like you belonged out there, and they were right there with you. It was…" He lifted his head to look right at Jamie. "I'm so glad I get to see you like that."

Jamie's chest felt warm. "Like what?"

"To see you perform at the highest level. You moved beautifully, all power and precision. I feel like I know you better now that I've seen you play hockey. I don't know, maybe it sounds silly, but now I see all of you."

Jamie kissed him, just a quick, teasing press of their lips. He drew back before he could get carried away, and felt Tyler's thigh press against the lump in his coat pocket. "Shit, I brought you something."

Tyler tilted his head to the side. "What?"

Jamie wasn't sure how he managed to pull the hat from his

pocket without dropping Tyler, but he pressed the lavender knit against his boyfriend's hard chest. "Thought you might miss this," he said.

"Jamie," Tyler said, looking at the beanie he'd worn since Jamie had met him all those months ago before his eyes found Jamie's face. His expression was so soft, so wrecked and happy that Jamie was tempted to kiss him. "I was prepared to sacrifice it to the hockey gods," Tyler added. "But I'm glad to have it back."

"How the hell did you get it all the way to the ice?"

"I bribed a stadium worker, obviously. Oh," he paused, and Jamie caught the mischievous sparkle in Tyler brown eyes—*fuck*, he looked just like Rowan. "There's a man named Don Schwartz who you owe a signed jersey. I have his address in my phone."

Jamie barked out a laugh. "I can't believe you," he said, shaking his head. "Did Rowan have fun?"

Tyler nodded, a tender smile on his lips. "The most fun. He shouted your name the whole time. The suite was awesome–Layla had a bunch of toys set up for the little ones and the food was amazing."

"I'm guessing he went down okay?"

"Yep. The Pack n' Play in the guest room is perfect, and he loved the stuffed muskie. I asked him what he wanted to name it, but he said he wanted to wait to ask you."

Jamie groaned. "That kid is going to kill me, Tyler. He's going to fucking kill me with how cute he is." He shook his head. "What about you? Did you have fun?"

"Yeah," Tyler said, nodding. "We hung out with Layla most of the time." He let out a quiet, amused laugh. "I never would have thought I'd feel so at home in a room full of women in coordinated puffy coats, but they are all great."

"That's all I want," Jamie said. "I want our time together to make your life better, or easier, or bring you some joy." He shifted Tyler's weight, his arms beginning to ache. "Baby, as much as I like having you up here, I need to sit my ass down."

Tyler wriggled free of Jamie's grip, and gave him a gentle

shove in the chest, sending him stumbling back onto the couch. As soon as Jamie's ass hit the cushions, his breath froze.

"Wait wait wait." He held up his hands, staring up at his boyfriend, his mouth going dry. "What are you wearing?"

Tyler's lips curved up into a smirk.

CHAPTER 26
TYLER
HERE, TOGETHER, WHEN WE CAN

Tyler was well-practiced in seduction.

When he was up on the stage at the club, he used his body to weave a fantasy. He knew how to lure someone in with a look, to put himself on display. He knew how to morph, depending on who was in the audience. The way he'd flex his jaw and roll his hips to entice women, or arch his back to entice men.

Now, standing in front of Jamie in nothing but a Sullivan jersey and a pair of green, lacy boy shorts, Tyler wasn't thinking about anything but the man in front of him.

Nothing mattered but turning *him* on.

"Fuck, you look good in my sweater," Jamie said, his voice rough and reverent. He braced his elbows on his knees, looking seconds away from standing and snatching Tyler up to have his way with him.

Tyler wouldn't mind that. Not one little bit.

"Spin." The request wasn't loud. Jamie didn't need to raise his voice to command authority. "Please," he added.

Tyler obliged, crossing one leg over the other and raising on his toes as he spun himself around.

Jamie groaned. "Baby, show me what you've got on under there."

With one finger, Tyler lifted the jersey just enough to expose the narrow hem of lace circling his upper thigh.

"Lace?" Jamie leaned back, his hands raking through his hair as his stare remained fixed on Tyler's body. "Oh, I bet your cock looks so pretty all wrapped up in lace."

Tyler felt alive. Alive and so fucking horny that it felt like his heart had dropped down into his belly, a beating and throbbing that was concentrating, building, making him dizzy with want.

He wanted Jamie to see him. He wanted to be wanted by Jamie, wanted to share his body with him in a way that went beyond just getting off and leaving satisfied. He wanted *everything* with Jamie, and, finally, he wasn't afraid.

The rough fabric of the jersey slid over his sensitive skin as he lifted the hem to show off the underwear. He heard a muttered "Fuck," from the couch.

Lace made made him feel beautiful, and nothing in the world compared to the feeling of the fine stitching against the most sensitive parts of his body.

It also made him horny as hell. He was already hard, his cock straining against the green lace as he advanced slowly toward his boyfriend.

Between the off-duty executive look Jamie had up top and the slacks stretched tight across his thighs, Tyler couldn't decide where to look. Finally he settled on those green eyes, which stared up at Tyler with such hunger and longing it made his skin burn.

"Beautiful," Jamie breathed as Tyler came to a stop between his splayed thighs. "You are so, so beautiful."

Tyler felt himself smile, threading a hand through Jamie's blonde curls. His hair wasn't quite soft, but Tyler loved how the messy locks felt between his fingers.

"C'mere." Jamie's hands tugged on the back of Tyler's thighs, closing the space between them. His breath was warm and the stubble on his chin was rough against the base of Tyler's throat.

Tyler stared down at him, unable to breathe, his body tight with anticipation.

Jamie's fingers grazed the back of Tyler's thighs until they reached the edge of the lace. "I love this," Jamie whispered, his tone adoring as his hands brushed the fine fabric.

A shiver trailed down Tyler's spine, and his thighs flexed.

Jamie looked up at him from under dirty blonde lashes. "I'm going to put my mouth on you now, okay, baby?"

Tyler nodded so hard his neck twinged. Jamie was the first person who'd ever called him *"baby."* He'd never been the kind of person who commanded an endearment like that. *"Slut?"* Sure. He'd heard that one before. *"Sexy?"* Yep.

But *"baby?"*

He loved the way it sounded coming from Jamie's mouth.

As Jamie's head ducked down, Tyler's fingers tightened in his hair. His teeth dragged over the lace, and Tyler pressed himself closer. It was electrifying, and he felt like he was hovering on the edge of control. When Jamie licked over the gusset of his panties, the hot, wet pressure of his tongue against his erection had him gasping, desperate for air.

Jamie took his time licking and sucking, and that combined with the steady leak of precum from Tyler's cock, had the lace soaked through. Tyler couldn't stay still, his hips rocking back and forth against Jamie's mouth as the pleasure built at the base of his spine.

"Hop up here," Jamie said, pulling away from Tyler's body and slapping a hand onto the couch beside him.

It took him a moment to figure out what Jamie was thinking, but seconds later Jamie had maneuvered Tyler's upper body to be draped over the back of the couch. He was on his knees, face buried into the leather cushion, with his back arched and his ass out.

Jamie tugged the panties down Tyler's thighs. "Fuck," he ground out, and Tyler felt the pad of his finger brush against his hole. "You, in my jersey, with my name on your back–*fuck.*" Tyler shifted backward, a silent plea for more, but then the touch slipped away.

Tyler was about to turn and ask his boyfriend *why the hell he wasn't fingering him* when his words were cut off by the hot slide of Jamie's tongue. He made a sound in the back of his throat that quickly turned into a whimper when Jamie's tongue pressed inside of him.

It was impossible for Tyler to stay quiet. His cock ached, desperate to be touched. Every breath from Tyler's lips was a cry, and he lost track of everything but his pleasure and the intoxicating rhythm of Jamie's tongue working inside him.

This time, when Jamie pulled away, Tyler whined at the loss of him. "Jamie," he pleaded.

Jamie's body pressed against his back, his wet lips brushing against Tyler's ear. "Are you up for fucking me tonight?"

"Yes," Tyler said, breathless. "Please, yes."

Jamie bit the side of Tyler's neck, and Tyler arched back into him, his naked ass meeting the erection trapped behind the placket of Jamie's slacks. Jamie groaned. "I'll need a little prep," he said, his voice rough and low. "Tell me where you want me and I'm yours, baby. I'm all yours."

"Lube?"

"Upstairs. Come on."

Jamie led them up the stairs and into his room. He clicked on the bedside lamp and produced a bottle of lube from the drawer, which he tossed to Tyler. Tyler snatched it out of the air, shamelessly admiring Jamie's clothed body.

Jamie exhaled. "I can't handle how hot you are," he muttered, his expression full of adoration and disbelief as he started to undo the buttons of his shirt. "I still can't figure out what you're doing with a guy like me."

Tyler scoffed, taking the jersey off and tossing it aside before crossing the room to join him. His hands worked Jamie's belt free, and then he looked up at his boyfriend. "There are a million attractive things about you," Tyler said, leaning forward to press a quick kiss to Jamie's furry chest. "But do you want to know why I really picked you?"

Jamie frowned, shaking his head.

"The mustache."

Jamie started to laugh, his smile so big that Tyler caught a glimpse of the gap in his molars. There was nothing but trust and affection in his eyes, and Tyler was hit with the full weight of having Jamie. He wasn't sure anyone had ever looked at him like that.

Jamie kissed him as he shrugged off his shirt, and Tyler raised up on his toes as their lips parted, tongues tangling together with growing urgency. Tyler pushed Jamie's slacks and briefs down, ready to see Jamie's body on display.

"Lay back on the bed," Tyler said, breaking their kiss and giving Jamie a gentle push. Tyler's hands shook with nervous excitement at the thought of coming inside of his boyfriend.

Jamie fell backward, his limbs spread on the duvet. Tyler took a good look at him, at those powerful thighs and long toes, at his shoulders and stubble-covered jaw, and his blonde hair fluffed around his head.

Jamie's cock was hard against his stomach. He was perfect in all the ways that mattered, and Tyler still couldn't believe he could have *this* along with everything else in his life.

Tyler hadn't thought there was room for someone else with Rowan holding so much of his heart. He hadn't been able to imagine the kind of person who would be willing to stick around for the crumbs of his attention and time.

Jamie had proved him wrong.

He'd shown up and stuck around. He had his own life, his own demands on his heart and time, but still, he'd shown up. And because Jamie had proven his investment in their life, in both of them, Tyler had realized he actually had room in his heart for more. For friends who showed up on Christmas to help him build an ice-fishing hut, and a community who came over with soup when his son was sick. He had space for the two women who had given them a home, who he and Rowan had come to trust and love like their own kin.

And Jamie. *Jamie.*

There was plenty of space in his heart for Jamie.

"Baby," Jamie said, a hint of desperation in his voice. "As much as I love the way you're looking at me, I'm going to need you to help me out here."

Tyler laughed, grabbed the bottle of lube from the edge of the mattress, and crawled up the bed until he was kneeling between Jamie's spread thighs. He squeezed the lube onto his fingers, and then reached down between Jamie's legs.

He loved Jamie's body hair, the patch of soft blonde surrounding his cock and trailing down below his balls. He found his hole and circled it with slicked fingertips. Jamie shuddered below him, his stomach flexing.

Tyler slowly pushed a finger in, watching Jamie's face for any sign of discomfort. With his mouth open and his eyes closed, Jamie looked completely relaxed. "Don't fall asleep on me now," Tyler teased, starting to work his finger in and out.

Jamie let out a soft laugh that turned into a gasp as Tyler pressed a second finger in. "Feels so good," Jamie breathed, blinking his eyes up at Tyler. "It's been a while. Since I bottomed. I'd forgotten how much I–*fuck,* I like it."

Tyler leaned down and pressed a quick kiss to Jamie's lips. "Want me to take it slow?"

"No. One more and I'll be ready."

Tyler obliged, adding more lube and working three fingers into his hole.

"Ready," Jamie said, his voice wavering.

Tyler removed his fingers and slicked his cock with more lube, feeling overwhelmed with want. Without prompting, Jamie grabbed behind his knees and held himself open. "Fuck," muttered Tyler, wetting his lips. "I'm going to lose it so fucking fast when I'm in you."

Bracing himself above Jamie, he gripped the base of his cock and lined himself up. He pushed forward, nudging at the soft whorl of skin with steady pressure until Jamie bore down, opening up below him.

It was exquisite, a tight squeeze that already threatened to send him over the edge. Tyler gasped, trembling as he tried to stop himself from coming so quickly. From letting go too soon.

"Yes," Jamie breathed below him. "Yes, baby. Yes."

Tyler drew his hips back, Jamie's ass clenching around him. He couldn't speak, could barely remember to breathe as he thrust forward, burying himself completely.

He kissed Jamie, needed to taste him and tell him with his tongue how good he felt. Jamie groaned, open-mouthed against his lips, his hips rolling to meet every thrust.

They were sloppy, all spit and tongues and sweat beading at the friction between their bodies. Jamie's broad, muscular chest covered in hair slid against Tyler's smooth, inked skin. Tyler wanted to erase every bit of space between them, keeping his thrusts hard and deep. Below him, Jamie grunted, his cock hardening and leaking against Tyler's belly.

There was a time in Tyler's life when he'd longed for sex to last forever, when the dream had been to fuck the night away without ever needing to pause.

Now there was something he wanted more.

He needed to see Jamie come apart, to watch him drown in pleasure at Tyler's hands. Then, at the end of it all, when Jamie lay boneless and spent below him, Tyler wanted to be the one who put him back together.

That was what he wanted.

"I'm close," Tyler warned as the pressure grew.

"In me," Jamie pleaded. A wet curl was stuck to his forehead, and Tyler licked a line up the side of his neck, moaning at the sharp taste of salt on his tongue. "Fucking fill me."

Tyler chased his release. He rocked his hips, seeking friction, reaching and reaching. "Fuck," he gasped as his cock throbbed, contracting before shooting deep into Jamie's body. He emptied pulse after pulse, his heartbeat everywhere all at once, his mind blank except for the exquisite pleasure of *Jamie, Jamie, Jamie.*

But he wasn't done. His work wasn't finished until Jamie found his release. He withdrew his sensitive cock, hissing at the lack of contact.

"Baby, what are you–*fuck*."

Tyler bent down and took Jamie's cock into his mouth. He bobbed up and down, his tongue flicking against the tight skin. With the taste of precum on his tongue, he swallowed, humming at the nudge of Jamie's crown against the back of his throat. Above him Jamie groaned, muttering curses and praise under his breath.

Jamie came with a hoarse cry, his cock pulsing in Tyler's mouth as he emptied down his throat. Tyler swallowed it all, taking every little bit of it until he stilled.

Tyler slowly drew away, Jamie's softening cock slipping from his mouth. Looking up, he saw Jamie, dazed and handsome and so exhausted that his eyes were barely open as he returned Tyler's gaze. A soft, lazy smile played across his mouth.

"C'mere," Jaime mumbled, making a grabby gesture that looked ridiculous coming from hands his size.

Tyler crawled up his body and collapsed onto the bed beside him. His head landed at an odd angle, propped up against the literal barricade of pillows at the head of Jamie's bed.

"Why do you have so many pillows?" Tyler asked, a yawn breaking through the end of his question.

Jamie turned to look at him. "I like pillows."

Tyler lifted his head and started tossing the pillows off the bed. He counted: one, two, three, four, five, *six* pillows before there was just one under his head.

"Do we need to get dressed? For Rowan?"

Tyler nodded, pushing himself up. They cleaned up in the bathroom before stumbling back into Jamie's room. He tossed a clean pair of boxer briefs at Jamie, and then pulled on a pair of old threadbare boxer shorts for himself. He'd found them buried in Jamie's underwear drawer and had claimed them as his pajama shorts.

"I'm going to check on Row," Tyler said, slipping out the door and down the hall. He eased open the door, careful not to rattle the knob, and tip-toed across the carpet to peek into the Pack n' Play.

Rowan slept like he always did–Bunny clutched to his chest, with a soft frown on his face. On his other side, the stuffed muskie Jamie had left for him was tucked close to his body.

Tyler watched him, checking the little things: his chest rose and fell, slow and even, and his blanket covered his body.

They were at Jamie's house, and Rowan was okay.

Tyler slipped back into Jamie's bedroom.

"How is he?" Jamie asked.

Tyler smiled as he nodded, climbing under the covers and sliding across the bed until he was in Jamie's arms. "He's perfectly at peace."

Jamie made that little humming sound he sometimes made when he was pleased, shifting Tyler so that he lay half-sprawled across Jamie's chest. His skin was warm, and Tyler burrowed in close, trying to get as much of Jamie's warmth as he could.

It felt so good to be there in Jamie's arms, content and sated, knowing Rowan was safe.

It was a reality Tyler hadn't considered could be his, and now that he was living it, he wanted to protect it. Wanted to treasure it, to treasure *Jamie* most of all.

Jamie's lips pressed against his forehead. "We probably won't get a lot of this."

Tyler craned his neck to look at Jamie. "A lot of what?"

"Nights together like this."

"I know," Tyler said, running his fingers over the hair on Jamie's chest.

Jamie frowned. "And that's okay with you?"

"Yes, because it's you. You're worth making time for, even if all we get are little moments. Even if we only see you for a quick lunch, or if we need to come by the rink to catch you after practice."

A soft smile spread across Jamie's face. "And I'll do the same for you, when I can."

"That's all we can do, right?" Tyler asked. "Be here, together, when we can?"

Jamie nodded, and tilted Tyler's head back to kiss him. It was a slow, indulgent kiss, deep, but without the expectation of anything coming after. When their mouths broke apart, Jamie said, "I need you to know how happy I am. With you. *Both* of you. Getting to call you mine, Tyler? It might be the best thing to ever happen to me."

"You too," Tyler responded, but then held up a hand. "I mean, Rowan's the best thing that's ever happened to me, but you are amazing, and–"

"Number three, remember?"

Tyler laughed, shaking his head. Above him, Jamie yawned. "Can I tell you something?"

Jamie blinked sleepily at him. "Anything, baby."

"I know we're not supposed to say big emotional shit after sex."

"We're not?"

Tyler brushed the damp, sweaty hair back from Jamie's forehead. "So I need you to know I've been thinking about this. And even though it's soon, probably way too fucking soon, I've been *feeling* it for a little while now."

"Baby," Jamie said slowly.

"I love you."

Jamie blinked at him, and Tyler got to watch as his words sunk in. He got to watch Jamie's lips part in a gasp, his eyes somehow widen and soften at the same time. And then Tyler got to enjoy the weight of Jamie's body settling on top of him as Jamie kissed him, slow and sweet and lazy.

Like they had nothing but time.

"I love you, too," Jamie whispered against his mouth when they parted.

"Are we idiots for thinking this will work?" Tyler asked, even as his whole body lit up with the heat of loving, and the warm glow of being loved.

Jamie's eyes crinkled in the corners, and the green seemed so bright and *alive* in the low glow of the lamplight. "Probably."

Tyler tried to imagine his future with Jamie, but found that it didn't matter. Not at that moment. Right then, it was enough that they were there, together in Jamie's big bed, choosing each other. "I don't think I realized how lonely I was," Tyler said. "And it wasn't like I was lonely for *anyone*, you know. I think I was lonely for you."

"We have each other now," Jamie said, earnest as always, and *fuck*, Tyler loved him.

"I want to be your teammate in life, in love, and maybe someday in raising Rowan." Tyler wasn't worried about his words being too much. Not for Jamie.

"I want all of it with you." Jamie kissed him again, like he couldn't stop. He kissed like he was ravenous, like he wanted to make a home inside of Tyler's body. When he broke away, Tyler was breathing hard, his body starting to wake up again.

"I'm going to treasure you, okay?" Jamie said, holding Tyler's gaze. "And I'm going to start by making you breakfast tomorrow before I leave."

Tyler grinned, pushing Jamie over to his side of the bed before sliding his body against his. Jamie's arm wrapped around him and pulled him closer. "How long will you be gone?" Tyler whispered.

"Eight days this time around."

"We'll be here, okay? We're not going anywhere."

"I know, baby." Jamie's lips pressed against his forehead. "Fuck, I can't keep my eyes open."

"Go to sleep, Jamie," he said, even as his own eyes started to drift closed.

The last thing Tyler felt before he fell asleep was the brush of Jamie's hand, soft and lingering, caressing the moth wings at the base of his throat.

ACKNOWLEDGMENTS

This book would not have been possible without my two friends and unconventional editors, who pop in and out of my process from start to finish. Zac and Morgan, I don't think words can sum up the gratitude I have for both of you sticking with me, and reading this story again and again, in all of the forms it has taken. Thank you to my alpha readers: JJ, Julie, Allison, Alex, Stef, Jill, and Anne: you all came in and your feedback and encouragement gave me the fuel and motivation to get this story over the finish line. Thank you to my dearest friend and fellow author Miah, who held down the beta reader fort and was always available to chat: every book you've been a part of is better because of you. To my sensitivity reader, Chase. You came in as a pinch hitter late in the game, and I am so so grateful to what you brought to this story. Thank you. To Ari for friendship and hockey knowledge–your friendship means so much to me. Thanks for putting up with me. To Len for the stunning cover artwork that has brought so many readers here, thank you for bringing Tyler and Jamie to life. To M. Anderson and Ian, your character artwork proved to be a source of inspiration throughout writing.

Thank you to the queer community for friendship, support, and the constant reminder that there is joy to be found in being yourself. Thank you to the group chat for keeping me humble. Thank you to my family, and especially to my child, who directly inspired so many of Rowan's quirks. Someday we will laugh about it together. Thank you to Tim and Michael from Wonderstate for making my maple lattes and laughing at my jokes.

And thanks to you, dearest reader, for picking up my book. Whether this is your first or the most recent of many, your time and attention means the world to me. Thank you, thank you, thank you.

ABOUT THE AUTHOR

Taylor E Weston is an emerging author of contemporary romance novels that follow real, flawed people navigating their way through love and the world. Her stories are people-centric, and include a realistic amount of eating and making out.

She lives in southwestern Wisconsin with her husband and son. When she isn't writing or reading, you can find her traipsing around her garden in rubber boots, talking about bald eagles, cooking with bacon, or making up stories about raccoons for her son.

Connect with Taylor at www.tayloreweston.com.

ALSO BY TAYLOR E. WESTON

Southeastern Alumni Series

Courtside

Southeastern Alumni Book 1

Courtside is an MF *almost* hook up-to-coworkers-to-lovers romance filled with big men with tiny dogs, breakfast tacos, annoyingly perceptive friends, forgiveness, and, ultimately, two people who choose happiness together — on and off the court.

Poolside

Southeastern Alumni Book 2

Poolside is an MM friends-to-lovers romance filled with vulnerable men who watch *Spartacus* together, accepting friends, healing, an opossum under a house, and, ultimately, two people who fight for a future together —in and out of the water.

Want something a little different?

The Grim, Me, and The Reaper Makes Three

An MMF spicy paranormal romance novella

Dying wasn't a part of the plan...

Tatiana was supposed to start dating again. She was finally supposed to quit her job now that she'd saved enough to buy the corner property on South Street and Ordell that she'd had her eye on for years. She was supposed to live now. She was thirty, flirty, and she was supposed to be fucking thriving.

Not dead. There was no room for "being dead" in her plans.

www.ingramcontent.com/pod-product-compliance
Lightning Source LLC
LaVergne TN
LVHW100520110826
845146LV00002B/715

* 9 7 9 8 9 9 0 5 6 8 1 6 7 *